For Joanna Rose –
A gift from Dan's
cousin, Via

Gwen

xx

she could
see
no good reason
to act
her age

Miri,

Hope to see you soon

D1117972

Joanne Greenberg

Montemayor Press

Millburn, New Jersey

For information contact:

Montemayor Press
P. O. Box 526, Millburn, NJ 07041
Web site: www.MontemayorPress.com

1 3 5 7 9 10 8 6 4 2

Library of Congress Cataloging-in-Publication Data

Greenberg, Joanne.
 Miri, who charms / by Joanne Greenberg.
     p. cm.
 ISBN 978-1-932727-09-8
 1. Jewish women--Fiction. 2. Female friendship--Fiction. I. Title.
 PS3557.R3784M57 2009
 813'.54--dc22
                                    2008044939

To Jeri Lynn

Who taught you all that courage and love?

Miri, Who Charms

Joanne Greenberg

Prologue

We're off Coal Creek Canyon, on a mountain road that's not familiar to me. In daylight, I might trace the turns we're taking, but it's night, and this police car has its windows tinted, making it even more difficult to see. I thought anxiety was supposed to sharpen the senses. Mine are dulled; I keep sinking away into blurred thought or sharp memory. Miri's sitting beside me, saying nothing. We're going to the place the rescuers have found, the cave where Miri's daughter and Miri's lover are lost or trapped or hurt or dead.

Now and then the officer—his name is Escobar—talks into his radio and hears crackle talk that seems to tell him that nothing more has been found. I think, stupidly, Can they search at night? and then I realize how tired I must be. The cave is darker than any nighttime darkness blessed by moon or snow or stars or the reflected glow of city lights. The anxiety blossoms into panic and I have to breathe and count the breaths to try to still it.

The trip so far has taken almost an hour. The roads are dwindling to trails. I let my mind go where it has wanted to go since we left Boulder long ago.

1

My girlhood couldn't have been as magical as I remember it. I see Miri and me when we were six and ten and seventeen, standing together bathed in the iridescent light of Denver's summer mornings. We're excited, planning an adventure, laughing, walking between our houses, or up in Miri's attic, on long, mellow autumn afternoons. I see us escaping, sharing secrets, winking at each other over the heads of parents, relatives, teachers, rabbis, congregations. Even when I come on the objective facts of those years, they dim before the joy of my private reality. I was ten when Adolf Eichmann was taken for trial in Jerusalem and Mrs. Pinsker and the Moshowitzes went to Israel to testify. I was in the synagogue when Mr. Moshowitz, after his return, stood up during the mourner's Kaddish and began to howl, "They made me remember!" until people moved close and two of them guided him away and walked with him. There were wars at home, constant and bitter. My mother and father weren't peaceful people. My sisters and I can recall years-long wrangles they had, and skirmishes between Mama and me, and battles each against all. I've packaged all that into a few donnybrooks of screaming and rage: The Shoes Fight, The Store Fight. These epic sieges were always drained of their anguish, eased, lightened by my escapes to Miri's house, two blocks away, where there was peace, blessed peace. Sometimes I ran, even crying, to Ada Mordecai's welcoming kitchen for Miri, glad to see me and full of diverting plans. When I couldn't escape, I could imagine being with her upstairs in the attic we had claimed as ours, lying on sleeping bags we'd put up there, to talk and as we grew into teenagers to listen to music and paint our toenails revolting colors.

"We both need boyfriends."

"Why? All the boys in our class are dumb."

"Because, Rachel, boys have to pay for things. They have to take you places and buy you things."

"But who would want to spend any time with them? All they talk about is sports. All they want to do is brag."

"We'll be together. We can talk to each other while they play and brag, but they'll have to take us out."

It was our friendship that gave me the idea of myself as privileged, bright, the possessor of a golden childhood. I needed the confidence born of that idea to fight my way into college and to persevere in the work I do now. Miri was never good at reflection. I want to number the days, as the Psalmist says, so I can understand how we brought this dangerous moment on ourselves. Then I might fix the mistake I made and get some height over what I feel for Miri now.

She was always beautiful and still is, a dark, vivid woman with long, shining black hair that she cut only last month. She looked like Scheherazade, and by the time she was twelve or thirteen, she had begun to have the beautiful body that made the boys choke up and go mute with yearning. I could have envied her then, but I never did—the difference between us was too great. My hair was the crimped, wavy mass that later would be called "Jewish Afro." I was taller, heavier than she, and clumsier. I had freckles on a skin that burned red in summer. People said I had a "nice face." When a girl is fourteen, a nice face is the last kind of face she wants.

We equate beauty with goodness. We can't help imagining ourselves living different lives if only we were beautiful.

Miri was a virtual only child. She had three brothers, but they were all a good deal older than she and only her brother Dan was still at home. In those days, I had a crush on him, because he was beautiful, too. I used to dream about him when I was nine and ten, as my lover or husband, but I think that what I really wanted was to be adopted into their family and have Dan as a brother. When we were fourteen, he was drafted and went to Vietnam, and came back darker, more practical, intent on marriage, children, and forgetting. He did all of that, marrying a very pious girl and moving to Israel with her. He's a rabbi now, more observant

4

than Hillel the sage. He sent Miri a picture of himself with wife and kids. I didn't recognize him.

Miri's father was Rabbi Ezekiel Mordecai, a biblical scholar and writer. He was one of those men who are deeply respected by the Jewish community not for what they do but for what they represent. He lacked what are now called "social skills"—he had little patience with the trivial details of daily life and a short attention span for his family, except for Miri, whose smile warmed his whole being, whose word made the morning. I see it now as a kind of idolatry; then I saw it as only her due.

"The more I read my newspaper, the sadder I get," he would tell us. "It's not only the outside world—our own people are bringing shame. Sing me the song you learned, Mirele, and take the pain away."

Even when he was annoyed, he never blew, like my father, into red-faced rage, pounding the table in answer to the screaming dramatics of my mother. His hands would come up and he would murmur, "*Tohu va' vohu*," helplessly, referring to the chaos God found in the universe before He gave it order. Then he would sigh, rise, and disappear into his study, emerging when a meal was ready or it was time to go to the synagogue. As angry as he got, Miri could always soften his eyes. "This idiot thinks he is an editor. What's the state of Jewish learning if this king of intellect allows such an article in his publication? Mirele, say the poem you learned," or, "Mirele, sit for a while." He was always courteous to me. He loved me because his Mirele loved me. In their strictly observant home, I saw only the quiet, the peace. I could always get past Rabbi Mordecai's polite exasperation or delicate scorn.

My house rang and shuddered, and not only because of my parents. I had two sisters who were angry also. Someone was always banging, calling, screaming; someone was always practicing bitter and hostile housework, slamming pots and pans, vacuuming like combat or raging up or down the stairs. My mother shouted, moaned, cried aloud to God. She even ironed noisily. Miri's house stood for me like an oasis, decorous and quiet. Our house was small, cramped, low-ceilinged, so that the noise of living rang around our ears. Someone was always

5

barricaded in the bathroom; someone was always pounding on the bathroom door. The Mordecais lived in a big house in the heart of West Denver, the old Jewish neighborhood which was vibrant with life in those years, before the dribble of Jewish people to East Denver became a flood. We lived two blocks from the Mordecais, but in a poorer area, nearer the noise and bustle of Colfax Avenue.

I've barely included Miri's mother, Ada Mordecai. That hurts because it's so typical. She was the hub of the house. When a wheel shoots sparks of life, or throws mud, no one notices the hub, where all the energy is concentrated, ego-effacing, efficient. At the time we were growing up, she was the consummate mother to Miri and to me. "Sweetheart, don't worry." She would hand me beets to peel or cabbage to shred. "Your mother yells at you because you're important to her. Do people yell when they don't care?"

"You don't yell."

"I'm not a yeller. God made all kinds, and some don't fit together so well. We can't blame God. The world needs all kinds. How we fit together shouldn't have to be His headache. Grate these fine."

The three Mordecai sons had all gone to religious school and, after that, to the yeshiva for a strict religious education, but by the time Miri came along, the money had run out, and so she joined me at public school. There were enough Jewish kids there in those days to all but close the doors for the High Holy Days.

Miri's glow was not only for our neighborhood, for Rabbi Mordecai and Ada and our little congregation. The teachers loved her. "Miriam, would you take this note to Mrs. Creevy in the third-grade room?" "Miriam, take Ronnie's mother to the library—here's his coat." "We can let Miriam be the announcer in our pageant."

Surprisingly, there was no envy, or none I saw. The kids liked her and took her superiority as natural, and they accepted me as her best friend—but that not without envy, sometimes, a look or a word here and there.

The result of our American education was that Miri and I were more assimilated than her brothers. We ate up Colorado

6

history, proud of the early Jewish presence in the state. The adventures of Otto Mears and other Jewish pioneers made us feel we belonged—Old Family, aristocrats of a tough, stand-up lineage. We forgot that a goodly number of these pioneers were "lungers," people who came west with the TB they hoped our clear, high air would cure. We were freer than the kids who went to religious school, less frightened of the life that was going on so energetically outside the enclosed piety of our neighborhood. When we were seven, eight, and nine, we traded food for forbidden comic books, which we took up to "our" attic, where we devoured them, and later, the romances that Mrs. Shrager, who lived next door to my house, read and sold to me for a nickel a copy. At twelve, we began to find ways to sneak out of Miri's house, and out of the neighborhood altogether.

"I want to go to the movies."

"How can you? It's Shabbat."

"That's when I want to go. It's impossible on a school day. Sunday, I clean my room and Mama takes me shopping, or we cook. After lunch on Shabbat, their guard is down. Papa eats, naps, or is in shul. Mama reads or has a nap. They don't care if they see me or not. Sunday, you work in the store. It has to be Shabbat, Rachel, and it has to be downtown, away from here."

A trip to a local movie would be impossible. The neighborhood houses had mostly closed by then, but to be seen going into or coming out of the ones remaining would have resulted in uproar. A bus went downtown, but we couldn't be seen riding, either.

"I have a plan, 'Chelle. I've been thinking it up and I'm sure it'll work. Every week, we do a mitzvah—visiting the sick. We take trays of cookies to the old-age home, the one on Colfax."

"This gets us to the movies?"

"Don't be slow, 'Chelle. We go in. We give out the cookies. We take fifteen minutes, tops. Good-bye and we're out the door, and we have an alibi for the whole four hours between lunch and supper."

"Number two. Money. Where?"

"Get your father to pay you for working in the store."

"Are you crazy?"

"Bottles, then, deposit bottles."

"All right, but what about the cookie trays? We can't go downtown holding cookie trays."

"Brighten up, 'Chelle. We leave them. I pick them up on my way home from school on Monday."

The plan, of course, required Ada Mordecai's enthusiastic co-operation. I cringe now when I think how eagerly she embraced it, giving her full attention and approval, buying the ingredients, helping us with the work of baking every week. I never realized until this moment what an imposition that request must have been. The cookies had to be made on Friday so as to be still fresh on Shabbat, when baking was forbidden. The Jewish housewife's busiest day is Friday, with cleaning, cooking, and baking for her own family celebration. Miri and I, oblivious to all that and the kitchen mess we made, got three full trays from her every week. We worked a scam that elicited praise from everyone for our virtue and charity. The deception was compounded as we entered the overheated, airless nursing-home world. They loved us. Withered arms reached out to us. Veined hands clutched at us in love. "Look, Rose, Bessie, Leah—here they are, the darlings. Come in; we've been waiting for you." "Sweethearts, a blessing, and here are all the cookies." "It's Reb Mordecai's youngest—yes—what's your name again—Miriam—and her friend. Who are you, sweetheart—Rachel, yes, I remember." Miri would respond with a big hug, even to the ones who drooled, which I couldn't make myself do. We delivered the cookies, stayed four minutes to be admired, and a minute after that we were out the doors and out of sight. The residents in the home were often too far gone to realize how perfunctory our visits were. They were always tremulously glad to see us and forgot us as we stood there. We only dimly realized our betrayal of them, or, if we did, forgot it as they forgot us, even as we were so eagerly awaited.

In those days, returning pop bottles for deposit was the traditional source of kid income. Miri got an allowance, but I roamed the neighborhood through the week and knocked on the doors of childless couples for the two-cent empties. I usually made enough for a child's ticket at afternoon prices in second-run theaters. When I couldn't raise the price of a ticket, Miri would raid the Rabbi's coat pockets for his change. We saw movies, dozens of them. We went to the arcades and the new shopping malls that were opening all over town. We were back before dark, our piety proven, pretentious, and phony.

2

We practiced the cookie ploy for over three years. I suspect my older sisters, Shifrah and Shirah, knew what we were doing, but they had lies of their own to tell, and on Shabbat both my mother and Miri's surreptitiously cleared plates from the table and washed them, made beds, tore paper towels from the roll, and used electricity when the men weren't home.

Our parents were very protective of us, but in different ways. The Mordecais wanted their only daughter to be modest and untouched by the world. My parents wanted help around the house and at the store, but they respected the Mordecais and were proud of my friendship with Miri. We learned to exploit our knowledge of our families to get school-trip permissions and, once, a ski weekend with a classmate. We went to plays, and spent summer days at Elitch's and Lakeside, our local amusement parks, without our parents suspecting anything. We went to Ada for the intellectual set of requests, stretching the definition of learning until it creaked with the strain. We went to the circus with a group from school and called it a biology field trip. We rode the rides at Lakeside and called it a physics project. We read books that would have made my parents shudder and reams of trashy romances, whose covers we replaced with wrapping paper, that we said were English assignments. To my mother, who was restless and dramatic, we played on our need for physical health—the young men in the yeshivas, who were to be our husbands, might themselves be slender, pale, and etiolated, but a wife should be "blooming," and without sunshine and activity, there can be no bloom. My father, who was, at that time, managing a pawnshop that dealt principally with Jewish ceremonial items, had needed my sisters' help, and, finally, mine. Miri took on that challenge. Luckily, the store was closed on Shabbat, but I didn't want to work there at all. To tend the store by myself would have been pleasant. There were long periods of inactivity for reading, daydreaming, or playing with the items that came in, but I worked under my father's eye, and his theory was that idleness is a sign of mental sloth. Why was I standing like a golem? Why wasn't I dusting the shelves, polishing, arranging?

"Look at these siddurs—holy books you treat like trash. A customer comes in, I should blow the dust off before I show them to him, and then ask a good price for them?"

Being the youngest had been protection enough, for a while. Shifrah had served six years in the store, and Shirah three. She was eager to pass the torch. I saw years stretching away in the airless place, dusting and seeing no one under sixty. It was Miri who formulated the tactics by which I was to be liberated from the store and from my father.

"Don't argue with him," she declared, "and 'Chelle, never whine or plead. They hate that. Be clumsy and eager. Be brainless and sweet. Use how big you are. Whenever you bend to get something, something else should fall. Then be sorry, and as you are picking it up, overturn another thing. Then be sorry. Smile at the customers and be pleasant and eager and take three-quarters of an hour to find the thing they want and three-quarters of an hour to make change."

Slowly, I did. I worked up a repertoire. Miri told me, "Always carry four things at once. At least two will drop and break." I was so eager to please the customer that I brought out all the books of the kind he wanted to see. Of course, I dropped half of them. Being siddurs, they carried the name of God in them, and dropping them created consternation. I tangled myself in prayer shawls when I unfolded them. "Oops." My father began to free me out of simple disgust.

Miri's being was expressed in action. Her school projects were stunning in their ingenuity and detail. I was dreamy in classes; she took elaborate notes. She learned how to ski, to swim, to dance. She was fearless and intrepid. Her joy in activity glowed out of her, radiant and warming.

So, with Miri's coaching, I was able to convince my father

11

that I was a clumsy nitwit, too inept to polish silver, dust, or make change. I kept Shifrah and Shirah from giving me away by simple extortion. Shifrah was seeing a boy from a nonobservant family, and they did lots of nonobservant things. Shirah kept a small wardrobe of miniskirts, low-cut blouses, and leotards in my dresser and wore them under the clothes she left the house in every day. With stiletto heels, lipstick, and eyeliner in a huge purse, she would slouch around with her friends, looking like a jaded hooker. To all my sisters' secrets, I was witness and co-conspirator, and their plans were balanced on my silence. When I read Dante in college and saw the phrase "The love that moves the planets and the stars," I thought that fear might do as well as love. Extortion had made me cynical.

The summer we were fourteen was the summer we met Art and Ab, two boys from school, who discovered us one Saturday at the Lakeside Amusement Park. From then on, we were a foursome, going as far out of the neighborhood as we could, alibiing one another, bent more on freedom than romance, having the fun I never would have known without Miri's ability to charm them, her quick, incandescent smile, her "Good. Let's go!"

We met the boys in secret, but being with them was innocent, even decorous, as I remember it. When we lay down together on our picnic blankets, it wasn't to have sex, but to moan at the unfairness of parents, rabbis, systems, the world. Art wanted to make a million dollars and give it away to people who would multiply it and then pay back some, and the project would grow, until it became a worldwide cure for poverty. He had it worked out mathematically. Ab was interested in science in a way I've never seen before or since—it was pure curiosity, an end in itself. When one wasn't saving the world and the other wondering whether his math problem could be proven by physics, they were love-struck over other girls. I was like a sister; Miri was out of reach.

Art wanted to break into the Friday-afternoon school dances at the high school. We got ourselves in. Miri wanted to ski; we called the boys. When we were fifteen, we talked Art's brother into taking us into the mountains over the Christmas break and to

White Sands in the summer. Miri was active in everything, but she was against all action relating to housework. Except for the great cookie caper, I don't remember any of the early years with her spent in the kitchen.

In the kitchen was Ada Mordecai, the quintessential Orthodox housewife. People don't use the Yiddish word *balebusteh* anymore—women's lib has starved its roots—but in those days that designation was the apex of a woman's aspiration. Ada personified the word; she was a marvelous cook. Her pots and pans looked like new. Her kitchen shone; order sprang from her fingers. She never raised her voice and never seemed at a loss, worried, frazzled, or angry. My mother was a howl of discontent. She railed at lost opportunities and a vanished self. I stayed at Miri's all I could. If one of the empties I picked up from the Liebers' back porch had contained a genie, my single wish would have been to live at Miri's, to be Rachel Mordecai.

Yet, now I realize that not all could have been sweetness in the Mordecai home. Noah, Elias, and Dan, Miri's brothers, must have chafed now and then under Ada's admirable order and competence. Of course, we took her gifts for granted. Now, it seems that women can barely see to the needs of one or two children. She performed miracles for four and a very demanding husband while keeping a strictly kosher home, cooking the long, involved ethnic menus, the traditional gefilte fish from scratch, the full panoply of holiday and Sabbath meals. She couldn't have been the intellectual write-off we made of her then. It's true that her conversation with us was confined to eating, health, and such soul-strangling topics as bowel regularity and the fit state of our underwear. "Rachel, take that slip off and let me sew it. A girl with a pin in her slip? A slut."

How we giggled at that. Our heroines weren't homemakers, but Hollywood stars—Jane Fonda, Liza Minelli, Julie Andrews. We would sit in the forbidden theaters and watch the forbidden movies for clues to futures we wanted to live, not the ones we were afraid we would be living, and if one of the heroines sniffled or slumped or let a stocking sag, we would both hiss, "Slut!" and giggle. I went into high school excited, rather than frightened, because of Miri.

13

High school caught us like a tornado. We fell in and out of love together as rhythmically as the moon-shivered tides, and not only with Jewish boys. Bobby DiSalvo, Lonny Clare, and Dan Symes all had my rapt attention in turn. Miri had passionate dream affairs with three Mexican boys, one after the other. None of the objects of our passion was aware of us or of what we conjured in his name.

As we moved through those years, I was asked out more often than Miri. Art took me to school dances, still a buddy. He was presentable enough. "Don't get any ideas," he'd say. Ab never took Miri. He never went himself. He was too tall, his hands and feet were too big; his red-gold hair, like mine, was kinky. His best feature was his voice. It had been lowering and mellowing year by year. The problem was that when he tried to speak to girls, it choked and broke. Other boys began to ask me out. Miri was too beautiful, too lively to be approachable, although dozens stood staring at her, all but moaning as she passed. Boys of low confidence found me pleasant because my confidence was even lower than theirs. She was still having to depend on the younger brothers of the rabbi's students. Boys were losing their virginity, but not with us. I remember only one of her admirers from those years, a clumsy mouth breather named Melvin. He's handsome now and a professor at the Baylor College of Medicine.

3

I had so convinced my father of my ineptness that he worried when I set the table. I stayed out of the house and at Miri's by becoming interested in a handful of nonexistent school projects that kept me from home, until my presence there was as rare as the visit of an acquaintance. By that time, people had seen Ab and Art with us and were making matches. Both families were acceptable, although Rabbi Mordecai wanted better for Miri. "Be careful," Ada told us: "men won't value what's offered too easily." My mother was eager, my father amazed. "You can get married quickly before he finds out how clumsy you are."

An intrusion from the outside world came in those years—the Vietnam War. Our community was riven by it. The problem of military service was more complicated for us than for Americans in general because of the exactions of Orthodox living. A draftee who didn't protest his call-up risked his religious life—food, hours of prayer, Shabbat, the whole structure that one of our prayers calls "the house of our lives."

Most of the local boys protested their inductions and were exempted, but some went, putting their spiritual lives on hold, and there were murmurings of disapproval in the congregations and wrangles within the families. Miri's brother Dan said that he would take off his kippah and go. I was at the table when Rabbi Mordecai said incredulously, "Whose fight is this, yours?"

"It's payback to America."

"Don't be ridiculous."

"Don't you remember Uncle Ephraim telling us how it was at Dachau when the survivors looked up into the faces of the American soldiers who liberated the camps? Don't you remember what he told us one soldier said? 'We're back. America took us, and now we're back.' A Jewish soldier."

15

"That was different; that was because of the Nazis."

"We're American; we do American things—it's Talmud, remember. The Talmud says—"

"Don't quote Talmud to me. You're throwing away your life."

"We don't just live here, Dad; we *belong* here." Then Dan left. The Mordecais were devastated. Rabbi Mordecai paced the floor, murmuring. We heard him in his study, going over the reasons why Dan should have stayed, or at least let the army come for him. Even in his grief, though, he never insulted, yelled, demanded as my father would have done. The dignity of his grief made me ache for him. One afternoon, I passed him in the hall on my way upstairs to Miri's room, and I looked up into his face with all the love I could give. He put his hand briefly on my head, my springy hair, and sighed, then took it away quickly, as if it had been burned. I was fifteen then, no longer a child, and, as a girl, couldn't be touched without the possibility of sin.

After all that, you'd expect the Bronze Star at least. Nothing dramatic happened. He served in fights he never told us about. His letters were all general. He came back withdrawn and darker-minded, telling us nothing. Six months later, he declared his family not observant enough and went to Israel. We argued about it all, my sisters and I. Because of my slight crush on Dan, I had been blind to Shirah's huge crush on him. She wept when he left Denver.

Most of the national anguish caused by the Vietnam War seemed to pass us by. The events of the time took place in an alternate universe outside our community, kept from us by our piety. The suicides of two Yeshiva boys and the news that a girl from an observant family had run away with a Latino store clerk rocked us more than the scandals in Washington or the threats of civil rights militants. We had armed ourselves with faith and law. Outside, people robbed, stole, were violent. Outside, girls had "experience." Outside. How it menaced, the ugly, evil, fascinating, thrilling Outside.

Our war was the Six Day War, which ate great holes in our neighborhood's sense of solidarity. Most of us cheered, some of us went to fight or to live in Israel, and some few stood against the rest of us, saying that Israel wasn't to be established until the

16

coming of the Messiah. Since the Messiah was nowhere in sight, the state was contrary to the will of God.

It's important that I remember how subjective memory is, all the spilled treasure of summer sunshine, of Miri and me dressing up, pushing against the boundaries of our enclosing world, giving birth to ourselves. Miri wanted to go to college.

"Listen, 'Chelle, it's time we were thinking about how we want to start making that happen."

We were out at Sloan's Lake, during the halcyon days of February. The snows had melted and a sweet breeze was warming us up for the sucker punch of the big March and April blizzards. The ground was too wet to sit on, so we were walking. I'd been exiled from the store that afternoon for having dented a silver seder plate and broken two of its little glass fittings. I had knocked the plate over while dusting. My clumsy act was only half an act by then. A gloom had settled on me because I saw the end of high school moving toward me like a rock wall into which I would soon crash and be delivered into a life just like Mama's. The prospect was killing my reflexes.

"We're going to Denver University," Miri said, "both of us. I have a plan." The plan was that we would both get scholarships and chaperone each other. The Mordecais wanted nothing that would interfere with the prospect of a good marriage for Miri. "They think you're sensible and a positive influence on me. You've already convinced your father that you're hopeless, scattered, dreamy, and clumsy. Who would want to marry such a girl?"

"Thanks."

"Work that, 'Chelle. Let them see that if you don't go to college, you'll end up on their hands forever."

"So we magically get scholarships?"

"We study the scholarships. There are special ones. Minorities—"

"Jews aren't considered minorities; you know that."

"By minorities, I mean—"

"My grades are good, but you have to be a genius—"

"You only have to convince them that you're special. No one wants a grind, a bookworm. Listen, tomorrow afternoon we go to

17

the library and we research what's out there, and we find which ones give the most money and we make ourselves into just the people they're looking for and are dying to see."

"I read there was a scholarship for unwed mothers."

"If that's all we can find, we get Ab and Art to get us pregnant and then we apply."

"You take Ab. I'll take Art."

By that time we were laughing so hard, we had to stop walking and hold on to each other.

The next day we went to the library and found dozens of scholarships listed, but only a few that would apply to us.

"You're not black; your father's not a union man; you're not a polio victim, not blind, not—no—here, an unwed mother." And we were off, choking back laughter in the glare of the librarian. "No—wait—look at this, Miri. Isidore Friedman: Jewish-American women interested in careers in the professions. Four-year in-state university. Tuition, books, fees."

"This is the one we want."

We found two other scholarships, less desirable, and we decided that Miri should go for one of those because Rabbi Mordecai would give her some help.

I spent that year walking my father through Miri's plan. I gave him reports from all my teachers, letters, recommendations. I showed him his own wife, exhibit A: my mother, a wrangling, miserable woman, whose ambitions and possibilities had been stifled and whose frustrations broke over the heads of husband and children in rages and weeping. It was a job convincing him that not all women raged and screamed and threatened suicide.

Miri's brother Noah married during that year, and a little later my oldest sister, Shifrah, got a nebbish of a man from New York. They left after the wedding, returning only to show off their babies. Two days ago, she called me from there to curse Miri, by which I realized that our misery had hit the national news. Noah's wife wrote a steaming letter, which I spotted and plucked out of the rest of the hate mail to answer myself.

At seventeen, I was happy, bound for the big world. At eighteen, high school was over. A real world loomed before me. I was terrified. I'd won my battle with my father, because he thought me ineligible for the life of a woman, but I had no real idea of what I wanted to study at the college I had fought so hard to attend, or whom I wanted to be in the years ahead. I knew my piety might weaken even more under the spell of the alluring, degenerate Outside, but I had no dream to aim at beyond the will to dream. I was, at that time, calling myself Raquel—not, as my father thought, to be closer to the Hebrew pronunciation, but because Raquel Welch pronounced it that way. I hear that she, too, came from a neighborhood where girls tied their hair back and were demure and tried not to be too bright.

Miri had her life planned down to the last detail. She would go to college and study medical chemistry. She would marry a research chemist and together they would do important research that would be of interest to the big drug companies, which would vie for the cures they discovered. There was a Nobel Prize in there somewhere, and apartments in New York and Denver, and a house in the Bahamas to get away to.

What would I do with my freedom? My father was still laying down rules, and one day when work was light at the store, he reviewed them. "You'll live home and help, after school, to get dinner. Saturdays you'll spend Shabbat here and Sundays you can come to the store, and you can forget about those sex classes."

"What sex classes? I'll be taking architecture courses."

I was amazed at what had come out of my mouth. I had no more idea of becoming an architect than a hard-rock miner, but I did know that I wanted something that would make me independent someday, earning my own money. Once the words were out, they established a faint outline of reality, and then, as I said them to myself, as I heard myself saying them, they took form and substance. I rode the bus into town to Denver University and then to the community college. I spoke to advisers there and collected catalogs and studied them. I began to see ways and possibilities, and Miri and I sat over the catalogs and figured.

My father wouldn't stand for my working for money somewhere while he was giving up my services at the store, however wretchedly they were performed. He wouldn't allow me to live at home and not be under his control.

19

"Stay *here* and go to work," Miri said. "You're going to win that scholarship, and you won't have to pay for rent or food."

"Won't your parents complain—my living with you, taking up room, eating?" I was dying to do it, hungering to go, afraid to seem too eager. If only—

"Papa won't complain. You're here most of the time anyway, and your being here means that I won't be tempted to move out. And you'll be my chaperone at school. Mama likes you."

"You're so sure of the scholarship—you're so sure we'll get in to DU."

One of the drawbacks of coming from a nonintellectual background was my overemphasis on the difficulty of college. Miri only laughed. "My cousin Sy—a forty-watt IQ, and he got in. Relax, 'Chelle." I was petrified.

Two things happened at that time: My father's pawnshop failed, was closed, and sold in what seemed like lightning swiftness. He began working at an appliance store downtown. Then, on a Sunday night—Art called. "Yeah, what? Never mind. I'll tell you. You want me to talk you up to Lila Cohen—"

"Shut up for a minute, will you? Sit down."

"I'm sitting."

"Ab is dead."

"That's not true."

"It is, Rachel; listen to me."

"He's out of town. He's back east. He's looking at universities."

"I know that. Let me talk, will you?"

"If I talk, I won't have to listen."

"He got a ride with someone going to MIT. It was snowing. The car went off the road and crashed and he's dead. His dad called me from there."

My first thought was, What can I do to make this not true? I said, "I'll tell Miri," and hung up.

I went to the house. Rabbi Mordecai was in his study; Ada was sewing for someone's baby. Coming in, it all looked so normal. The family was gloriously present, but still somehow apart, separated from what changed all the time and went suddenly difficult and fearful. When I told Miri, I was shivering.

20

We went upstairs and sat in our childhood place in the attic, where there was still the embarrassing evidence of our past selves. We talked about how impossible it was that someone young could die, someone young whom we knew. People died on TV or in newspapers. That was a fact, not a reality. We talked about how we had met Ab and Art and the places we had gone together, about the day I fell and broke a rib, and how we practiced what I would tell them at home. We cried and laughed, the way you do, sitting shiva at a death, although there were only the two of us. I felt I was burying my childhood. It would be years before I discovered you do that all your life.

"Do you remember how we hurt his feelings when he had that awful crush on Marian Fine?"

"Do you remember when we tried his father's schnapps and all of us were sick?"

"They were more like my brothers than my brothers were," Miri said.

We went downstairs and told the Rabbi and Ada, and there were brought up short for our past secrecy. They were kind and sympathetic, but they had no idea that Ab was anything more than any other schoolmate, someone we knew, and our shock and sorrow were at the insult to our own immortality, not sorrow suffered at the loss of a friend.

Art came with us to Ab's funeral. The three of us stood at his grave and wept, and when we visited the family's more formal shiva, I saw his parents shrunken with his death, as though the volume of his body had been cut from theirs. As I stood, a little cramped from the low seating boxes the funeral home always sends for mourners, I had a sudden feeling of release. Look at the randomness, I thought, the riskiness of the world. It's not safe anywhere. I might as well step out on the ice as huddle by the shore. Papa's business failure had freed me. I could live at Miri's, work for wages, and put myself through school. It might take ten years, but I could see it being done. Papa had raged and been bitter at the store's demise; my sympathy for him rang like a counterfeit coin on the pawnshop's glass display case.

I got a job for the summer as a camp counselor. The kids were liberal Jews from Reform congregations. I liked the more open, freer Judaism, and I loved being in the mountains.

Denver University said yes to the fall term and I had lined up a job at a Target, restocking the store at night. Shirah married that July and I came home for the ceremony. Miri would be going to school with me, and if I lived at her house we could study together and I could really live the fantasy of being a Mordecai.

We planned all through Shirah's wedding, at which I barely said a word to anyone else, being taken up with my own exciting future. The affair was very modest anyway, boring. The ceremony was in our living room; the reception in the backyard of our next-door neighbors—cake, tea, and a bottle of schnapps my father shared with the men. I realize now that the glow a younger sister is supposed to halo about an older one, I had offered to Miri. Shirah, even as a bride, stood on two big feet in my estimation, ordinary as the hand-me-downs I was still wearing. Another counselor at the camp had driven me to town for the wedding and had to pick me up before the reception was over. "Write to me," I shouted to Miri as I left. She nodded. Miri wasn't a good correspondent. I wrote three letters to every one of hers.

ఇ.   ఇ.   ఇ.

Officer Escobar seems to be lost. He's been in almost constant crackle talk with the rescuers, and beside me, Miri is vibrating with impatience. "Miri, they haven't found Tamar and Val yet. We'll only have to wait once we get there."

"We've been waiting for days, and now this. No wonder they haven't been found before this; a bunch of incompetents was looking."

Escobar has located a place to turn around and is edging the car up and back to negotiate the narrow space. Miri shouts through the heavy mesh that protects the driver. "How far out of our way have we gone?"

"Not far," he says in his easy, gentling voice. "A mile or so. I missed the turnoff back there. Headquarters said it was marked, but I didn't see it. We'll be there soon."

Escobar has taken us because Miri refused to do what the sheriff requested—to wait for news at home. "I know you wouldn't want to be in the way," the sheriff told us, "and up there, you would. We'll get word the minute we've gotten to them, and the minute they're out. Please stay here."

"I'll drive myself if you won't take me," she said, and we all knew that she meant it.

"It's complicated." He was still trying to placate her. His hands were spread as though to calm, to quiet. "It's dark, and you're almost sure to get lost, and then we'll be sending men off the rescue to look for you. Please think again."

"I'm going," she said.

"All right," and his hands made a gesture of helplessness. "I'll have Officer Escobar drive you."

I think of that exchange as the car bucks over the ruts we had just endured on our way in. We would never have found the place on our own.

I doze a little. It was early evening when we started, but there have been sleepless nights since Tamar and Val went missing, and only catch-up naps and half sleeps, one ear open for the phone call. Time had become purely subjective, stretching and contracting to the shape of our fear.

After awhile, I hear Escobar say something and I jolt awake. "Here's the turnoff. You couldn't see the marker from the other side, but here it is. I'm going out to fix it so it'll show up better."

He opens the door and a wall of cold air falls in on us, shocking us and causing our breath to go smoky. I begin to think the sheriff was right and that we should have stayed home and waited. We've been in the false climate of the heated car and forgotten the mountain weather at night in April. It must be thirty out there. Thirty-two degrees Fahrenheit isn't freezing at this altitude; that's more like twenty-six or twenty-seven, but even with the dryness it will be wolf-cold at the site, and we came away in ordinary outer clothes—Miri in her blue trench coat and I in a jacket, fine for a quick walk around the block, completely inadequate for a long wait outside a cave. No gloves, no hats. I want to kick myself. Escobar gets back in the car and we bump onto a road even more rutted than the one we just left.

4

I came home in late August to find that the Isidore Friedman scholarship was waiting for me: tuition, books, and transportation. I ran to Miri's house to tell her.

She'd been working a summer job at the local library, and Ada welcomed me to wait in the kitchen and help with dinner. She was making holishkes, stuffed cabbage, each so square and even that they looked factory-made. She kissed me and set me to rolling dough for noodles. Ada was the only cook I knew who still hand-rolled the thin, thin soup noodles that were all but transparent in the bowl.

"Aren't you happy about Miriam? It's a wonderful match. She grew up in a scholar's house, after all, so she understands what sacrifices there are to make. Best of all, she'll be here, she and Jacob, not flown to the coast, and I'll be able to help her." She was crooning as she worked. "When the babies come—"

"What," I said, not a question. I was holding the rolling pin in one hand. She didn't see the shock.

"Roll," she said, "before the dough dries out."

"Miri's going to college," I said, not a question. "Miri and I are going to college. I came to tell her I got the Isidore Friedman."

She looked at me, beaming. "Miriam is going to be married. Isn't that wonderful? Roll. When you're done, I'll cut, and then we'll have some tea and eat a little of this coffee cake. It was amazing how it happened."

She launched into the details: that he was from New York, that he was everything any girl would want. He was brilliant, came from an illustrious family. He was wealthy; his people were making a fortune on some chemical process or other. On his own, there had been a book, biographies of the top scholars

25

of Talmud. All that, and so good-looking, a kind man—you could see it in his eyes. Most important, he loved her. A cousin had been to Denver to consult the rabbi and had seen Miriam. He had gone back and told Jacob. Jacob had come out in July, and at first, Miriam was shy and hesitant—any young woman would be, but even someone as stubborn as she could see the advantages in such a marriage. He had told her that there was no reason she shouldn't go to college. Education for women was one modern idea with good in it. Jacob Zimet, a fine-looking, healthy man. Many people valued the soft, wispy scholar who held his side when he breathed. She herself had never believed in that ideal, no. "Roll, Rachel; the dough will crack under the knife if it's too dry. Here—let me do it."

I waited for Miri to come home and tell me her mother had gone mad. When she came, she saw me, and before I could open my mouth, she said, "'Chelle, it's not what you think."

"What is it, then, and what do I think?"

She began to explain. It was a good match, she told me. He had indeed promised her a college education, and not class by class, one semester here and one there, eking out the degree, dependent on scholarships. "Jacob is nice and he doesn't expect me to spend my life in the kitchen. He gets along well with Papa. His parents are paying for remodeling a house for us—it's four blocks from here, a nice house with room for his study and his Torah and bar mitzvah classes, and I won't have to creep around the way Mama does, so as not to bother him."

"Nice house?" "Jacob is nice?" What was she talking about? Nice wasn't falling in love—nice wasn't something you give up long cherished dreams for. Mixed emotions, it's called. I called it shark soup. I felt betrayed, but how was I supposed to feel? Why shouldn't a friend fall in love and marry? Surely part of what I was fighting was envy, part plain selfish annoyance at the ruin of our plans. Once again, Miri had leapt ahead, twinkling and graceful, above the ordinary expectations of duller people. Miri's dreams had all been about freedom and what she would do. Of course, the meeting, and the marriage, had been arranged, a custom she had dedicated her life to escaping. Still—didn't arranged marriages often work out well? Wasn't he going to be part of her ambition, strong enough in himself to let her succeed? She saw my face and laughed. "'Chelle, you're living here— that won't change. I talked it over with Mama and Papa and they want you to come here anyway. We'll still study together, here or at my house. You won't suffer by my being married, really. It'll help all of us."

I told her about the scholarship—the Isidore Friedman, the best one, the one we wanted, and she jumped up and ran to me and took me by the shoulders, spinning me around and shouting a praise cheer we had learned in the third grade.

Afterward, I went home, muttering to myself like one of the street people we were beginning to see in our neighborhood. Why did I feel cheated? Why was I depressed? Was it envy, and feeling guilty for being envious? Or was it disappointment at not being able to go to college with Miri? I had no trust that her husband would let her go. Promises made before the glass is shattered are swept up and thrown away with the fragments.

But the next day, I went back and listened to Ada's exultation and congratulated Miri. They were so excited that I couldn't help being drawn in. The wedding. The mother-in-law. Never mind the groom, what was the mother like? Plans, gowns, tears of joy. When was the wedding? October, after the High Holy Days. So soon? Even with all the promises, a house, a college education, I knew that sunlight and adventure were going to draw away from Miri, and that she would disappear into the flattened world of 1970s Orthodoxy. Miri would become her mother and maybe my mother, howling at the search for sluts' wool under a dozen beds and tarnish on the candlesticks. Slowly, inexorably, it would happen.

Jacob Zimet was good-looking in a hulking way. I met him two weeks later at Miri's house and learned that the original plan had been for them to be married in Denver and then move to New York. Over the weeks of courtship, Jacob's asthma had been revealed, and Miri declared that Denver's fresh and health- ful air would surely be better for him than the smog of New York: Miri's magic. The wand never trembled in her hand.

Everyone here knew that Colorado was no better for asthma than anyplace else, and that the idea of its fresh air was a myth.

We all knew that Denver's air was as polluted as Manhattan's. Jacob's mother came to check out the bride. Miri charmed the old lady and floated the asthma-cure story on a waft of vapor. Didn't Denver have the best respiratory hospital in the country? Jacob's mother was anxious for her son. Did Denver really have libraries? Telephone service? Mail delivery? Did buses run on roads? Were there necessities for Jewish people here, kosher butchers, synagogues, boxes of matzo in the stores? A mikvah? A cemetery? I was almost crushed with laughter. I bit my cheeks and stifled my giggles and stopped hating Jacob at that minute. Miri smiled and everyone in the room smiled in response. Miri's charm worked with women as with men; she wasn't provocative or bubbly. She radiated responsiveness. Jacob's New York provincial mother and judgmental sisters were drawn to Miri's beauty, her health, the rapt shine, the glow of her approval. Are we not brighter, wittier than we thought we were? Are we not happier? Isn't the world lovelier now? Jacob himself was trailing Miri with his eyes, saying next to nothing, and as my anger left me, it was replaced by a slight condescension when I looked at him.

At that first meeting, I saw that Miri had laid the ground rules. Their marriage contract might be in Hebrew, but it included her education and a profession if she wanted one. "Yes, Miriam," he said, and "Yes, Miriam" again.

Knowing Jacob as I do now, I realize how much more of a mensh he is than I first believed. I try to see behind all that's happened since I met him, love-struck as he was. Remembering him in those days, I can see that "Jacob" then wasn't all Jacob's fault. He had been an "illui," intellectually precocious, and Jews have too soft a spot for precocity in their children. We idolize the little boy violinist, the rabbi in miniature, who has memorized the book of Leviticus and can stand up in a bar mitzvah tallis and sing it in half an hour. Jacob had been raised with an army of such partisans. Look what adulation did to Caligula. Figure we got off well.

I would come to understand that Jacob's asthma might have been made worse by a psychic throttling that had brought him here, where there is, literally, less pressure in the atmosphere.

Jacob allowed himself to be talked into the move. Miri's incandescent smile fed him, watered his roots. He bloomed in her presence. I heard his breathing ease as he sat at their table. The wedding was to be stunning.

I started school, fearful but eager. Miri's college plans were on hold until after the wedding. She began a hectic full-time round of shopping. Every day, it seemed there were things to be bought and ordered and fitted and fussed over. I went with her when I could, to pick out silver patterns and stationery, invitations and gifts for the guests at the reception, linens and household equipment. I helped her measure furniture and think about rugs and carpets, all the things we had sworn to each other we would never interest ourselves in doing. Miri sailed headlong into a maturity of acquisition and household choices. Cotton sheets or cotton blend? Ada Mordecai, the "Oh, Mother!" of a thousand heavenward looks and condescending giggles, was suddenly necessary for her advice, her fussiness transmuted into wisdom.

Miri was measuring her new in-laws also. "Jacob's family thinks this Denver move is temporary. His mother told me we'd be moving back to New York in a few years. She needs to know that he'll be living here, that we're not *moving* to New York to be with his family, so the more we remodel and the bigger we make the wedding and the more work he has here, the better. We make it sweet, we make it healthy and a good living; we make it convenient. Done and done." She clapped her hands one time and flicked the fingers, the way Ada did, flouring a bread board. "My idea is that after a few years here, maybe we can go to *California!* 'Chelle, are there Jews in Hawaii? Did I tell you he's been hired by the synagogue as head of Hebrew education? His parents were trying to say that the books he wants to write can only be written in New York, where the research resources are."

Those were the days before computers came and revolutionized the way study is done. I was back at the basics of Miri's life-to-be. "How are you going to keep house and go to college?"

"I'll manage it. After the wedding, you can move into my room at home. You can come over and study with me, every evening if you want. Mama and Papa are ready to have you.

29

Mama hated the idea of all her kids gone. You'll ease the pain by being here. I've thought all this out, 'Chelle. Everything that's happening will be good for you, too."

In the meantime, aluminum or stainless steel? What kind of mattress? What kind of headboard?

Miri's prospective wedding lit fires at home. Why wasn't I thinking of marriage? I'm still ashamed of the way I stood in the kitchen and shouted to my mother that I had no plans to marry and recreate the family I had grown up in. "You yell and scream at the way your life was ruined, that you're in hell, and now you want me to join you there."

"Your friend Miriam got herself a wonderful match, a scholar, but an earner, too. I hear the family's very well-set. She won't have to lift a finger. You can marry a man like that, a man who's not bitter; when they're successful, they're not angry and bitter all the time, and then life is good for everyone."

5

The words I remember my mother saying and the words I said and the way we both felt sound and feel antique to me now, echoing a time long past, but I know that in every cultural movement only some few of us rise or transform ourselves. The rest squat where we are and dig in for a long winter of siege. I had daily accounts of Miriam's progress, as though I hadn't been seeing her myself, lists of the gifts that were coming in, updates of information on the Zimets. My mother prodded; Ada exulted. I felt the awful weight of it all. Why a service for twelve if there wasn't the expectation that Miri would entertain lavishly? Why all the armentarium of a traditional kosher kitchen: dairy sets, meat sets, Passover sets doubled, if she weren't to spend long days in the elaborate preparation of the traditional foods?

I went to the Mordecais' often, and usually Jacob would be there. I liked his smile, his happiness, which spread to include everyone who loved Miri. He was glad to see me. In those days, men didn't touch women who weren't their wives, but his eyes warmed me with welcome. What was surprising to me, then, wasn't Jacob himself, eager, happy, hopeful Jacob, but Rabbi Mordecai, who, except for his chats with Miri, had sat mostly silent during the years I was at his table. He blessed, sat, ate, rose, and returned to his studies with a kindly but always preoccupied vagueness. Now he waited with his prospective son-in-law and became voluble and expansive on all kinds of subjects, scholarly and ordinary. His hands rose and fell in the discourse; his eyes were bright and genial, with a life I hadn't ever seen in them before except when he'd turned them on Miri. Watching the family then, I began to form my ideas about relationships that would affect the way I followed my professional work years later. I learned little from what he and Jacob said, but without being conscious of it, I began to study what I hadn't begun to learn in a formal way: what architecture spoke of, the ideas of seclusion and privacy, of company and community, and the elements of rooms and spaces designed for human use.

I also saw a look of puzzled concern on Ada's face as she studied Miri. These dinners were times when the prospective bride was meant to be intent on her fiancé, discerning his likes and dislikes, watching, reading his moods, listening deeply to his opinions, which, whether she agreed with them or not, would be the ground tones of her life. Instead of this, Miri took part in the discussion and seemed to notice nothing about which foods Jacob liked, which opinions he held, what made him comfortable, what distressed him.

Three days before the wedding, Orthodox New York emptied through a funnel pointing west. I was astonished as Ada told me of the number of rooms required at hotels and about the arrangements for kosher food. "Oh, yes," Miri told me, laughing, "by train and plane, by oxcart and stagecoach, by riverboat, barge, and ocean liner. Air transports darken the sky; the huge doors open and parachutes blossom in the air. They're coming; they're all coming."

The Mordecais certainly couldn't have borne the cost of such an enterprise. The Zimets must have done most of it, and gotten the worst of the deal.

But at last I would be at a real wedding. Shifrah and Shirah had married from our living room and we had to call neighbors to supply the extra plates, cups, and chairs.

School started and I was caught in the dislocation between the days of the Observant Jew and the secular season. Rosh Hashanah was on a Tuesday, a school day. Yom Kippur was a juggling act, as well. I bounced between school and synagogue, out of the rhythm of both, unwilling to sacrifice either entirely to the other. The all-or-nothing model of Orthodoxy collapsed.

After the High Holy Days came Miri's wedding, and it filled the synagogue. The gifts heaped two long tables in the huge downstairs hall. There, I watched a little old lady peering at the underside of one of a set of plates unwrapped for show. She stopped me, an age-spotted hand on my arm. "Ruchele"—the Yiddish affectionate diminutive of my name—"it's a blessing, isn't it, a *mechaiah*, your friend, and such a good match." She looked vaguely familiar. I smiled and moved to go on, but she spoke again. "I remember the two of you, so sweet, such lovely little girls, every week, *bikur cholim*—visiting the sick. My mother, may she rest in peace, used to tell me how wonderful it was, how you came with all those things you baked. What a mitzvah it was, a holy act, the two of you, with your sweet faces. All the old people waited all week to see you."

I felt like cringing, like weeping. I thanked her and moved around the clusters of other gawkers. Upstairs, I circled the groups in the sanctuary, and outside, standing in the warm glow of a Colorado mid-October Indian summer day, I felt miserable and invisible. Romantic love, Shifrah's husband had told me, was an American obsession. For observant Jews, he declared, expectations were understood and met, and from that, love came. Good luck to you, Shifrah, and many happy returns.

At the ceremony, I found myself weeping, and so was given credit for tender feelings I didn't possess. Other weepers embraced me, Jacob's aunts and mother, Ada, and Miri's aunts. We women stood on our side of the shoulder-high board that separated us from the men and watched Miri come down the aisle between us and do the traditional walk around her intended. Her veil wasn't so thick that we couldn't see her looking straight ahead. I have seen brides devour their grooms with their gazes as they circled them, adding a thrilling erotic note to the traditional proceedings. Downcast eyes weren't Miri's habit, but she kept them level, so we didn't know what she was thinking. None of what she did seemed real to me.

Beside me, Shirah was whispering. "She's doing the right thing, Rachel. Did you see the table downstairs? Have you seen the house they fixed up?" I gave her a look I had been using too often lately. Maybe someone would rush in with the news that the Messiah was coming down Colfax Avenue, headed west, and we had to get out there before He was away and up into the mountains. Maybe the wedding would be broken up by a dybbuk, a wandering ghost inhabiting the groom or the bride, or both. Let those spirits get married instead. Jacob spoke his vow. Miriam spoke hers. Each said that he and she would be "separated" for each other according to the laws of Moses and Israel. The glass was shattered, Jacob all but jumping on it. Mazel tov.

She found me sitting on the floor in the synagogue coatroom, which, in the warm weather, held only someone's forgotten sweater. I was crying, and Miri, in a perfect Miri moment, bridal gown and all, sat down beside me. "How could you?" I croaked. "And don't tell me this was sudden passion."

"I told you I had it all figured out," she said, "and it's okay, really, 'Chelle. Jacob can be worked around. He's better out here than he was in New York, and as he gets more success, he'll be even better. Look at my father. Did you ever see him so happy? Look at my mother; she's got the son-in-law she wants and all of us safely married. I'll be in college full-time and we won't have children until I'm through. You'll move into my room and be fussed over and you and I will stay best friends and we'll study together. All of us will be getting what we want. Later, California."

She took me in her arms and hugged me. "I know you think this is a mistake, and that I'll drown in the house among all the dishes, pots, and pans. It won't happen."

"Promise me."

"I promise."

"You have to go," I said. "They'll be looking for you."

"Let them look; they'll never find us here."

We both leaned back against the wall, Miri, in her cloud of tulle, me, blowing my nose. We sat, resting and talking and then for a few minutes half-adoze, and then she sighed and rose and gathered her wedding finery around her and floated out into married life.

6

Miri and Jacob went to Key West for the honeymoon, staying at a resort for the Orthodox that was glatt kosher and carefully observant (twin beds and toilet paper pretorn for Shabbat). She sent me a postcard of the place showing the rooms and the elegant buffet, tasteful as any in Europe. "Beautiful beach," she wrote on it, "wonderful eats. They even imported three old ladies to sit on the porch and stare at me to see if the wedding night had accomplished its goal. No, I'm not. I'll call you when I get home."

I'd told my father I wanted to study architecture. I'd said it out of need for something to say, and because I'd said the word, I began to say it to myself and then to an adviser at Denver University. Luckily, no one asked me why I had chosen that study, and years would pass before I could put my reasons into words. Isidore Friedman, my scholarship benefactor, was long dead, and the administrators of his grant met with me only once a year. I would send in my grades and write an essay each year stating what I had accomplished and what I planned for the year ahead.

But something denies the impersonality of such a situation. Miri and I laughed about our foursome, she and Jacob, Isidore and I. She emerged from the honeymoon happy and not pregnant. All the wedding prep had put her a quarter behind me at DU, but there were still many classes open to her. She spent the weeks until the quarter began furnishing the house. People had begun to visit almost immediately. "Don't they read their Torah?" I complained. "Isn't there supposed to be a time allowed for the newlyweds to be alone?"

"That page fell out of the book," Miri said, "but I'm not suffering. I wouldn't want you to stay away."

I'd been going there to escape the anger and ugliness of failure at home. Twice a day, I would start to tell my parents I was leaving for Miri's house; every time, I would be stopped by some compunction, until I realized that I was hoping for a blowup by my father or a hysterical outburst by my mother that would end with her saying: "You don't like it here? Leave us, then." When I was at the newlyweds' home, I helped Miri, who kept moving furniture at whim. Jacob was called in for the heavy stuff, but the third time Miri enlisted his muscle for the couches, he said, "Decide it and then call. If this is a bodybuilding enterprise, I'll summon my students and they can all help." He was smiling as he said it. I think he was delighted with the work—the first time, I'm sure, that he was ever summoned for anything but a scholarly opinion or a demonstration of brilliance.

"Stay for supper, Rachel," he told me, "or I'll end up doing the dishes."

I liked him. He enjoyed us and our playfulness together. Sometimes when Miri's parents came, Rabbi Mordecai would listen to us and grumble about women's chatter, but I could see that Jacob drew a secret pleasure from our take on life. He was turning into a very social man, one who enjoyed looking down his table and seeing groups of guests. "So tell me, Rachel, how are your classes in school?"

"All intro stuff, survey of this and that. The classes are huge and they glop out the knowledge like the servers at a steam table."

"So being a woman helps there. You'll separate the fat and the gristle from the meat, make stew, and from the bones a nourishing soup." He gleamed at Miri. "Mirele, what kind of student is Ruch'l?" He was playing Talmud with her. "Is she the sponge, the funnel, the sieve, or the strainer?"

We both answered at once, but I said "funnel" and Miri said "sponge."

Miri started at the university. She was taking a full program and coming home late, but the elaborate meals of the early weeks of marriage continued. There were holishkes, sweet-sour and rich with tomato sauce. There were helzels with kashe, crusty challahs soft in the middle, chicken soup with homemade noodles. Where were they coming from? I knew Miri to be even less interested in cooking than I was, but when I saw those absolutely mathematical pillows of stuffed cabbage leaves, I knew that Ada must be coming over to help Miri when guests were at the house and that we were dining on the leftovers. Jacob's relations often visited, and in surprising numbers. They were all too pious to stay in hotels. That spring and summer, there must have been thirty of them, some staying for a week at a time. I helped when I could, but I began to realize that Ada was doing all the cooking and that she was taking Miri and Jacob's wash home, returning it ironed and folded. The sheets went to a laundry.

"If I'm running a hotel," Miri said, "it's necessary to have a staff."

"But every day—"

"We worked it out together. Mama couldn't make all that food just for Papa alone. She makes double pans and brings one over, or I pick it up on my way home from school."

I looked over and saw the helzel, stuffed chicken-neck skin, redolent with onion and garlic, lying in the neat rows. On the counter, a braided challah cooled. It had none of the bumps and knobs my mother produced in hers.

I was still waiting at home, afraid to make my move to the Mordecais'. I knew the change would make a monthlong marathon of gossip in the neighborhood, folded into the blintzes, bubbling in the stews. I slept at home, I studied at Miri's, I ate Ada's meals.

Miri had told us that she would be studying accounting and finance. The idea was that with those skills, she could take what Jacob earned and what he was to inherit and build a solid, dependable wealth. The women in Jacob's family had often managed the finances and done well for their families while the men studied and wrote. Yet, as the quarters progressed, the books I saw on her table were texts on physiology and cytology, not the simple survey course I was taking.

"Science is more interesting than fiddling with numbers and trying to make equations come out right," she said. "I dropped bookkeeping and took this lab course instead."

37

"What does Jacob think?"

"He doesn't know yet."

As I look back at those years, I realize that secretiveness wasn't an occasional convenience for us, but a consistent pattern in our lives. Miri and I hid plans, ideas, activities, first out of a need to flout the rules of our parents' piety, and then to accommodate our own causes, freedom, cowardice, laziness. My sisters had hidden their lipsticks and miniskirts. Ab and Art had been secret smokers. I hid when I felt a reason, but Miri's secrecy was a natural response, used beyond the need.

"When are you going to tell him?"

"I'm not lying to him; I'm simply not telling him the details yet. And I will take the courses we planned, later, but 'Chelle, biology, genetics, biochemistry—it's all so exciting. Remember how great it was in high school?"

I didn't.

We were busy and happy. I was studying drafting and the history of architecture and taking a structural class, where there were thirty men and four women. I went out with two of the guys, but nothing came of it. My mother was incredulous.

"Architecture? Your classes must be full of men. Can't you find someone in any of them?"

"I guess not."

"If you put some makeup on . . ."

Miri was also getting static. She must have been getting it heavily, because I was having to answer for her in synagogue and supermarket, at the bookstore and the dry cleaner's. "It's your punishment for staying in the neighborhood," I told her.

"What are they saying?"

Of course she knew. Jacob's cheering section, the bar mitzvah mothers and the ladies of the sisterhood and all the relatives, his and hers, had begun to wonder when Miri would become pregnant. They stopped me in the street and cornered me when they saw me. "Your friend—such a lovely girl, and Rabbi Jacob, what a wonderful family they would make. How long is it, a year? And what about you, Rachel, not a man in sight yet?"

By that time, Rabbi Mordecai had recovered from his first heart attack, a light one, a tap of warning, the doctor had said, but the diagnosis had sounded like doom in his ears and he became more demanding than before and more impatient. He wanted a grandchild, two, three perhaps. His present grandkids were all far away. Ada didn't nag Miri, but I could see that she, too, was measuring her, counting weeks and months. I listened to Rabbi Mordecai all but disown Miri's eldest brother, Noah, when he learned that Noah and his wife drove to the synagogue on Shabbat. The rabbi had hoped for a dynasty of scholar exegetes. Elias, married and then divorced in California, had become a computer whiz and was designing something that would make him wealthy. Now there was only Jacob, who came up to Miri's father's expectations, but after six months, no pregnancy, after a year, no child, no boy.

Jacob himself must have felt some of this pressure, but he was so bird-happy that the comments and suggestions rolled off him and he took all of them as a sign of his belonging. "Mirele, Mrs. Kovner says you should sleep with potato eyes under your pillow."

"Why not Mrs. Kovner's eyes instead?"

"She means well. It's the old-fashioned way—lots of babies quickly. Really, you know, I think that idea comes from the pogroms in the old country. We're here now, so we don't have to reproduce before the Cossacks try to kill us. Ruch'l, pass me some more of that potato pudding."

The blowup that moved me out of the house and into Miri's came halfway through my sophomore year. The university was deep in town, and my father began to complain about my being out at all hours. My scholarship committee had given me praise for my grades and my declaration of a rigorous major. I was proud of my accomplishments, proud that my professors felt that I had the makings of an architect. My father demanded that I stop night classes. Weeping with rage, I fled the argument going to the Mordecais', and moved in the next day. I would spend the following year and a half there, in Miri's room, whose two windows looked out on to a backyard where two beautiful cherry trees supplied me with blossoms and Ada with cherries for the Passover wine. There were lilacs there, too. I got a little table and floor seat and studied out there on mild days. I was as happy as I had ever been, maybe pretending to be Miri, a Miri thrillingly conscious of how blessed it was to sit under the lilacs. On Tuesday and Thursday afternoons, I studied at her house.

"Miri, you smell terrible."

"It's the path lab—the stuff they use hangs like a cloud. I usually get off the bus a stop or two before I need to and walk home. This time, I was too tired. Stay for dinner, 'Chelle. Jacob is out tonight and I was going to cram for a test, so we can work together all evening."

"What's the inducement?"

"Liver and potato knishes—Mom's."

"I want to remember how luscious these smells are—what Ada brings over here, the roasting meat and fried onions, bread-baking fragrance, dark-bake odors, sugar smells, butter smells. When I was a kid, I'd get them before Ada opened the door. The places I design all banish food smells for potpourri. In modern kitchens, you have to arrange space for the fans that take away all those delicious odors."

"I like our houses neutral, not remembering what we ate last night."

"Miri, when I'm dying, I won't see a bright light at the end of a tunnel; I'll smell Ada's kitchen on a Shabbas evening."

Because of Rabbi Mordecai's condition, the food I ate at their house was "healthier" now. To get Ada's best, I had to eat at Miri's.

I sat in her kitchen and looked around. She had been in the house for over a year, but the kitchen wasn't hers yet. Upstairs, the rooms used by all those relatives had the same impersonal, pleasant blandness. There was no part of Miri in them.

Miri's home was in the attic. She had a thick rug and two Japanese floor chairs, stacked sets of boxes of raw wood that served as bookcases and filing cabinets. She had a typewriter and another small table. But for the rug, the place was austere, but it was definitely hers, as she liked it. She had told me, "No one can take this room over, no matter how many of them come. I keep the door locked."

That statement made me sad. The servant life was falling over her like a burka. The attic refuge reminded me too much of the attic we had furnished in her father's house, our secret place there.

"On Friday, Jacob's cousins and the three boys come, but not to this room." She gave a little grin, one I could remember on the face of a ten-year-old. We had gone to a candy store just out of the neighborhood, where people bought food and never questioned the origin of each ingredient. We had purchased fifteen five-cent marshmallows (gelatin, an animal product) covered with milk chocolate (a milk product), and eaten them all on the way home. They were delicious. Had I done that alone, would I have savored that taste?

Over dinner, I described my classes and my joy in what I was learning. Architecture is at the same time the most visible and most subtle of the ways people organize themselves, I told Miri. I gloried in the excitement I was feeling. "Look at how you can use more of the space to give both privacy and a sense of openness. Now, if I were designing the spaces in this house . . ."

Some of the work I do now is a response to Miri's old cry for privacy, a place of her own. Miri herself has changed; that big house in Denver so fussed over, so decorated, is now being lived in by others. The ways we took to become the people we are, are now paved over or gone to weed.

Because I lived at Miri's parents' house, I was in on all the holiday celebrations there—Shabbat, Purim, Passover, the High Holy Days, Sukkot, and Simchat Torah. On the days Jacob and Miri came to the Mordecais' house, the men would go off together to study or nap a little between services. At those times, I watched Jacob to see if his new status in the community was freezing him, but it didn't seem to be. His growing status relaxed and quieted him. In the first months of his marriage, he would leave the room with his eyes whenever Miri left it, even if for a moment. Later, he would turn to me, smiling, and say, "Mirele looks happy, doesn't she?" Then he would tell me about the brilliant Katz boy, or the funny mistake the Katz boy's cousin made. His kindness wasn't imposed; it was, I think, a function of his happiness.

The car has hit a rut and Escobar mutters a curse. The bump throws me sideways and pain from my bruises is so sudden that I cry out. Miri and I had a fight before we left, a violent one— thrown plates, pots and pans swung out, and a fierce joy when they landed. In our rage, neither of us felt much pain, but as this trip has continued, the protecting narcotic of emotion has worn off. I'm aching all over. It's been worse, of course, since Escobar left the paved roads and began our trip on this trail. He is driving faster than he should. The car bucks and rocks up and down, side to side. Now and then, he loses the trail and has to turn on his low beams to get a wider spread of light.

Miri hears my little yelp of pain. She, too, has bruises. I've felt her moving to ease a sore arm and shoulder. The car bounces again and throws me against her and we both cry out this time, so that Escobar says, "You ladies doin' okay back there?" He hadn't seen the brawl—another officer had come in on that—but I'm sure he's been told to watch us, two middle-aged broads who get into catfights.

"We're okay," I say.

Beside me, Miri snarls, "Don't answer for me, Rachel; I didn't want you along."

"Like you've been such a success at running this," I say. "You don't want me here, but the cops do—ask Escobar. If you have to insist on your rights and demand to be here, ask any of the cops how happy they'd be, having to put up with you alone."

"Your being here was their idea, not mine. We've had too much of you in our lives, Rachel."

Our voices have risen. "Listen, Miriam, you selfish—"

But Escobar slews over into a rut, and I can hear him wrestling with the steering wheel. He shouts back at us to shut up, and we subside, muttering.

She had no right to say these things to me. We were friends, best friends, protecting and defending each other. We were—we had been—loyal and loving.

7

Miriam had been married to Jacob for two years. Jacob was at the synagogue most Tuesday and Thursday evenings, and I was at their house regularly to be with her. That time was the happiest of my young womanhood. I loved the warmth and order at the Mordecais'. I loved studying with Miri, Jacob's friendly acceptance, the opening of my intellectual world, and the dawning call of my profession. I told Miri about my days and she told me about hers.

"It's almost like reading kabbalah," she told me. "Listen to what this book says: 'Our beings are fragile and tough. A fifth-of-a-second pause in the electrical charge sent into our hearts between forty and one hundred and fifty times a minute, varying with demand almost instantaneously, can bring on arrhythmia and death.' How does that pause come to be, 'Chelle? Do you know that a bone repairs itself in the form it once had? How come? Why are some cancers quick and others slow? What decides? What are the secrets?"

I sat with her on those evenings and watched her, and thought, Miri herself can light a room. "Do the people in your classes know you're married to a rabbi?"

"Some do. One of them in my cytology class said it was a waste. They all seem younger than Jacob, raw, peeled, in a way. If the people in this neighborhood knew how well the local boys stack up, they wouldn't worry so much about my virtue."

"So people here still nag you?"

"God yes. 'How come I don't see a little stomach on you, darling? Married how long now? Isn't it almost three years? Isn't it time to do something for your parents? When I was married two years, I already had my Chaim, and my Dvora was on the way. Have them now, darling, and you'll all grow up together.'"

"Enough. Has it been that relentless?"

"Only three times a week everyone asks me when. It's one more reason Mama should do my shopping. The questions my pathology professor asks me have some dignity at least."

"Miri . . ." I turned my eyes to the textbooks on the table next to us. She had them in a pile: cytology, *The Disease Process,* hematology. Beside us on the table was a crisp-edged, flaky streudel. She began to cut it. "How long will you be able to keep your study a secret from Jacob?"

"It's necessary, 'Chelle, or I wouldn't do it."

"Won't he come in one day and find you working and ask what relationship hematology has to accounting? You do smell sometimes from the lab. Won't you be spending whole shifts in the hospital?"

"I do them now. As long as I'm home to smile at his relatives and pull a kugel out of the oven, he doesn't ask. I do our bills and keep the household accounts, and it's worked out so far."

"He leaves it all to you?"

"Think of our growing up, Rachel, when you were over at our house. My father lived his ideal life. He studied Talmud by himself and with groups of scholars. He wrote books about the books he read. He never studied the weather—he would be surprised to look up and see it had been snowing for two days. Earthly systems, politics, war, art, modern history, medicine were all outside his interest. The Holocaust was an event that made him lift his head briefly from his texts, but it only made him more convinced that anything outside of Jewish Law was a termite mound."

"And Jacob?"

"Jacob is aiming for just that elevation. It's the ideal, after all, the way life should be."

"That elevation seems off to me—the writers of the Talmud were all practical workingmen; some were laborers. Your father—"

"Knew what season it was by the portion of Torah they were reading in the synagogue. The Talmudic writers were a different breed from its readers."

"And Jacob?

44

"Jacob dreams of being free of extraneous worries and practical things. When he learned that Rabbi Gemaliel used to cut the vegetables for the Shabbat stew, he came home and cut two carrots and peeled three potatoes and went to his study."

"Not telling him seems dangerous. Aren't you afraid it will come out?"

"It's hiding in plain sight, 'Chelle. If he wanted to know, he'd look." She smiled at me. "And before I leave DU, I will take a bookkeeping and accounting class—I really will."

I didn't see Jacob as being consciously oblivious. I thought his not noticing Miri's work was because he had so much to do. He taught four or five classes, studied with Rabbi Mordecai and others, and saw the division of labor—men's days and women's—as he had been taught.

Miri also saved her excitement about her studies for me. "The cell is a miracle, 'Chelle—it's life with everything packed inside. Listen to this," she pulled me in, greeting me one Tuesday evening. "I've been reading about a bacteria—it says, 'virulent in blood samples, its effects toxic.' It's been seen in the blood of wealthy Japanese men and rigidly kosher and observant older Jewish women." She led me to the table. "There was an outbreak in Jerusalem that killed one woman and sent three others to the hospital. The two other recent outbreaks were in Kobe, at a geisha house, among upper-level Japanese industrialists, but not the geishas themselves."

"I'm at a loss." We sat eating potato pancakes, so crisp that they all but scratched the plate. "Was it only Jewish women?"

"Only strictly *frum* Jewish women."

"In summer?"

"No," Miri said, grinning. "For the Japanese men, it was in summer."

"I've got it!" I turned to her and waved my fork. "Japanese men take long, hot baths, and Orthodox Jewish women go to the mikvah. Something in the water!"

"Lots of people go to the mikvah, men and women."

"You know the answer?"

"I do."

"Give me a hint."

45

"It's related specifically to a one-week period involving the phases of the moon."

"Passover."

"Right."

"Then I have it. The geishas all make matzo brai fried up with onions and eggs for their clients. The eggs go bad and the men get sick. What's the answer?"

"Sushi."

"How could I have been so dense? All Orthodox women eat sushi at Passover."

"Visualize those Orthodox women, 'Chelle. There they stand, chopping the fish for gefilte fish. Watch them."

"Oh, God, they're *tasting* it to see if there's enough salt, enough of whatever spices each one uses. They taste it when it's raw to see— Oh, Miri, raw fish!"

"Right. I put that together, and how I loved it when the light went on. Sure, another guy had figured it out, but I love the mystery in pathology. How did these cells get here? Why do some die and some thrive? Is this harmless biote suddenly toxic? The dead can speak, and viruses can, as Jacob would say, discourse."

"Why don't you let Jacob in on what you're doing? It's not as if you were into black magic, gibbering spells in a corner. You'll soon be earning money doing it."

"Jacob has money and it doesn't interest him. The accounting I'm supposed to be studying is about law, about order in a domestic universe in which he's only interested as a consumer. In the meantime, Denver's growing and inquiring minds want to know. I'm in demand."

I loved being Miri's confidante, her only one. I loved being a keeper of secrets, watching, knowing, being on the very inside of things. It's the fun of being a conspiracy addict, knowing what only the insiders know.

On Yom Kippur, they name all the sins. I wonder if I ever heard them name that one.

46

8

The lie ruptured in a single afternoon a week after Miri had told me about the raw fish. She called me at the Mordecais' when she knew Ada would be out.

"The virus has invaded," she said. "The ballet dancer has tripped on her own laces and fallen flat on her face, just like that."

"What's happened?"

"Come on over. Jacob is at school."

She was seldom out of the pathology lab, she told me, but that afternoon, she had been carrying a tray of blood samples from the pediatric floor, downstairs. The senior pathologist had been afraid of an outbreak of a virus in the ward. Walking into the elevator, there was Mrs. Becca Isaacson, flowers in hand, making a visit. "I stood there, frozen and not three feet from her, and my tray started to shake, those glass tubes and the slides of blood all stuttering in their little slots. I tried to think of something I could say—there I was in a lab coat with the name tag on it, and 'Pathology.' I wasn't visiting the sick; I was *working* there. She saw it and I knew she saw it, and by the time I got home, half the Jewish population of the Rocky Mountains must know it, and the news is now traveling into Wyoming."

My mother was in on it two days after Mrs. Isaacson's hospital visit. She cornered me on my weekly appearance. "Your friend's been playing games on her husband." Her tone rang with accusation.

"What games? Which friend?" I felt as though I had fallen through the ice, and the lie wasn't even mine.

"Miriam Mordecai Zimet is *who*, and *what* is God knows what. Becca Isaacson saw her being some kind of hospital person, doctor, nurse. What was she doing there? I thought she was supposed to be in college."

"She is. She's studying to be a pathologist. I think she'll do that, or be a medical examiner."

My mother turned her hard look on me again. "So you knew all along? You're not lying, are you?"

"Am I training for a career? Yes. Is Miri? Yes. What's so bad about that?"

"She's supposed to be married, being a mother, making a home. The college thing was to keep her doing something until the babies come."

"Those days are gone," I said.

"That career thing will cook her goose," my mother said.

I look at the Orthodox community now and see changes there that, for all its denial of change, are huge and pervasive. Observant women are working at skilled jobs and daughters are as likely as sons to go to college. What my mother said in the mid-seventies, and didn't herself believe, seems quaint now. I need to remember that the world of my neighborhood was still reeling from its horror at the sexual revolution let loose in the Vietnam years. It had drawn in tighter, turned itself into a knot of refusal. When my mother speaks to me out of those remembered wars, I cringe with embarrassment for her.

Jacob found out on Shabbat. When the sun was down, Miri called me. "I'm coming over. Jacob knows."

"Won't he want you there?"

"I'm giving him a chance to assimilate all of it. I shouldn't have to see him before he's ready. Don't tell my folks—let me do that."

"I wouldn't touch that one."

"What are they doing?"

"Your mom's ironing in the kitchen, watching *Lucy* reruns with the sound off. Your dad's in the study. He left the table about half an hour ago."

Miri was there almost before I hung up. "I flew here on my broomstick, and I think Jacob might divorce me."

I must have looked shocked. "Jacob said college was okay."

"The trip has changed. It's been over two years and no child. I've deceived him about what I do all day, and, according to him, in the worst possible way. In my handling of diseased pieces of flesh, no matter how small, dead flesh, I've purposely been endangering the potential being that should have been forming in me. I didn't tell him I was taking the Pill, either. Who wants a baby while she's in college? I am bringing the threat of plague into our home, he said. When I told him that was nonsense and that I wanted to continue in my career, he all but froze in disgust."

"Did you defend what you were doing?"

"I told him how much I loved the work, how vital it is, that it undergirds all of medicine. I told him I could spend all my life, a good life, doing this work and never come to the end. He says that about the Talmud. Why shouldn't I have my Talmud? It isn't fair."

"Do you want to stay with him?"

"Sure, I'm willing, but I don't want to give up what I've fought for, what I worked for so hard."

"You hid, Miri. He must be angrier about that than about anything else."

"What he said about bringing disease home—it was so stupid."

"I don't think he meant all that—he's a modern man."

"He's a modern man who wishes more and more that he was medieval."

"You can't believe that—he was hurt. You hurt him and he hit back."

"'Chelle, I won't give this up. I'm going on, married or single. I run Jacob's hotel and carry a full load at school. He should be proud of me. He should stand up and cheer."

"He won't do that when he's been kept from it all this time. Listen, Miri—why don't we work on this? I can get the names of some pathologists who are observant Jews. We might even get them to write or call Jacob."

"His objection isn't based on being Jewish, but on being Jacob. He's always been protected and coddled. When he has a cold, the sun stands still."

"Why don't you want to work your magic on this? You know how to sweeten things, how to move people. Why not now?"

"I'm tired of faking, of smiling, of running a hotel."

"You don't run a hotel. Ada does, and you've always charmed everyone silly. You can charm Jacob, too."

"He wants kids. Lots of them. He wants a normal life, he says, and he gets to decide what normal is. When I started college, I didn't know how much I wanted to do this, so it didn't matter. Now I know, and it does matter. It matters a lot."

"Rachel?" Jacob was on the phone. "I can't come over there and you know it's not fitting for me to see you alone. If I meet you at some local place, there will be talk. I need to speak to you."

"It takes only one Becca Isaacson with a mouth on her like the great white whale."

"Do you know a place where we can meet?"

"Bandimere," I said.

"Where they race the cars?"

"One of my classmates races there. This Sunday afternoon, they're having a demolition derby. I doubt if Becca Isaacson goes to those. Dress appropriately."

That Jacob came at all testified that his love overwhelmed his anger. I'll give him this: His outfit was his idea of a workingman's togs—a T-shirt, baseball cap (they hadn't started wearing them backward yet), and an old pair of gardening pants held up by suspenders.

"All you need is a wad in your lip and you'd fit right in."

"A wad?"

"Chewing tobacco."

"My grandfather took snuff," he said.

"In his cheek?"

"Listen, Rachel; it's too noisy here."

"Sound rises," I said. "We go and sit under the stands."

We ended up in Jacob's car. "She lied to me, Rachel," he said.

"I know. I kept warning her."

"'Warning her'? Am I a bomb in the road?"

"Miri doesn't take to confinement very well, to rules."

"I love her, and I want her to remain my wife. Can you tell her? I try, but I see her face freeze when I start to talk to her."

50

"You said some hard things, Jacob, about bringing diseases into the house."

"Not into the house, into her body. What I said sounded wrong, even to me, when I said it, but we've been married for two years and no baby, and she was working with the worst kind of plagues and germs and taking the drugs that do God knows what to her body to stop it from its natural work."

"What if Miri found she couldn't have children, what then?"

"Then we would weep and adopt. Israel has children left parentless in wars."

"That's not Miri. You want a Miri doll, not the person herself."

"She lied to me, Rachel. She deceived me, every day, every night. She took a pill to keep her sterile and empty. She nodded yes and yes and had no intention of making a family. Yes and yes and hated Shabbat, with all the relatives coming."

"She says you made a servant of her."

"That part is true. What's also true is that she made me so proud and happy, I wanted everyone to see that I was more than a book, a student with a better memory than the other students had. Talk to her, Rachel."

"A marriage counselor?"

"Inside the community, everyone would know. Someone outside the community—they look at me and see a zealot and a cult person, all but a lunatic."

It never occurred to me that I'd been reading Torah wrong all these years. The biblical Jacob needed both Rachel and Leah as wives. Laban's treachery in substituting Leah so he could get another seven years of work out of Jacob was a side issue. Jacob needed one to love inordinately, another to be married to, with all that meant.

"Talk to her. I can hire help for her—cooks, maids. When the babies come, I'll get people to help. She can go to school. She can be a scientist."

Men are accustomed to fixing things, pushing buttons, making happen what they think should happen. If I hadn't caught the real sorrow, the real confusion in Jacob, I would have been embarrassed, appalled by his naked need. "We want men to be open," I would tell Miri later, "and then, when they let us know how they feel, we criticize them for it."

We heard the clamor of a high moment in the derby from far away. Someone screamed; there was a protest of tires, a crash, and then another.

"Please, Rachel, please."

"I'll talk to her."

The car bumps along and I wonder how the rescuers could have found this cave, how Val and Tamar found it. The thought confuses me. I remembered Tamar saying they had stumbled on it, a sudden, serendipitous discovery. What were they doing up here, so deep in the mountains? I'd always trusted Val, who had never been reckless—I'd been caving with him myself. He'd been careful, very careful, and he wasn't ambitious, because I would have caught it in him. His dreams for Miri were for marriage, and for Tamar that he would bring her along as a caver, probably as a caving partner later, when she was in her teens, ready, trained. His love, his passion, was all for Miri. How had they discovered this cave?

More talk from the radio and Escobar keeps contact, but we can't hear what he's saying, because his soft voice is lost under the pounding of our wheels on the trail. He calls back to us. "Not long now. We ought to be there in ten or fifteen minutes."

Miri grinds her teeth and whispers harshly, "He's so proud of himself. He blundered onto the right road and now he thinks he should get a medal."

We're still angry. My arm is throbbing and she hasn't spoken a civil word since we left Boulder. My own anger is mixed with sadness, exhaustion, anxiety, and hope, a whole bouquet of emotions, many of them contradictory. It comes to me that part of Miri's charm is the purity of her feeling. Ambivalence makes us strain, work too hard or give up too easily. Uncertainty clouds our eyes, makes our gestures graceless, our smiles waver. We strike people as being inauthentic, phony. Miri is sure. Her lines are clear and straight as the part in her hair. This charm of hers isn't only her beauty. I always knew that.

There are lights ahead. The car has jounced against some sort of bank and lurched a little bit sideways, and there they are, lights and fires, a brave little outpost against the surrounding night. No wonder ancient people worshiped fire. Escobar, to my amazement, stops the car, turns back to us, and says: "I need to talk to you before we come on-scene." He gets out and moves around to my side, opens the door, and slips in beside me. On my left, Miri groans with impatience.

"I need for you to know," Escobar says, "that the more you demand for yourselves, the slower the rescue's gonna go. If you really wanna help, you'll stay where the captain says and do what he tells you. I haven't radioed us in yet because I wanted to clue you in to what you need to do to help us. Cap'n Hale is in charge over all. We've got people here from Boulder Grotto Cavers; we've got the Boulder County Sheriff's Department, and Clear Creek Rescue in support. We've got a medevac chopper on standby and a Clear Creek ambulance, if the weather makes an air evac impossible. That's lots of people. When you get that, you get a complicated scene, and you don't want to do anything to make it worse. Do you understand?" He looks at Miri and softens. "You're the mom, and naturally you want to know everything that happens. Don't demand the officers' time or extra attention. Believe me, we all feel for you. The press will be coming soon, and if you really want to help, you'll take the weight off us by keeping them busy. Okay?" We nod. "Let's go."

The unwanted mother and the even more unwanted friend bump into the camp and park outside the ring of light. "Stay here and stay warm," Escobar says. "I'll come and get you when Cap'n can see you."

I put my head back against the seat and try to remember all the moves that got me here.

54

9

Miri and Jacob were divorced three months later. I saw him alone one more time.

"Not the auto race, please, Rachel."

"No—Ada and Rabbi Mordecai go to her sister's this Sunday. Why not come over then?"

We were in a strange situation. Miri had moved out and wouldn't go back to her parents. I was with them; she was in an apartment near the school.

"I'll come, but I'm not ready to see them, not yet."

He sat uneasily in this house where he had had some of the happiest times of his life. "Is she sure, Rachel?"

"I think so, yes."

"I know you've been in the middle of all of this, trying to be a good friend and a good person. Why didn't you tell me?"

"I couldn't. It would have been gossip—"

"All of a sudden, they get pious."

"Why didn't you look at the books she was studying?"

"I feel like a terrible fool."

"She was trying to do it all—be what she was supposed to be and what she wanted to be."

"I can't stop feeling that she lied and betrayed me."

"I'm sad about it, too."

"I still love her. I only want what's real between us. She wants to make a career? Let her. She can keep house and have babies, too. Why not? People will help her. The woman—"

"You ran a hotel."

"She never told me she didn't want to live an ordinary Jewish life. Why did she deceive me?"

"Do you really think she can be a pathologist and keep the kind of home you're used to, and have a large family, and keep all the holidays with all of their demands?"

"That's our lives—that's what our lives are."

He looked at me in such open grief that I felt my eyes sting. His love had been simple, direct, taking utterly for granted a whole list of presuppositions and expectations, to which Miri had never signed on. He was humiliated, bereft in a landscape he didn't recognize. In our snug, closed world, men and women did not see each other alone. He had broken that rule in his terrible anguish. Watching him suffer was all but unbearable. We were sitting at Ada's table. I had made tea, which I had forgotten to pour. I reached out and covered his hand with mine. Gently, almost tenderly, he removed his hand.

Miri didn't miss one of her classes or a day in the lab. Because the divorce was uncontested, the Jewish procedure was simple and quick. The secular divorce took longer and cost more, but its matter-of-factness surprised me. Shouldn't they at least ritually tear up a pillowcase?

I was in court for the decree looking covertly at Jacob, who was pale and was wearing an unpressed shirt that was a little yellow. Ada was no longer doing his laundry, Clorox and then sun-bleaching in her backyard. Afterward, Miri and I went for coffee and then to her lab at the hospital. "Look at me," she said, and, half singing, twirled in a circle and lifted her arms over her head. "I'm free. 'Chelle, you should get married and then divorce. Then you won't have to listen to everybody giving you bad advice. When you divorce, they give up on you. Mama looks sad, but mostly, I think, it's because she's upset at what people are saying."

There she stood, smiling and relaxed. Her joy overtook my picture of Jacob's drawn face as he sat in court, his agony apparent and wide-open. He had been given the house. "He'll be lonely there," I said.

Miri grinned. "Sure, for a month. I can hear the tectonic plates of the continent shift as we speak, with the gathering stampede of widows and divorcées on the move. I was married for over two years and he got what he wanted every day—home-cooked meals on time, a willing bed partner, laundry done, and an observant household."

"But Ada made—"

"It didn't really matter to him who did his laundry or made his dinner. He never asked me if the system was working well, if eating at five or seven or eight would be more convenient for me, or if he could help by picking up the clothes he left on the floor after stepping out of them. Would it be better to tell his relations to come on the weekends or during the week, or after Pesach? He never asked. And I knew that I would be the one to raise the children, too, except for the occasional helpful criticism from him if they made noise. I'm my father's daughter, after all. Don't you remember that damn quiet?"

God no; I remembered the luscious quiet, the sweet calm and order of Miri's house, the neatness, the smell of good cooking that lay like a blessing on those who came and didn't carry with it the undertang of unwashed clothes or leftovers moldy with disinterest. My mother's argument with the world was long and loud; she hated housekeeping, and although we lit our candles precisely at the minute published on the Jewish calendar hanging in the kitchen, the Shabbat Shalom, the peace of the Sabbath, was drowned in anger and chaos. When I'm overtired and overburdened, even today, I can send my thoughts back to Miri's house, where they rest gently in memory, where I walk its rooms and sit at its Shabbat-set table and contemplate the world that Shabbat should open to all its children.

Miri was moving ahead. "Jacob has the house, yes, and in fifteen minutes he'll have a wife to put in it. I'm ready to find an apartment, and it won't be here, in the neighborhood. A world is waiting for me outside this ghetto, and I want to be part of it."

I, too, was coming to the end of the happiest time I had lived so far. The college year was ending and I would soon leave the Mordecais' home.

Miri's idea about Jacob's future was right on the mark. Three months after the divorce, he was remarried. He brought his bride to that house, where she fitted in without an edge or a bump. They began to have children almost immediately and he continued with his classes and his studies and after some years, began to write the short, closely reasoned tractates that are now circulated on the Internet: JacobBenAaron.com. We heard that one of his daughters is studying to be a physicist.

I believe it was my memory of the stillness and calm of Miri's house that made me move toward a career in interior design. Some architects—Frank Lloyd Wright for example—want complete control over every element in the residences they envision. Most are happy enough to cede to the client or the designer the more mundane elements of their grand plan. As a designer of interiors, I work with both architect and client. If the stairway is turned in this direction, there's space saved, but in this direction, easier access, and in this, a style statement. Which would best suit the client? When I graduated the following year, I went to work for Cromelin and Metzler, PC.

Miri's half of the divorce was more difficult than Jacob's. Of course, the entire community blamed her, and Ada looked at her with sad eyes. She got a room near the hospital and threw herself into her studies with all the strength of that headlong will of hers. I was busy, too, and after my graduation, I found a small apartment in the not-yet-gentrified downtown.

Miri eventually moved to Boulder, where she worked in the pathology lab at the community hospital. I didn't see her in those early months except when she came in for the mandatory holidays. Ada always called me, and I went eagerly, happy with the greeting she gave me. "Come in, Rucheleh. Oh, you look so sophisticated in that suit. Here, you can take in the soup dish, but be careful; it's a little too full. Did you hear the Bernstein girl had twins? Oh, and Mrs. Slonski—the old lady was in her jewelry store and a boy came in to rob it. He pulled a gun. She gave him such a kick, he fired the gun into the ceiling, and by the time the police came, the boy was begging for his life and she had the gun. Come, Rucheleh, say the blessing with me." Rabbi Mordecai was more reserved. I think he saw me as an accomplice.

I realize now that they needed me there so they wouldn't fight with Miri, blaming her, and so that Miri wouldn't become angry and defensive. As it was, there were looks, a word now and then, a long sigh, a face averted. These said enough. I was there to keep a peace I wanted as much as they did. I was there to reflect the love I had for all of them, and that was fine with me. Rabbi Mordecai wanted to be critical of Miri, but he couldn't bear to maintain the role. Miri would smile as she described an event at the lab or a moment in her research, and he would warm to her. I would think, There are few better things than love and welcome shining in another person's eyes. Ada was a harder victory, but even she couldn't maintain her disapproval for long. "Mirele—do you ever see the patients, maybe the little children, when you get the samples you study?"

"Not often. The samples are usually taken by the techs or a special nurse, then delivered to the lab."

"You've saved lives, though. Do you ever find out if you have saved a life?"

"It's a group effort, what happens. I'm part of it, and I'm glad enough for that."

The Mordecai boys were far away. I realized that Ada had no other home for the love that had been awakened by her motherhood. At those holiday times, Miri and her parents were building a truce.

Rabbi Mordecai seemed to have none of the squeamishness Jacob had had about her work, so Miri sometimes described it to us, although she said that at her level at the pathology lab, the jobs were routine—the usual tests, the expected results. I remember one evening, the discussion about hepatitis B and reports from England and Germany concerning it. The virus was most present in male homosexuals. Could it spread into the general population and become a plague?

"Like syphilis?" Rabbi Mordecai asked.

"Yes, and with a large population of hosts, the virus tends to mutate and strengthen."

"Are you studying it? Could you be harmed by studying it? Madame Curie died from what she was studying. Perhaps Jacob was worried that such a thing might happen to you."

Miri shook her head. "I'm not studying it. When I come across it, I send a report to the researchers who are working with it and to the Centers for Disease Control. Trust me; the lab technique is excellent. We have no germs flying around."

"But people die of that," I said. Miri shot me a look.

As we talked, Ada was up, brushing the crumbs from the table with her cupped hand. I had bought her a little crumb sweeper to do the job, and she had exclaimed over it. "What a gift, imagine, there's something for every need." I never saw her use it.

Rabbi Mordecai was interested in the new virus. I was surprised at his openness and curiosity. Had he changed, or was he accepting us as worthy discussants? This was an advantage I now see that he had seldom given Ada.

"People do die, but the possibility of my catching any of the diseases I identify is remote." Behind me, where she was waiting to clear my place, I heard Ada stifle a sound and make a quickly whispered plea, reflexive as the crossing of themselves that pious Catholics do. "I love to be where I am," Miri went on. "It's like being an anchoring thread in a spiderweb. The web trembles, and I know it. A piece of dust, a fly lands, and I'm alerted."

There were only four of us at the table that evening, so it must have been after a holiday. That must have been Rosh Hashanah—there were leftover apple slices, and a honey cake, already cut.

"Do you want to do research?" Rabbi Mordecai asked her.

"Oh, no, that's a hundred percent of one thing for twenty years. That's not the web; that's the fly." And we all laughed.

So, I realized, they were already forgiving her. Their forgiveness would be even easier with Jacob married and his wife constantly expecting. It helped that other girls in the neighborhood, the daughters of strictly observant families, were beginning to go to local colleges and take courses not directly linked to domestic things.

When I saw Miri next, she told me she had bought a house. I was excited. "Let me design the inside," I said; "let me get my hands on it." I was full of ideas. The place was not in town, she told me. It was an old farmhouse, the largest of four that had probably been a family compound of some kind. The big house dated back to 1905, and the other houses to the twenties and thirties. "Two stories, and a big attic, more than I can use, but the price was right because of the neighborhood." I should have wondered at that.

10

I went up to see the place on one of the windy days Boulder has, when gusts tear along the granite teeth of the front range, beating their way through dust and snow and finding the weaknesses in everything built by human hands and screaming at it and buffeting it and breaking it apart where they can. I drove through town and north to where the houses were separated by weedy fields. Here and there a relic building or broken chimney told about former failures. I took the turnoff on Miri's map and drove a mile out on a dirt road, where I turned right, and there was a ruin of a place with the large farmhouse Miri had described, like a whale beached in a storm of driftwood. Miri had said there were three other houses. There they were, but she hadn't mentioned the trailers, shacks, wrecked buses, and junked cars spread out from them. Dust devils pulled at the unpaved road and rode in tracks between the shacks and trailers.

I was appalled. Why had Miri, who had grown up in a tree-shaded, sound-muted, ordered neighborhood, chosen these bones to gnaw on? I pulled up at the side of the road and took in the place.

Some ethnic builder had designed it—it had a foreign look to it, something in the height and placement of the windows, and an off-center door. I found the basic form oddly pleasing, but there hadn't been any upkeep for years. The paint had been beaten off it and there were sagging shutters on those windows that had shutters at all. The yard was weed-grown, but as I approached the front door, I saw that someone had graced the entrance with a lilac bush, now bare and stringy from drought.

Miri was at the door before I knocked and she opened it with a laugh. "I won't get Jacob's relatives here anyway."

"It's a wonder you get mail and phone service," I said, but the crack about Jacob's relatives made me smile.

She pulled me in, and we both began to laugh.

The place was a mess. All the need for neatness, order, and scrupulous cleanliness demanded by her profession must have been kept at the lab, because the rooms here looked like a train wreck.

"I haven't gotten settled yet," she said, "but I wish I had a picture of your face when you came up the walk. I'll get to this sometime," and she waved a hand limply in the direction of the unpacked boxes and the clothes on the floor. "It all ganged up on me."

"Ada would have a fit," I said.

She picked up a dirty cup that was by the feet of a sprung couch. "The neighbors are friendly, real people, easy, except for the couple in that house across from me. They're drunks and they'll eventually kill each other or leave. I'm not crazy, 'Chelle. Boulder is growing and it has no way to grow except north and east. Eastward, there's heavy snow and the wind, and in winter it scours all those plains. North, and against the mountains, is where people will want to build. I'm putting all I can into land here. By the time the boom comes, I'll have acreage to sell."

"Where did you get the money for this?"

"It didn't take much, but Jacob made a settlement when we were divorced and I got some from a trust my grandma set up years ago."

"Can we clean this up and stop your clothes from fighting on the floor?"

"Oh, and something else," Miri said. "I've decided to change my name. I'm listed at the hospital as Miriam Marigold. When I took back my maiden name, I thought I might as well fix it up."

I tried not to laugh. I had stopped calling myself Raquel, but Marigold? "Why not a tougher name—maybe Snapdragon? I think you'll need it."

She was late choosing a new name, but prescient about the growth of Boulder. Miriam Marigold is now a very rich woman. The farmhouse has been remodeled and brought up to code. Its electrical system is state-of-the-art. It stands on a ten-acre parcel with beautiful windbreaks on three sides. Around it is a development of fifty houses, each on its aggressively green square of lawn. Miri owned eighty acres by the time she was finished, and sold the parcel for a figure near two million. She's not protected from everyone's rage, however. Yesterday, kids came riding by the house, hooting and throwing things.

We spent the day cleaning and I tested the place for soundness and was surprised at how well it had held up. Of course, the walls on the inside were constructed of old-fashioned lath and plaster, stabilized with horsehair. They were cracked and stained and the floors rose and sank in waves, but the people who built it had come from a tradition of heavy framing and deep foundations. The cellar was stone-lined and solid; the supporting structure was of heavy oak, beams brought here from the east.

"You should try out my valuable training," I told her. "Your kitchen is inconvenient and so is what they used to call the parlor, where they entertained the pastor and displayed the dead. Let me refit you."

"No time," Miri said. "I do my day at the lab, warm up something or eat it out of a bag, read something light and stupid, and head for bed. I'm thinking of buying a Crock Pot so I can put dinner on in the morning and have it ready when I get back."

"Not with the wiring you've got in this place," I said. "At least get someone in to replace all of it, and do it as soon as you can. You've got three spaghetti junctions in the kitchen and one under the bed in your room. It's a wonder you don't sleep with your eyes wide-open." I would argue this for almost a year, before an electrical fire in her kitchen drove her to its first repair in fifty years.

And the mess? I don't know if that was the real Miri, or whether she was declaring another kind of freedom, a freedom from order and predictability in her life as an antidote to the order necessary in her work. Which parts of our personalities are set at birth, which random and unpredictable?

I asked her how she felt about not being rich anymore. Except for the divorce settlement, and against legal advice, Miri had asked nothing from Jacob. "I want to keep it simple." She had done just that. Jacob had the house and all it contained. Rabbi

Mordecai and Ada, feeling betrayed, were giving her only meager financial help. "No blintzes, no streudel, no kugel, no knishes," Miri told me. "I now eat like the neighbors."

"Do you miss any of that old life, the food, the order, the community, anything there?"

"No, none of it," she said, but I thought she answered too quickly.

After my first visit to the house, I began going on Sundays. Miri's back yard looked like an area for army training. When spring came, I helped fix it up a little and we even planted some more lilacs. She seemed to be doing work on the place to please me. Some of the plantings actually survived the following winters, although now I doubt if she ever went out to sit on the benches we put there, especially positioned for watching the sunset and the few stars that now hesitantly claim the evening. On those Sunday afternoons, we read together or dozed or talked, but I rested, really rested, from clients and fashion and nervous associates and ringing phones.

Miri threw herself into work and went back to school for a master's degree. She would, in the next years, get a master's and a Ph.D. in pathology and write a handful of papers on mutations of crossover viruses and other topics I don't understand. I loved my work; Miri vibrated in hers like a tuning fork set to 440 vibrations a second: concert A.

That winter passed and the spring. Miri's routines were improved with a promotion at the lab. Her talk was mostly of what she was seeing, studying, learning.

Because of Miri's work, I knew about hepatitis B, and when the Gay Men's Health Project joined the experiments to study it, I was able to discuss it knowledgeably with the gay men I worked with.

By that spring, I, too, was doing so much work that I was given my own secretary, and relieved of some of the routine duties I had been stuck with. I began to dream that in five or ten years I might go out on my own. They were nice dreams—I would take only those jobs that were a challenge to me.

Like any firm in which there are several partners and associates, ours had office politics, favoritism, gossip, and power playing. I would have become embroiled in all of it but for Miri and the Sundays and special holidays I spent at her house, working in the yard, fixing the place, or just sitting and talking or reading, or napping. Now and then, I shared office gossip and politics with Miri.

She was encountering her own brand of ego trips and power plays at the hospital, and we would find ourselves comparing notes and motives. I came to know the structure of her department and the names of the combatants in it, and she of mine. She could ask, "Has Metzler gotten over his hissyfit at your contradicting him in that meeting?"

"No, but he had to admit I was right. I think he's having an affair with the other associate and he's afraid I'll start the word on it."

"Did you see them?"

"Yes and no. I went into the conference room on Thursday, and they were there, both dressed, but standing very close to each other, and when they saw me, they jumped back the way you do from a rattlesnake. She went red; he went pale."

"Human physiology is a wonderful thing; all my professors say so." Miri was smiling.

"The situation isn't as funny as it was when it happened," I said. "I'm getting that raise and new work, more creative, and because of what happened, I have to wonder if the raise and the new responsibilities are based on the work I've done or whether they were given to me to shut me up. I want my success to be real, and now it's all clouded over with doubt."

"You can do the work, so who cares how you got the promotion?"

"It smells, Miri—he made it smell."

"Success is a great deodorant. I think Elizabeth Taylor said that."

There are lights, people milling around in the cold, equipment and trucks parked outside the circle, defining it. Yet, I have the feeling that the chaos is purposeful. Having come from thoughts of the chaos of Miri's house in Boulder, I'm sensitive to the difference between purposeful chaos and the chaos of disinterest and neglect. A large man is coming toward the car in which we are sitting. I roll down the window and feel the chill of the mountain night. He looks in and his face registers surprise.

"That all you got to wear?" We nod. "Okay; I'll get you some blankets. The problem is, we might be all night at this—all night and God knows how long into tomorrow. Snow's predicted up here—not much, but enough to make you damn uncomfortable two foot away from a fire. We're not going to be able to keep our car motors running that long. I sure wish you ladies had stayed home and let us do what we're trained to do."

He hails a passing shape silhouetted against the light. "Go get Escobar and have him come back here and turn off his motor. Never mind—I'll do it," and he reaches in and turns the key.

Miri leans over me. "Have they found her?"

"No, not either of them. This is the cave, though. He marked it, and the caving people have been in there following his markings. Their van was found a little way down the trail."

"Where's the entrance to the cave?" Miri asks.

"Oh, it's about a hundred and fifty feet to the south and down. This is the closest level spot."

It's getting cutting cold in the car. We creep out and go toward a butane heater that has been set up near some kind of staging area where lengths of rope are coiled, along with caving gear and tarps; two litters and boxes of other equipment are being readied. There are blankets also, neatly folded, and we take two and go over to the fire, pulling up two of the stoutest boxes to sit on. We huddle in the blankets and wait.

"We shouldn't have come," I say. "We're in the way. We're of help to nobody and they'll have to keep us warm and fed and toileted. We're hogging space at this heater that the rescuers may have wanted to use."

"They'll need us when Tamar comes out—" She shivers. "We'll be absolutely necessary then."

There's that glowing, golden confidence, whose other side is arrogant self-will. People with such confidence walk their courses, turn their heads, and see they are followed by whole battalions of apostles.

II

The partners gave me a party, or, I should say, they let my changed status provide an excuse for a party. In those days, friends of friends showed up at such events, and by the time I put in an appearance at mine, there were lots of people there I didn't know.

I feel cast adrift dealing with crowds at parties. I thought I'd have a few drinks, eat some of the snacks, and do an early fade-out, but I learned that there was to be a cake with my name on it, congratulations, and toasting. The hostess told me all that would happen at around eleven. I'd have to be there to receive all this from a roomful of people, many of whom had no idea who I was. I figured I could sneak out to a movie and return in time for the cake cutting. Then I thought: Why not take advantage of the size of the house and simply wander off to find a secluded spot where there may be books or magazines, and where it would be easy to disappear and read for the hour or two before having to reemerge in front of the cake?

I was going in search of the secret door when I passed a knot of women and got caught up in a rivulet of their conversation. "This is funny," one of them said. "I had to come to Denver to meet people from Boulder Community Hospital. Where do you work, Marge?"

"Radiology. I've seen *you*," and Marge indicated a tall woman at her left.

The third woman said, "I'm in the ER, yeah, coming and going. What about you?" She asked another woman. They were making a circle.

"I'm in the path lab," the fourth one said.

I was about to stop and tell them that I had a friend in the

69

pathology lab, but I didn't get the chance. "Path is right. One of your assistants is so busy they should name a mall after her."

"I know who you mean, but I don't think it's all her fault. She's a very good pathologist; we're lucky to have her, and it won't be long before she'll head the department. She just happens to attract men; some women do. I wish I did. It's not as if she flirts a lot, and she's never out of that lab coat. They come to her—it's like a pheromone, or the light on a glowworm."

"Pheromone my ass. They come because she puts out. Did she ever meet a man she didn't like?"

I stopped dead for a second, and thought, I'll have to ask Miri who that is. I think my face flushed, but I still hadn't spoken. I moved closer to be included in the conversation's circle. I stood there and let the talk wind past me. I felt light-headed, but there was a cold feeling in my fingers and more heat in my face. There must be other women in the path lab. Why should they be talking about Miri? Then someone said, "The Marigold. It blooms all season and it's open all night!" And they laughed and I stood there. The rage that came stopped me from saying anything. What could I say to their smug faces? Then I realized that if I leapt to Miri's defense, bad would be made worse. Even as I seethed and went red behind my eyes, the conversation moved on like a tornado that touches down, does its devastation, and spindles away in a matter of seconds, leaving its chaos to confound logic and good sense.

No one seemed to notice my upset. I stood there, wondering why I hadn't spoken. Then it was too late. A person wades into these moments slugging or doesn't get in at all. I felt I had betrayed Miri.

Some time later there was the cake, with congratulations and laughter that I heard as through a curtain. I had found a quiet room, but instead of spending the time reading, I wasted it spinning defenses for Miri. My Sundays with her testified in her favor. I should have spoken about those long, leisurely Sundays. Surely if she were entertaining carloads of men, her time wouldn't be measured out so generously to me. Even in Miri's household chaos, I'd seen no evidence of a male presence, no reference to a man or men in what she did or how she acted.

Where were the phone calls, the cars parked outside her house waiting for me to leave? Where were the excuses about why I shouldn't come up this or that Sunday? Where were the shaving soap and razor in the medicine cabinet, the uneaten candy, the flowers dying in the vase? The only men we talked about were Jacob and occasionally Art and Ab, the boys of our girlhood. Ab was long dead, and the last I'd heard, Art was some kind of engineer, married, living in Denver. Miri herself had been in degree programs, one after another, tough, demanding studies. Where would there be time for all those lights and pheromones these women were describing? Miri wasn't doing candlelight and wine with attractive men. She was doing spotlight and microscope in an empty lab at night, and resting with me on Sundays.

Of course, I thought, it was jealousy. I wasn't jealous of Miri, but many people were, and not only women. I realized there must be men also who thought she had advanced too far on looks and charm, men who might brag about having made it with her. All the sexual games and gossip and the ego trips of junior high and high school don't stop; they might have followed Miri into the lab.

How could I find out? Did I want to find out? Miri was my friend, my best and oldest friend, and the safest thing I could do would be to try to forget what I had heard, ascribe it to the envy of people less brilliant and lucky than she was.

But it sat there. The next Sunday, I went up to Boulder, and it was still sitting there, and in its presence I found my usual words sounding hollow and artificial, like a bad phone connection. We never discussed our social or sex lives and I realized that, too, as I listened to myself make conversation. Finally, I said, "Miri, do you go out much? Do you get to meet many men?"

We were sitting in the shade of the north side of the house, where the porch sagged and the view faced the road. Across from us, neighbors came and went and the trailer squatters behind the dilapidated house drank and bickered or drank and dozed. They had hailed us, friendly enough, when we'd first gone out, calling to offer us a beer. We waved and called out, "Maybe later," and pulled our chairs up to the porch rail.

71

She looked at me quizzically and then said, "I get a lot of sex, but not a lot of pleasure." She was wearing shorts and a sleeveless blouse. Her body was still lithe and smooth with no bulge anywhere. Her feet were bare, and I thought they were her only imperfect feature, with bunions beginning and corns here and there. She was resting them on the railing. I waited for the surprise to leave my voice and then I said, "Where do you find them?"

"None are serious," she said, stretching, "and you're more particular than I am. Mine are men wishing they were divorced, men wondering if they're gay or not, men wanting a mistress but too cheap to buy one. Sometimes the sex is good; usually it's not."

"Then why do it?"

"I got used to it. Jacob and I were nice and regular, all according to Jewish law. There's no law now, but there's habit, and you hope one of the men will be worth the Pill and the effort."

I was shocked. My friend, to whom I had confided everything, all the anguish when dawning love went sour or lovers turned out to be married—all the confidences I thought were shared, looked back at me, grinning. I felt stupid, angry, betrayed, and Miri seemed not to notice. I got up and went into the house, and to the bathroom, an unventilated, miasma-smelling place, to seethe and stew for a time. Maybe she didn't want me to see so uninviting a part of her, to imagine the clothing parted for quick moments in the hospital linen room, or a jab up against a wall.

After I had calmed down a little, I went back. Miri was still sitting, chair tilted, her feet lifted over the porch rail. She'd been dozing.

"They weren't part of your life, were they?" I said.

"Huh?"

"The men. You don't tell me about them because they have no reality for you."

"No, they don't," she said.

"I wish I had somebody," I said.

She murmured, "So do I," and we sat there for a long time as I thought about it and watched two boys throwing stones at an abandoned car.

12

That was the summer of surprises. The mornings shone; the nights were sweater-cool, the rain a blessing. I'd wake up and lie in bed on Sunday mornings until nine, dress leisurely, and go out for a bagel and whitefish at the kosher deli, which was barely hanging on near the old neighborhood, its demise as leisurely as its service. There, I gossiped with the waiters and waitresses, some of whom were my parents' ages, and I let them mother me. It was at the Sunday-morning deli that I learned about Jacob Zimet and his new wife and their children, and kept tabs on Reb Mordecai and Ada and even on my parents—the parts of them they would never share with me. After breakfast, I'd take my walk and meet with my "dog friends," the group that took their pets for a regular airing at that time. We'd amble along, chatting. Eventually there came to be a group of eight of us laughing and celebrating pet holidays and events. I was the only member of the group who was not a dog owner.

After the walk, I'd drive to Boulder. Miri had begun to change other parts of herself along with her name. I didn't hear any more about her sex life, but she was dressing Boulder-style—lots of earrings and dangly jewelry, pants and men's shirts, sandals and a wide-brim black hat like Navaho men wear. On her, it all worked. She had become vegetarian, too, almost carelessly, as a way to cook less. We got used to playing with combinations of food in salads and sandwiches—mushrooms and olives, peanut butter and peaches, capers and eggs. She told me pathology stories and I shared great moments in interior design. Some Sundays, she was exhausted and drained and would lie there like an invalid on the porch, dozing and waking while I read, fading off in the middle of our talk. She attributed her lethargy to work on this or that bacterium or virus she was studying, and diseases associated with it. There was a new form of hepatitis. By that time, some people in my office, and in the interior-decorating, fabric-design, and lighting-design firms we dealt with, had also developed what was then identified as AIDS, and had begun to sicken and die. Their situations gave our talk an urgency and point it hadn't had before. Nothing was academic anymore. Miri said, "We're all at sea here. Research is coming in; people are learning slowly what this thing is. Medical research is long, slow, and complicated. You don't see viruses under an ordinary microscope."

"People are dying."

"I know. I'm not in research, but the pressure there must be horrific. My own work is stressful enough. Thank God for these Sundays."

"Thank God? What am I, chopped liver?"

"On rye, with lots of chicken fat and a dill pickle on the side."

It pleased me to think that Miri, too, was renewed by our Sunday afternoons together.

Time passed, and I don't remember any trauma about the fact that we were now in our thirties. We were happy enough as we were, and we both, I think, looked forward to small joys and solid professional advancement, with no essential change in the way we were living. We were unprepared for being overwhelmed. Both of us fell in love.

I'd been working in what was practically an all-male enterprise, but finding no one and no one finding me. My parents had given up hope of my marrying by then. I myself had seen marriages begin and marriages end. I'd watched the gay world reeling from the effects of AIDS, and the disease begin to move into the straight population, deflating the huge balloon of sexual liberation that had barely risen before us. The eighties were the years of funerals and of dozens of revealed secrets in my profession. Three of the men I had thought of as possible lovers turned out to be gay and dying with lovers, a sad surprise.

My deli's Sunday-morning bagel eaters had begun to drift away also. Two successful kosher places opened up at the eastern edge of the city and took a chunk of the trade away. The regulars in the neighborhood were enough to keep the place going, but its glory days were over and a quiet descended, punctuated by the coming and going of staff, younger now and less knowledgeable about the community, and less interested in it.

Their unconcern left the diminished clientele obliged to chat with one another, so the habit of sharing tables began even when the place was half-empty. One day, a man I had been greeting for some time came to my table and asked if he might sit with me.

"Sure."

He was tall and thin, but not gangly. His hair was beginning to gray and be eaten away on the top. His eyes were alive in a somewhat round face. And I thought, Not a Jewish face.

"Niall," he said.

"Rachel," I said.

He was a cop. "I *was* a street cop," he said, "but now I investigate complaints brought against officers on the force."

I told him what I did, and he asked intelligent questions. We'd been sitting together for two Sundays before we got to last names. "Rachel Yovel."

"Oh," he said, "Yovel—it means jubilee. What a great name. I'm Niall Finn."

"I laughed. "Don't tell me they gave you that at Ellis Island."

"No, I'm a sure-and-begorra Finn with a great-grandmother from the auld sod."

"How did you know what Yovel meant, then?"

"I know lots of Jewish stuff," he said, and grinned at me, "and all because of the little savage I was as a kid. Rabbi Feldman died last year and I'm left alone with the story. I tell it in his honor. My mother's still alive, but deep in Alzheimer's. It's in her honor, too."

"Okay," I said, "let's hear it."

He took a breath and looked at me and then let his gaze drop. I waited. "I was—there were three of us, a set. We were twelve, I think, or thirteen, and someone got the idea of breaking into a synagogue and stealing the treasure in gold and silver that everyone knows the Jews hide there. This was in Chicago, and if you knew the neighborhood, you'd laugh yourself sick. Treasure, ha." He was still looking down. "Well, we got in. My buddy

76

knew how to break windows without making a crash. Because we couldn't find the gold and jewels, we got mad and pillaged the place." He took another breath and looked up at me to see if rage had replaced interest. "The police got us the next day, all three of us, down at the station house, and our mothers were down there, two of them yelling how their darling boys were innocent, and my mother asking me, 'Do you have anything against those people?' 'No, but . . . '

"'Do you know them at all?' 'No, but . . .' 'You don't know anything about them?' 'No, Ma.' 'Then why would you do such a thing?' 'I don't know.' Her voice didn't rise. She was a yeller, my mother, but not that time. 'It's ignorance that's done this,' she said. 'The police told me that one of you urinated on something in that building.' 'That wasn't me. I . . .' 'No matter; Hate, that's up to you, but to do something like that, to be a part of that against people you don't even know, without hate? I'd call that pig-ignorant.' She called the rabbi the next day. It was Rabbi Feldman. We went to his study; my mom waited outside.

"I expected him to rage at me, hit me, even, and I was ready for that. He looked at me as if I were a puzzle he could solve if he tried, and his first words were, 'How did such an idea come to you?'"

I was listening closely, imagining the scene.

"But he didn't yell," Niall said, "only the questions. 'Please try to remember.' He acted as if he were trying to make us partners in an investigation. 'What exactly had happened that day? Was the decision one person's? Who thought of robbing a synagogue?' I knew those questions were a golden way to lay all the blame on the other guys, but somehow I couldn't. The rabbi had given me the respect of being serious with me. I was a kid and he was treating me like an adult, even like a colleague. We talked for over an hour. He asked me if I knew any Jewish people. 'No—I go to St. Barnabas. There are Jewish kids in the neighborhood, but we don't hang out with them. We're with our own and so are they.'

"My mother was out there, waiting all that time. She told me later that she'd heard our voices, a murmur, one low, one higher. She, too, thought the rabbi would give me hell, hot and hard, but when we came out, his hand was on my shoulder. He went to her and said, 'Your boy here tells me he goes to parochial school. Do you go to Mass on Sunday?' I was surprised that he knew about Mass. My mother told him we usually went to the ten o'clock. He asked if there was an earlier Mass and if I might come to the Sunday pre–bar mitzvah class he held for the kids and their parents. It was from ten to eleven.

"My mother said I'd be there, and I thought part of the deal would be ratting on the other kids. When I asked him about that, he looked puzzled, and then he said that the police had a good-enough case against all of us without any of us affirming or denying. There were laws we had broken. I would receive whatever punishment the state had in mind. That was the state's business. His business was my inner life."

Niall patted his pocket for a cigarette and then remembered he had given them up and looked around a little helplessly. I shrugged. I had given them up, too.

"I was in the class for a year. We talked about ethics, history, holidays, ceremonies, some of the questions raised in the Talmud."

"And you learned what Yovel meant."

"That, and some Yiddish and some more Hebrew. Mostly, I learned to ask questions that couldn't always be answered, or that could be answered in many ways, and some that were answered paradoxically."

"What happened to the other boys?"

"We all paid fines. We all spent a month in juvenile detention, going to school in the daytime and then reporting to the lockup. Tiernan is a high school principal in Chicago now; Keely got into drugs and died of an overdose."

I left late for Miri's.

Niall and I had breakfast together twice more before he asked me out for the evening. He told me he had married at eighteen and been divorced at twenty. He was wedding bell-shy.

13

We courted. No one says that now, but I like it better than the usual trivializations: shacked up, had an affair, lived with each other. We didn't make love for two months after we began going out.

I wanted and didn't want Niall and Miri to meet. She was beautiful and charming and often willful—and one look would move him to her in as natural a way as seeds are blown downwind, gone.

Then, one Sunday afternoon, Miri told me that a man was coming to visit. "What kind of man? What kind of visit?"

"Henrik," she said, "Sanseverino."

There he came, in a utility truck with a company name on the side, all but shaking itself to ruin on the washboard of the unpaved street. When it pulled up and stopped, I asked Miri where she had met him.

"We had an argument at the supermarket."

I watched him coming up the weedy path to the house. He seemed almost to run, to bound. He was full of energy, small, compact, dark, like Miri, and with an outdoor tan. He seemed delighted to meet me. During the afternoon, I learned that he had been to college for a while, majoring in philosophy, but had switched to engineering and then left college and studied on his own while working at a long string of jobs, from gardening to clerking in a bookstore, horse handling, and selling stocks over the phone. He sounded happy with all his choices. With Miri, he was tender and playful and utterly unlike Jacob Zimet, whom, I realized, I still missed.

Some of what he said bumped slightly in my mind, as it met unplanned resistance. All of his jobs had been different. He had lived in forty places. Where was the center? But I was also charmed. He went into Miri's carelessly tended kitchen and, cheerfully commanding us as trainees, created a grand vegetarian meal. "Miri, you've got to outfit this place better. No steamer? No spices? How can anyone cook without paprika? Here, cut these fine."

I felt a bump, like a speed bump in a parking lot. "What are you doing now? You should be cooking in a tony restaurant."

"I did that actually. Then I was doing estate evaluating, but I got tired of dealing with greedy people and with *things*. I started doing more work outside, garden design, landscaping, and I've also been running Outward Bound programs with special groups, cancer survivors, learning-disabled kids, people like that."

I said I thought he'd be good at that, and I meant it. Charm goes a long way, even while the charmed one is hanging from a rope.

We sat and ate and talked the afternoon away, and I enjoyed myself more than I'd thought I would. His years at this and that had given Henrik wide knowledge, but he never pontificated or acted in a condescending way. I found myself sharing experiences, some funny, some frustrating, about clients and architects, and I ended up by inviting Henrik down to one of the jobs to see what I was doing.

Because of Henrik, I thought it would be safe to introduce Niall to Miri, and I indulged in some of my old dreams of us as part of two couples, four friends, something more lasting and deeper in all our lives, enjoying the fun we had once had when we were in high school with Art and Ab. I hadn't seen Art in years. I had heard he was married.

Niall said he would like to meet Miri and Henrik. He'd heard many of my Miri stories and was curious about her and interested in what I told him, but he warned me that people thought about policemen the way they did about priests and nuns, rabbis, mathematical geniuses, and mafiosi; special care was to be taken. "Cops are people who are seen to judge other people's behavior," he said. "It seems to bring out the worst. Remember, too, that I carry. If I hug her, she'll feel the gun."

80

"Try not to wave it around and yell 'freeze!' like you do all the time."

I called Miri and Miri talked to Henrik and we met two weeks later, on a Saturday evening for dinner and a play, and again a week after that, at Miri's for a long Sunday afternoon. Even though I was on the watch for anyone's discomfort, I was happy with the way things went. Niall's ease with people, his inclusiveness, dispelled whatever emotions his being a policeman evoked. We joked around, laughed a lot, and went out to the big field behind Miri's house, where the men created a game they tried to teach us, a combination of tag, Prisoner's Base, and Who's Got the Button. On our way home, I said I thought the day had gone very well. "You see, they were very natural around you."

Niall smiled. "You're right. Henrik's a good choice for her, I think. They seemed okay with me. Good consciences, I guess. People usually go tight with cops. There's stuff left over from the sixties, too—pigs, fuzz. I think it's how come cops are comfortable only with other cops. It's nice for me to get into the wide world. I had a good time."

We went out together often after that, and now and then I spent time alone with Miri. Niall never showed any signs of love interest in her, which was a great relief to me, although not before some weeks of anxiety. "Do you think Miri's pretty?"

"Beautiful—I'd say beautiful."

"And attractive in her manner?"

"I'd say a little hectic for me, keyed up. I can see her pulses."

"You've looked closely enough to see her pulses?"

"Cops are trained to notice things. Miri's exciting. She's got a lot of charm."

"And me—what have I got?"

"Something quieter, deeper, plus a good ass and great legs. I think you care about people more than she does. No hard evidence; it's just a hunch."

Niall didn't bring me candy and flowers the way Henrik did to Miri, and it was Henrik who planted the line of cottonwoods that would provide the windbreak and protection from snow that the house needed and then would later annoy the neighbors. There was something steady and satisfying in Niall, like a good meal or a good house: well situated, with fine views, but not advertising itself or calling down the lightning.

We married the following summer, and in the fall, Niall Finn converted to Judaism and we moved to North Denver, which made for an easier trip to Boulder, where Miri and Henrik were living. I was supposed to become pregnant right away with a boy who would grow up and marry Miri's daughter. When Henrik joked about this, I said, "Then you two better get married. It's bad form to marry in your ninth month, even though I don't doubt there's a company that makes maternity wedding dresses." They laughed and held hands under the table.

My family considered Niall an outsider, convert or not. "*Finn,*" my mother would say it as if it were a curse word. My father called me Mrs. Finn. They stared at Niall with distaste. We visited them when we had to and with Shirah taking care of them, I felt less guilt about seeing them as seldom as we did. Rabbi Mordecai and Ada were our stand-in parents. Ada said she had long considered me a daughter. Why not? I'd all but lived at their house when I was a girl; I'd lived there in my college years while Rabbi Mordecai bloomed in the presence of his son-in-law and Miri moved away from them all. The old couple genuinely liked Niall, even though I felt their pain about Miri. She had divorced a good man and taken up with someone they didn't know, a *luftmench*, a man who made a living from thin air. Now and then I tried to get them to see the Miri I saw, a gifted professional, a home owner who was even kosher, in her odd way. "She's a pure vegetarian, so she never mixes meat with dairy or eats tref. As for Henrik—he's tender with her and heaven knows helpful and loving. I can't think of a better man for her."

"Then why don't they marry?" Ada would snap, and Rabbi Mordecai would say "Hah!" and change the subject.

We liked going to the Mordecais' for Shabbat evening. Rabbi Mordecai would pretend he hadn't seen us drive up. To hurry, our using the car was a break in tradition, but we now lived too far to walk to his house. Niall breathed in the aromas of the dinner to come, grinned, and said, "Thank God for the sense of smell: aromatherapy."

82

I laughed and told him that the spice box was for Havdalah and we hadn't done Shabbat yet.

Ada's cooking for the rabbi's heart took a Shabbat break by declaration from the patient: "Shabbat has no heart attack. Baked potato is chol, everyday food. Latkes are Shabbat food, and fry them in chicken fat." Her latkes were feather-light and delicious. This break in the heart-healthy regimen lasted until havdalah, the ceremony ending Shabbat. It was also Niall's favorite, the celebration of the simple luxury of perceiving light, warmth, the sense of smell. I liked being part of Jewish life without disappearing into it. Neither Ada nor Rabbi Mordecai criticized our level of piety.

While we ate, I talked Miri up when I could. She and Henrik were actually making something out of that bare patch of earth in front of the house and Henrik had a plan to use sun and wind to heat and cool the big old place. "And she's doing important work at the hospital. I've heard people say she'll be head of the department one of these days."

"What kind of work did you say he did?" Rabbi Mordecai's tone was peevish.

I said, "Landscape design—that, mostly, now. Miri is buying up the land around her, and when the city starts moving north, Henrik will be in a perfect position to design the landscape of developments going up there."

"And before that, and before that? Is Miriam supporting him?"

Niall and I looked at each other. "I wouldn't go that far," Niall said.

"It sounds familiar—in these cases, the woman gives, the man takes. How much does he take?"

Niall said, "He's a lightning bug, not a firebug. He darts from thing to thing, but he's not dishonest."

"How do you know?"

"I ran his sheet."

Our heads came up. "You studied his record?" Ada seemed horrified.

Niall looked around at us. "I suppose that's not done in civilian life, but it's what cops do. The tools are right at hand."

"And you found—"

"Nothing. Nothing bad. He was cited twice for speeding five years ago and then again last year. There was a fraud investigation of a company he worked for ten years ago, but he took no part in the fraud and was cleared immediately."

"And taxes?"

"The good news is that there's no evidence of finagling or paring on taxes. The bad news is that I don't think he has ever earned enough money to owe the government much. I think he's a very interesting person and his studies make him great company. People get suspicious of that; I did, I admit, but don't worry. I don't think there's anything there."

"I'm guessing I broke the holiday mood," he said later.

"Good guess. Now they're wondering if you looked *them* up."

"The rabbi borrowed heavily to finance that huge wedding of Miri's. It's almost all paid back, now."

"Niall! What about me?"

"You? You're more likely to show up on a pigeon list, which was why I had to marry you. People like you shouldn't walk free without a keeper."

"You think I'm softheaded."

"You trust. God bless you. The world would be darker without people like you. But . . ."

We had married as modestly as Shifrah and Shirah. I had to eat the derisive words I'd uttered as a teenager. Before the wedding, we flew to Chicago to visit Niall's mother, who, to his pain, no longer recognized him, and who seemed to think I was her sister. Niall cried on the plane back to Denver. Rabbi Mordecai married us. There were twenty people, including two from my office and four of Niall's colleagues. Miri and Henrik came, and as always, she turned heads as she entered the room. Then I smiled and Niall looked at me with a little wink that made me melt with love.

In law, a Jewish wedding is as bare and basic as any on earth. In custom, it's replete with symbols and layers of meaning four thousand years deep. We edged toward the limit of bare and basic, much as a second marriage would be, or one in which the couple was very old. Niall had been married before; I had no patience for outfitting myself and making extravagant plans. Now and then, my mind went back to Miri's elaborate and gorgeous wedding: gown and veil, white shoes, champagne, loaded tables, people dancing all night. We had cake and tea, and the next weekend Niall took me to a big old hotel in Silverton.

I realized as we made love that I'd held back some small part of total giving, total taking, letting go.

"My God," Niall said afterward, "I thought I was getting a kitten, but she grew up a tiger."

14

Here were the foundations laid by hand. Here was the framework of what we thought would be our lives. We saw a house we liked and bought it. That fall, Niall built a succah for the holiday, and Henrik and Miri came to help. We all worked on the knockdown wicker structure, but by the time Henrik was finished with his plans and he and Niall had erected the thing, it was almost too beautiful to take down at the holiday's end. We spent three nights there, two with Miri and Henrik, bundled against the Colorado autumn in down quilts and heavy sleeping bags, laughing and talking in the dark. The neighbors were fascinated and we invited them to sit under the hanging pieces of fruit and the sheaves of wheat and the branches of myrtle Henrik had woven like pieces of art. There we ate and drank and chatted easily, picniclike in October. The neighbors loved the succah and they took easily to Henrik and were awed by Miri. When the holiday was over, we all decided on an even bigger succah for next year, a neighborhood affair, even though only the Silvermans were Jewish.

For Passover, we went to the Mordecais' seder the first night and spent the second with Shirah and her family and my parents, who sat gloomily at the holiday table and criticized Niall Finn's eyebrows, shoe size, and existence. "Wait till you give them a grandchild," I told him. "You'll start looking better."

Henrik was showing a real talent for landscape design and I began to think that his trouble all along wasn't that he lacked talents but that he had too many of them, and didn't know which of a dozen gifts to cultivate. Miri was strong in the lab but never balanced a checkbook. Her physical coordination was splendid, but she had no eye for art and a tin ear for music. I don't think she could tell the difference between hip-hop and Haydn.

She told us that research on the AIDS virus was beginning to yield slow results. Miri was not a researcher or a virologist, but she was staying at the lab evening after evening, under pressure to meet the need for more knowledge of the disease. There were also travelers from exotic places bringing problems home to her in Boulder, spirochetes and parasites from around the world. "People on humanitarian missions sometimes get more than they bargained for. Terrible things go on in the blood," Miri said. She seemed to thrive on the work.

Her world was life and death. I was designing interiors for Denver's new rich. Some of the demands promoted gracious living; some were hymns to vanity. All those high ceilings declared the owners ready to pay any price for fuel and air conditioning.

"Henrik, why not come with me on a project and see what you think about the garden." We were digging holes for the new cherry trees in our backyard to replace the ones we had planted the year before that had been eaten away at the roots by voles. "I'm doing a house with an interesting inside-outside potential. Wanna take a look?"

"Sure," he said. He was smiling at me with surprise and delight.

"You won't have to plant anything—I want to show them a nice integrated design."

That nice integrated plan won us the Compton Prize for residential architectural design. The garden was a wonder in scale, given dimension with trees and big rocks, groves, and small open spaces. The walks, sunny here and shaded there, protected the exposures for all but the coldest days of the year.

As it evolved, I watched Henrik take on all the problems that came up, solving them with immense flair and creativity. The whole site was no bigger than an acre, and I was amazed at what he was able to do with it. We weren't halfway through its implementation when people began coming to see what was happening.

"He may be a genius," I told Niall. "The plan doesn't look daring, but it's full of new ideas. It just skirts being pretentious by the clever use of small flowers and ground cover and the spontaneity of the whole thing. The house is ordinary enough, almost generic—a McMansion—but this one feature makes it unique. He's got noise reduction, and with what I've done, there's a sense of both space and intimacy. When it's finished, the whole flow of outside-inside will be so easy that there won't be excessive care needed to maintain it. Can you get a day off to come and see it when it's done? I swear, Henrik sat in the middle of it for two weeks, just conceiving the effects I had going on in the house."

"Who's to do the actual gardening?"

I waved regally. "Henrik has mapped it so well that any competent landscape man can do it. I can't wait till it's finished."

We went to look; Henrik brought Miri. The clients let us walk through the house while I pointed out this and that feature. We went out to the garden. My design had stressed accessibility from almost every room in the house. Even Miri, who was all but unaware of her surroundings, was charmed. "We all wish we lived here," she told the clients, who beamed.

"Four other jobs," I told them when we were on our way to lunch at our house, "and people will be photographing our work for architectural journals and garden magazines."

"Not every client will want so much inside-outside," Henrik said. "Privacy is becoming a big fad lately—walls, gates."

"When they see what you've done, they'll think again."

"What I like about this work we're in," he told Miri, "is that each one of these projects is different. Rachel has it right that I get bored with the same things repeated. There's lots of room for differences here."

"The next project will be a challenge," I told him. "The clients have an art collection, so they'll want lots of wall. I've done all I could to keep the place from looking like a museum."

"Do they have sculpture?"

"Oh, yes, placed in the middle of the floor—all the ambience of a garage sale."

"Take me there," Henrik said, "give me a look."

We were in *Architectural Digest* and *Fine Gardening* for that one, and I had to put off three commissions because I didn't want to crowd Henrik. An afterthought backyard became an outdoor gallery, niches among plantings of trees and shrubs, a dozen surprises along a meandering path with benches for viewing.

"And we ran heating under the walkways so people could go out there in the dead of winter," I told Niall.

We were on TV during the week of the Home Show and Henrik was perfect: modest, down-to-earth, making the case for aesthetics without any of the overblown language that turns people off.

I was happy to let him do the presentations. He was handsome and energetic. He gave me all the credit I could have asked for. We got dozens of calls from people inquiring about our work.

Those days were thrilling; they were fun. There were new ideas from one or both of us all the time.

Niall watched our enthusiasm flower and saw some of the drawings we were making for yet another client. "You sybarites are having a grand old go at it," he said, "really wowing a poor old flatfoot like me."

We hadn't talked about what might happen if I started making money that exceeded, maybe far exceeded, the steady but modest salary he made. "If I start shaking down the big bucks, maybe I can bribe you," I said. As soon as I spoke the words, I wished I hadn't. He'd been dealing with a knotty mess in the department involving extortion, theft, and robbery by police officers who were running a criminal enterprise that involved men he knew. I saw his face go tight. "Oh God, Niall, I'm sorry."

"I know. You forgot. Christ, I wish I could. I'm glad you forget. I think hearing you, Henrik, and Miri at work helps me get some balance. My part of the world's a swamp. It's good to look out of the swamp, but sometimes I think civilians like you are deaf and blind and walk past open manholes, getting by on luck alone."

"What I do must seem trivial to you—where the bathroom goes, why the kitchen sink should face this way, why the kitchen cabinets need to be here and not there."

"I don't judge that. Good things make life nicer. Come to that, good policing isn't noticed, either."

"But lots of it is grim."

He grinned at me. "Darlin', someday when we're rich enough, I want to hire you to design our house."

"So my making lots of money doesn't bother you?"

"Archie Comstock has a Rolex. Archie Comstock just bought a house near Cherry Creek."

"Didn't I meet him when we were playing volleyball at the department's picnic?"

"You did indeed, and he's going to be playing volleyball down at one or another of our correctional facilities at Cañon City. It's nice to have a Rolex and a loft in LoDo. It's even nicer to have those things with money you don't get at gunpoint."

"Niall Finn, me boyo, you'll have a house with a sunken tub and a garden with a heated walk."

"A *mechiah,*" he said.

But, on the third of Henrik's and my combination projects, things started to go wrong. I was doing a lot of other work along with our shared projects. I'd left Henrik to do his part without the three or four long meetings we'd had before. When I did get to him, I found he hadn't produced anything. "There's been a drainage problem. I'm working on that," he said.

"Let's meet on Thursday. Will it be handled by then?"

"Sure," he said.

But it wasn't, and it wasn't until I shepherded him through the process. We finished late. Clients hate it when projects take longer than expected. They want to move in. Some have sold their former houses and have to stay in hotels or with friends.

"Rache, you're bucking for an ulcer," Niall said. "Maybe this was just a tougher project than the last ones—you mentioned a drainage problem."

Henrik's complaint was that he was too mired in petty details. Couldn't the garden people come into the process earlier?

We tried that on the next project and found the process cumbersome and the garden people unhappy. Costs went up. The fourth project was delayed even longer than the third.

I realized that the plans he was drawing were becoming abstract and grandiose. I didn't even show his next design to the clients. When I took the plans back to Henrik, I expected, and dreaded, the argument we would have, but he shrugged and

90

cheerfully admitted that the ideas were impractical and their costs far beyond what a client would pay.

"Why don't you try again?" I asked him. I silently blessed Niall for telling me to wait before getting Henrik's signature on any long-term partnership.

"I don't want to redo this one," Henrik said. "I've got this larger vision. I'm going to submit a plan like this to the city. We need a bigger, better park than Chautauqua."

"He wants Muir Woods in Boulder," I told Niall. "Birnam Wood coming to Dunsinane."

"Wherever he wants his woods," Niall said, "I don't want you up a tree. Can you get another landscaper to step in?"

I did, and walked him around Henrik's three projects to show him what I was looking for. The result was passable. He picked up features that he copied, a literal translation, earthbound, one might say. He lacked all of Henrik's flair, originality, and spontaneity.

Henrik, meanwhile, had gone on. We'd made nice money together on our three projects, and he'd taken his part of the profits and invested them in some local stocks. These he began to study with the same depth and intensity he had given to the gardens. Miri didn't seem to notice, or, if she did, she didn't mind that with such a constant change of center, the centers would give out. Niall chuckled; I thought Miri's tolerance was a virtue, one I should cultivate.

He'd left our venture with such charm and openness that I couldn't be angry. Ours was the only business breakup in my experience where the partners stayed friends.

"When he hits oceanography or deep-sea fishing," Niall said, "I'll be surprised. Until then, it'll be just the usual."

During those two years studying stocks, Henrik also made necessary repairs on Miri's house—typically for him, with ideas more splendid than what he would actually implement.

"The electrical system here is nineteenth-century," he declared. He planned an elaborate rewiring of the whole structure, and for months, holes in the wall at floor and eye level awaited their outlet assemblies. He completed the kitchen, though, and with a bank of outlets on each wall, anticipating all the household appliances that were to come. The wiring in our house was inadequate.

Niall hung his head. "I did shingle my uncle's roof when I was in high school," he said, "and I put up these shelves. Granted, the guy at the store said it was a Sunday project, but it took me most of two weeks."

"You have a good heart," I said smarmily.

"Pffft!" Niall replied back at me.

In March, the sluggish department, forced by Niall and three other inspectors with threats to go federal, began to move. Thirty-six police officers, ranging from patrolman to lieutenant, were indicted on as many as sixteen counts each of theft, burglary, extortion, conspiracy, and destruction of evidence. "The cases are good, sweet pea," he told me, "but I'll have to make sure they stick like ticks."

"Oh, not another six months where I don't see you."

"I'll try to be as quick with it as I can."

"Miri's asked us out for dinner on Saturday."

"I'll be at the office, but I can come to Boulder from there, and we'll have Sunday together if I have to kill to get it."

"I think the invitation might be for congratulating you. You've been too busy to notice, but your gorgeous puss has been on TV, in the papers, and on the Internet. The news has been on all the talk shows, too."

The restaurant was new, Himalayan, and had just opened up in downtown Boulder. There were enough vegetarian choices for Miri, and plenty of meat and potatoes for Niall and me. The food was delicious, the spices giving subtle new flavors and undertones to the stewed lamb.

I remember how good it all felt, laughing and talking together, congratulating Niall, and kidding him about becoming commissioner. I hoped it would help to take away some of the pain he was feeling. Four of the men arrested had been more than acquaintances; one was a friend.

We had wine, and Niall had Indian beer. "Listen," Miri said, "I can't wait for dessert." She held her glass high above her head and, speaking slowly in a voice that alerted the two tables near us, said, "Here's to my healthy, happy pregnancy."

"Miri!"

"Yes—it's true. Surprise, surprise. I waited till I was sure."

We all applauded. The two couples at the near tables applauded and raised their glasses to her.

Then, of course, there was all the kidding about Niall and me, about how I would have to become pregnant soon, and Henrik declaring that he would redesign the upstairs rooms, and we had a mock argument as to which of us was best suited to do that. Henrik ordered some more wine, and we drank to him, and he stood and bowed to the two tables that were now cheering us.

We saw them home afterward, standing at their door in the cold, hugging them, kissing them, excited in the glow of their elation, watching them go through the door and into the lighted hall, his arm around her, her head on his shoulder.

On the ride back to Denver, we were silent, savoring the evening, and Niall said, "Well, I guess we'd better get started ourselves, if we are going to provide their kid with a marriage partner."

"You're not feeling cornered, are you? I hope not."

"No," he said, "life is moving us on, that's all. It'll be a good balance, which, God knows, I need. Help me tonight, Rachel. I need you. I'm aching and angry and sad."

The next afternoon, I was in the office redesigning a bathroom when Miri called. She was at home. She had come back early from the lab, feeling a bit queasy. Henrik was gone, and there was a note on the bureau, from which his brush and keys, watch and loose change, and a small cast-metal model of a mail truck were gone.

"Sorry," the note said. "I wasn't cut out to be a father. No promises were made. Good luck."

15

Miri's immediate response was rage. I knew the weeping would come later, but now it was all a cleansing fire. He had left his outworn hobbies and shed personas all over the house: garden-planning equipment, books on the stock market and genealogy, a box of scrolls to be filled in, carving equipment, camping equipment, boxes and skeps for an aborted beekeeping scheme, elaborate kitchen gadgets, waders, snow-shoes, fishing gear. Some of the things were valuable—I remember a beautiful drafting set I would have liked, but she had everything carted away to the dump. I sat with Miri in her kitchen every evening that first week, and we raged together and then ordered from the only place in Boulder that would come out so far: Moroccan. To this day, the smell of a certain spice evokes those memories: tang of sorrow, leaden anger, helplessness, and the small, unspoken admission: We knew; we always knew. Why were we surprised?

The year before, Miri had finished her doctorate and had been made acting director at the lab. This change in position had changed the nature of her presence there and of her friendships.

"They all saw Henrik," she said. "Sometimes he'd pick me up and we'd go out for dinner. No one will have the nerve to ask me what happened, but everyone will have a go at what they think happened. When I start to show, they'll get it right."

"How are you feeling?" I was staring out the back kitchen window at the decaying mounds of snow in Miri's north field. "Are you getting morning sickness or the weepies?"

"I'm too mad to know," she said.

I let Niall comfort me.

"She'll be all right, Rache, and about Henrik—just say I'm

94

shocked but not surprised. He had all the staying power of an Irish setter. Go see her, but please—next month will be April, when I'm done with the crap down at the department, and before the trials start, I want us to get away. I thought California—snorkeling or surfing or something."

"Miri won't need a shoulder by then. She'll soon be busy with her pregnancy and other people will come forward to help. Ada's stayed away as long as Henrik was there, but as soon as she finds out he's gone, which I'll make happen very soon, she'll come."

Deftly, tactfully, Niall gave me room to be alone with Miri. "Girls' days," he called them, and I knew that she had been easier for him to take when we had Henrik's moderating presence. The mix had changed; it became more difficult for him to get up on a Sunday morning and say, "Let's take some lunch to Boulder," or "Let's invite her to a show." It was a few weeks after Henrik had taken off when Niall said, "There's a nice guy in drug detail, Bernstein—you remember I told you about him. I think he and Miri would get along well. Divorced; kids live with the wife. Let's have them up for an after-noon."

"You're matchmaking, and she's pregnant and she's still raging and fighting in her mind with Henrik—they're still together, in a sense."

"I just thought— Yeah, you're right."

A few days later, he said, "We could have maybe ten people, and include Mike Bernstein, not all couples, so it wouldn't seem so obvious."

"Only like a rock through a plate-glass window."

I had to laugh. Most of Niall's friends were cops, and Miri's tolerance of authority was minimal. She had harsh judgments about Law Enforcement and its professionals, and while she exempted Niall from these judgments, there was little room in her catalog for authority figures. "She'll have to find someone on her own," I said. "In the meantime, there's a baby and that's got to take first place in her plans right now."

"She'll keep the baby, then?"

"Oh, yes. Single motherhood isn't the nightmare it once was.

It's tough, but not impossible." I spoke with more certainty than I was feeling.

I think the lab people must have been sympathetic. Miri told me she didn't take her personal life to the office, but the statement was laughable. She was looking hollow and bereft. Her glow, the mischief and joy, didn't light her face and her movements lacked grace.

"I wish I could help her," I told Niall. "It hurts me to look at her."

"You help her already," he said, "and she'll get over this. The guy never advertised himself as steady or dependable, and he did live off her, more or less." He saw my look. "I'm just being honest."

"Everything you say is true and none of it matters. She loved him. She was wonderful and glowing and happy with him, and they were together for four years."

"I know, but guys like that puzzle guys like me. What do women see in them?"

"Who knows?" I lied.

Slowly, Miri woke to herself a little. There were body changes to marvel over, and the dread and promise of April arriving, with its heavy snows. We could feel the ground drinking the water of their melting and see the cascades from the mountains beginning to roil richly in the creeks and streams. Trees began to bud. We all stretched and smiled and lifted our windows to smell the new air.

It was mid-April before I gave up on Henrik and stopped dreaming that he might realize what he had lost and come back. I think Miri must have harbored some of those wishes, too. Half the hospital was staffed with single mothers working their way through divorces or abandonments, and some, not as many as there are now, but some by choice, for the children they wanted. Back in our old neighborhood, Miri would have been an object lesson to all the young girls. Here, she belonged.

Yet I felt that something pliant and playful was gone. I thought at first it was the weight some women lose in their faces, a spareness early in pregnancy, an intensity and focus that planes the features close to the bone and leaves the eyes wider in their hollows.

Her house went back to the pre-Henrik days of dishes left in the sink and clothes wardrobing the floor, but she was more and more careful of what she ate and the water she drank. Coffee left the house, tea, and cocoa left—how I missed *that*. The ordinary vegetarian diet became rigid and rule-bound. Nothing she ate could have been grown in ground where pesticides or herbicides had ever been used. She allowed for no food additives and shopped only at special stores that could promise those conditions, and even there, not this rice or that wheat. It all reminded me of the so very perfect kashrut her father and Jacob had demanded, even more than the kashrut of our childhoods.

Her new law meant, of course, the end of our friendly dinners out, or ordering in when we were tired. Niall told me that I was on my own with her when dinnertime came. "She wants to visit us, fine. I'll put up with a vegetarian meal. But I'm not willing to harvest the carrot myself to make sure of its past life. I'll go over there for an afternoon, but we pack our own lunches. It's almost summer; we'll put in a garden up there and eat that. She's making herself very hard to get," Niall said, "for the future, I mean. Unless she opens up after the baby comes, she'll find the going very tough."

I had toned down his matchmaking instincts, pleading for him to wait until the baby was born. "On the contrary." I was smiling. "For every left-handed, clothes-dropping, opinionated, beautiful, and energetic woman, there's a right-handed, neat, laid-back, maybe not so beautiful but fascinating man."

We were tossing Miri's options back and forth from our positions on two air mattresses in a blue-green pool, which we would soon leave for a sprint to the much cooler ocean, where we wouldn't have to be shocked by the chill. The 150 feet of the sprint would cool us perfectly. We had been vacationing in Panama City, Florida: the Redneck Riviera, off-season. The weather was Florida-hot, but the best hotels were empty and had dropped their prices. We were enjoying a special travel package, and had three days to go on our week.

"Every day here saves us the money we would have spent in Paris," Niall was saying for the third time.

"Of course," I agreed, "the art museums are certainly comparable, the cathedral is magnificent, last night's Mozart concert thrilling, the local Arc de Triomphe, a triomphe that Paris could never match."

I had promised our week would contain less about Miri than it turned out to do. Niall had come through the police department shake-up and was facing testimony at the trial of all the officers named in the criminal ring. That would happen in May. He wanted to shut the thought away, and ditch Miri's problems, too, which didn't leave us much to talk about, since most of our thinking was hung up on what was happening to those people in Denver and Boulder. We swam and fished, took tours out to see the local sights, and went sailing, and I stopped using the Pill.

"If it's a girl, we'll have to name her Panama. We've already made love in the ocean twice."

"Whales do it there with great success," Niall said.

Coming home, I felt again how deep into life we all were. I was busy, fully engaged; Miri was trying to reassure people not to panic about contact with anyone who might have AIDS. She was on TV the week we came home, urging reason and pleading for a damping of the hysteria about the illness and its sufferers. Her charisma gave her words a force and conviction that their logic alone wouldn't have supplied. We watched her interviewer begin involved questions, but someone in the director's booth chose Miri's face even as the questions were asked, because the camera moved in on her and that luminous, intense aliveness; her beauty and urgency came at us unmediated for her full two minutes.

"Thank God she's not running for office," Niall murmured.

I was surprised. "Haven't you ever seen that light in her?"

"I suppose I have," he admitted. "I just wasn't zeroed in on it. I wanted to be sure you knew who I was in love with. Be glad she's arguing for tolerance. Be glad she has a good cause."

98

16

It was May, then June. The long days gave me lots of light for Sunday afternoons with Miri, and we returned to something like our old schedule. On Sundays, Niall stayed in Denver to do a series of house repairs. He bought himself a headset so he could work and listen to baseball games. I always made it home for a late dinner and saw that his afternoon had rested him. The trials were over, the department slowly reconstituting itself. Complaints were down.

I was working hard, visiting Miri, and probably overtired, which was why I was due for one of my spring colds. I felt one starting that Thursday. Why couldn't it wait for the weekend at least? I left work early and went home to try to head it off with a warm bath and the evening in bed. I was sleeping deeply. There was someone at the door. I went there half-asleep, still putting on my robe. I thought it was odd that Frank Elliot should be standing there. "Frank, are you looking for Niall?"

He put both his arms out and took both my hands. He said, "Rachel."

It was Thursday. It was June 13, and Niall was dead.

He had left the peril of the streets for the safety of the administration building and Internal Affairs. For years after, I played the scene, and for years after, I spoke aloud in the night to his killer, an ex-cop whose life had been blown apart by addiction and debt, and who had gone to the building when everyone was leaving work. He had shot a secretary and Niall and two other officers, none of whom had had anything to do with his dismissal from the force. He had wounded three other officers and been shot by a rookie on his first day of service.

"You couldn't have known how good a man he was," I cried

99

to the TV picture of the shooter, a man our age, worn-looking, aggrieved. To the picture in the newspaper, I shouted, "I loved him. You took him away. Why didn't you turn the gun up and shoot into the air?" He hadn't. My scene, the endlessly running scene where he dropped the gun and fell to the ground, was never played.

There was a full regimental funeral, with all the rituals and presentations, and the coffins were borne by all the top brass citywide. I stood with the two other widows, both with children, both younger than I, half-dead myself.

The shooting made the national news and the intrusion of the media kept me from grieving properly for some time. They wanted me stalwart, brave, and willing to tell a freeze-dried story. All they got was a shock-eyed ghost, mute with grief. For weeks, I was followed and called. The police had set up a support group for the widows and families of slain officers. Wasn't I going to join it and share? they asked. No. Wasn't I going to support gun laws, safety regulations, better security? No. I would go back to work soon, I hoped, designing kitchens and bathrooms in pretentious houses. I would try not to drop tears on the printouts. "I will not sob on the job," I told Miri.

The force is very good at death and funerals; its people were wonderful to me and to the other widows. The blue support system did a fine job for all of us, especially for the kids, becoming surrogate fathers for a time. When the next storm came, an off-duty cop was up fixing my rain gutters, but it was Miri who came and stayed with me and took the calls, and who walked me out in the big open pasture in back of her house, walked me through sunrises doped with sleeplessness and sunsets with tears. By the second week, we could walk the outer boundaries of the field without my stopping to break into sobs.

The worst of it was that while my spirit broke itself apart, my mind closed down in self-protection. I turned into a zombie, one of the open-eyed dead. I put food in the oven and forgot to turn the oven on. I walked the world, picking things up and putting them down in other places, aimlessly. I locked myself out of my house, and almost reported my car stolen because I had forgotten where I parked it.

My work was so submerged in detail that I was afraid of returning to it, and so for a month I didn't go in to the office. I was terrified to think that I might confuse one set of plans with another and make some humiliating or costly mistake.

Miri took me shopping so I wouldn't blank out in the supermarket, weeping or lost between the tomato sauce and the canned peas. I was grateful but I did realize, however dimly, that she had her own worries.

"Aren't you supposed to be home, resting, taking care of yourself?"

"I don't approve of sore breasts, swollen ankles, fatigue. Women get those symptoms from chemical fertilizers and pesticides."

"What about mood swings? I seem to be the only one crying, lost, sniveling, blubbering."

"Refined sugar can cause mood swings. Who knows what mental problems are caused by all the impurities in the air, the water, the food? Preindustrial women took pregnancy in their stride."

"I've never seen a preindustrial pregnant woman, I guess. Have you had ultrasound and amniocentesis?"

"Ultra, yes, amnio, no. Who needs all that? What I need is science, and I need you, 'Chelle. It's time for us to go to Denver to tell my parents about my pregnancy, and being a single mother."

A month had gone by since Niall died. I looked at Miri and noticed her swollen breasts under the black sweaters she wore. Black made her look wounded, vulnerable, and romantic. It made me look sallow and ill. "You mean you haven't told your father and Ada, yet? My God, Miri . . ."

"I don't want them screaming at me."

"When have they ever screamed at you?"

"Well, I don't want that *look.*"

I saw Miri's courage and yearned for it myself. She had been left, abandoned, and so had I. Abandonment made her crisp and angry and independent. It had made me weak and needy and stupid. Miri had begun to allow no authority in her life higher than her own will or even her own opinion. But it worked. For Miri, the chutzpah worked.

We went to see Ada and Rabbi Mordecai. Even though Niall and I had visited them only six weeks before, they seemed smaller, shrunk a little, and with a pang I remembered only then that they had been at his funeral and his shiva and had sat with me for a while. I had barely noticed them there, in the sick haze of my grief.

I so wanted the familiar warmth and generosity of Miri's home, Ada's energy, Rabbi Mordecai's ironic certainty. They seemed to know it, and they tried, but I could see the effort it took. The rabbi paused over the blessing before we sat, a blessing he had been saying all his life. The food was all the healthy, low-fat, salt-free, taste-free, pleasureless, blue-milk cuisine of the heart patient. Later, we marveled at the many uses of the soybean.

The conversation was also low-fat. Too many of us had too many areas of our lives that were off-limits. Reminiscences of Niall would wait for a time when they wouldn't automatically bring a wave of weeping. Miri's recent years with Henrik created a zone of silence. News of family could take us only so far, and my family's disapproval of Niall and of Miri's "lifestyle" had made those relationships dutiful, formal, and stiff.

We ate. Ada murmured a word or two about Niall and I fought tears, and then Miri told them that Henrik was gone.

"And I see you are going to have a baby," Ada said. "How come you didn't tell us months ago?" Rabbi Mordecai's head came up. He hadn't noticed.

"I was working. I was busy. Time passed. I'm here, now, and now you know."

I breathed and noticed I had been holding my breath.

Everyone was silent and then Rabbi Mordecai said, "And the man—he didn't want to convert and he didn't want to marry?"

"We liked him," I said, "Niall and I. We thought he was a nice man." They all got that—not good or loving or fine; Ada winced.

"We never met him," Ada said, and that was the first time I ever saw Miri lower her eyes.

It was only for a moment, and then she looked straight at Ada and said, "He was nice, yes; most parasites are. They attach themselves delicately, without causing pain, and they suck the blood of their hosts painlessly and drop off only when they're sated or when the host dies." Rabbi Mordecai looked amazed. I wondered when Miri had begun thinking this. Niall had said something like it to me about Henrik once, but he had hoped Henrik's obvious love for Miri would overcome those propensities and that time and inertia would slow him down. "I've seen my future in the microscope," Miri said, "parasites disguised as symbiotes."

Both of us were now unattached and it seemed natural that we would return to the way things had been five years before: the Sunday visits, the calls back and forth, a feeling of being girls again, even though I was now a widow and Miri in her sixth month of pregnancy. I had just been given an office, name on the door and all. Miri helped me furnish it, since I was still sunk in misery. Her own house was a shambles, with hospital castoffs, family castoffs, and garage-sale items from lower Boulder. She took me to shops and urged me to choose fabrics and colors. Without her, I might have disappeared into my work, and the work wouldn't have been enough, and because of that, the work also would have gone dry and poor. Our friendship saved me from emptiness.

17

It also seemed natural that Miri's pregnancy would assume a greater importance in our lives than it would have had Henrik and Niall been with us. The changes in her body and psyche became the news of our day. "Come up on Sunday so you can tell me what shoes I'm wearing. I can't see my stomach. My lab coats are all stained in front because they rub against the table when I lean over. I never knew that happened to fat people."

"Have you been sick?"

"I must have eaten something sprayed with pesticides."

Niall had bought a new car the week before he died, the only new car we'd ever owned. All of its first year's problems were supposed to be covered by the warranty, but whenever I took it into the dealership to be fixed, I was given lame answers, bad service, and suggestions that the car's stopping spontaneously in the middle of highway traffic was somehow attributable to my bad driving.

"The car's in the shop again. Towed," I cried to Miri, "and they won't get it back to me for two weeks at least." Then I burst into tears. "Niall's dead. They know that because they see it clinging to me—vulnerable widow. I can't call Frank Elliot again. He was Niall's friend, but he has his own family and his own troubles, and Miri—I feel so helpless and stupid and they know that and they can let me sit here for weeks and charge me because they say what happens is my fault."

"Hold on," Miri said. "Let's see what the two of us can do together. If that doesn't work, we have other weapons. I'll call in sick on Monday and we can both go in."

At the car dealership, I saw, not for the first time, her conscious use of that radiance she could summon. I watched her open it to them, a revelation of delight in their existence, like Miranda in *The Tempest*, seeing men for the first time in her life. Of course, she murmured, turning luminous eyes on them, they couldn't know the importance of my car in my work, but that was now made clear. Surely they would want to help me in my need. A beloved husband had bought this car and had died, leaving it to me. It was his banner over me, his wish for my protection. They and they alone could ensure that legacy and make it real.

Not all this was spoken, of course, but all of it was suggested, first to the manager of the repair department, then to the mechanic. She wasn't kittenish or cute and, to my surprise, she wasn't sexy. She reminded me of a movie saint, urging people to their better selves, convinced as much by her beauty as by the force of what she said. We left them staring after us.

"Do you know what you do, and how you do it?" I asked her as we drove back to Boulder.

She shrugged. "I just let them know how important it is, what I'm saying to them."

The car was fixed in a day. I'm still driving it.

Now and then, she would talk about Henrik, and her anger would wake up again, and my love and loss would make me weep. Miri could rage until I reminded her about the child she was carrying. "He gave you that. He all but remodeled your house. The kitchen was a disaster; look at it now. You have the beginnings of a garden with a Japanese-style hedge that cuts the noise. There's that line of trees. Henrik gave a great deal of himself." Then, I thought about my gifts from Niall, and my years as a policeman's wife. I had an outlook on life that I never would have gotten on my own. I was tougher, less impressed by talent and more by competence and steadiness. My friendship with Miri and her pregnancy, which I was sharing vicariously, strengthened me.

So we balanced each other as good friends often do, making up for lacks and bringing out strengths in each other.

Miri began to buy all the land behind the farmhouse, month by month, and when an aunt died and left her a bequest, she had taken the money and purchased the eighty acres to the north and another eighty to the east of the farmhouse—scrubland, wind-scoured and treeless and with no water. She bought the three houses near her, but all the other dwellings on the patch were squatter shacks, outside the city's grasp of codes and statutes.

Then, very suddenly, the land situation changed. The city extended itself to incorporate miles of open land to the north, including Miri's area, and three developers approached her. The neighbors around her, the easy, slatternly bunch in the shacks across the road and in the decaying smaller houses of the compound, disappeared, leaving their wrecked buildings and junked cars behind them. Miri sold but only her land on the east, and in two months the acreage was platted, graded, streets put in, and water and sewer lines laid down. In a year, Miri's house would be at the edge of a suburban development. The developers had been eager for the land and Miri ended up being financially very well-off indeed.

So all that summer, trucks went lumbering past, down the new road to the scraped and leveled building sites. Houses grew as though overnight. Miri and I sat in perpetual dust clouds and noise, and only on our Sundays did the boom abate, and even then, there were parades of cars with people looking to buy the prospective houses.

As Miri rounded and softened, as we bought furniture and hung curtains in the room next to hers, she began the motherdreams: "Chelle, this girl, if it's a girl, is going to be free. I can't wait to set her free. It'll be better with no men around to tell us what to do and who to be. Life will be better for her than it was for us because there won't be the conflict and fighting."

"Your parents didn't fight," I reminded her, "not like mine did."

"No"—and I saw her face go set with emphasis—"and they didn't fight because my mother gave in, all her selfhood, everything to my father's whim. When I think of what I let them talk me into, that awful marriage to Jacob Zimet, I want to scream. Nothing like that will happen to this child."

"Miri—" I was about to remind her how she had welcomed the marriage, how she had assured me what a good idea it was. I

106

closed my mouth. She was my friend and she was struggling to rebuild her life.

I didn't laugh or mock at the dream she had about the child. We both had a vision of a wonderfully contented baby, child, girl, woman, confident as I had never been, beautiful, of course, satisfied but not smug—in short, perfect. "And you'll be happier to have a girl than a boy?"

"Oh yes," Miri was all exultation, "the traditional dream is all wrong."

I began my slow recovery during those summer and autumn afternoons. Niall and I hadn't had the family we'd dreamed of. When I'd stood at the police ceremony with the two other widows, both with children by their sides and one of them pregnant, my shock and misery had held a subtle whiff of relief; there were no children to confront with the rawness of this loss, no worries about money or raising them alone, no single-mother tangle, and no pregnancy to worry about.

My sister Shirah was having babies, too, at that time, but I was closer to Miri than I was to either of my own sisters. I shared Miri's pregnancy, sympathizing with the physical changes, understanding the sudden tears and laughter, the hormonal roller-coaster ride.

We went to maternity shops and bought whatever looked good. We laughed with the other women who stood there and compared stomachs and diets and exercises. We used the stores the way men use bars; we let down, we spent money, and laughed about it. At home, the mother pictures began rolling in the theater of the mind. "What if she's born deformed? I don't know how to take care of a very sick child."

Miri was labile and vulnerable then, prey to sudden bursts of feverish energy and long hours of slowdown, sudden fads and fantasies.

We went on baby binges. We bought layettes and blankets and a crib, a dresser, a bath set. Shopping lifted me up into a realm of thoughtless, golden visions. I'd been spending the time in endless one-way conversation with Niall's killer. I muted those conversations with baby dreams. We blissed out buying little mobiles and tiny shirts and cute outfits and soft sheepskin mattress pads and stuffed bears.

Miri didn't want classes. I started doing exercises at home with her and found them good for me, too. I shared the community of the pregnant with her. Women greeted us in the supermarket. What month was she in? What gender was the baby to be? She was proceeding very scientifically with her pregnancy, but she had a tape recorder that played Bach and Mozart. She would balance it on her abdomen so the sounds could reverberate into the womb and let the fetus "hear" the harmonies, which was supposed to awaken the child's taste for good music. She played tapes of Chinese and Spanish poetry. "No Hebrew?"

"I don't want her sectarian in her religion. You're not suggesting that she be limited the way we were, stuck in a box?"

"The chances of that are slim, but it seems a waste to give her Lorca and Li Po and not Isaiah."

Why was I arguing? I didn't believe that any of the things Miri did for the fetus in utero had the least effect. All those attempts at influencing what was to be, causing this or that, making choices for the unborn child, seemed to me to be demands made even as Miri spoke about freeing her daughter.

I was also reaching out to catch the changes in Judaism. The women's movement had hit the old ways amidships and there had been an explosion of new and creative rituals, practices, and interest in widening our perspective. Women outside our little Orthodox enclave were wearing the tallis and tefillin and the kippah, prayer items once worn solely by men. They were learning to chant and celebrating the new moon, a woman's ceremony. Miri barely seemed to notice these changes and they slid by her almost without comment. The very intensity that focused her interest like a laser sometimes darkened that eye to everything else.

Then she stopped talking about Henrik. I was the one who spoke of his part in the child to come. "His bone structure's great, you'll have to admit, and he has a good IQ. I never saw him sick." I was standing at the sink in the kitchen, looking out the window, refreshed by the long field the four of us had walked in, now unkempt in its dry cover of weeds and haylike grasses.

108

"You have a good profession and security you could never have had with Henrik. Are you still calling yourself Miriam Marigold?"

"It's on my checks."

"You're not going to change the spelling of Miriam, are you?"

"Who used to call herself Raquel?"

"Touché." Never keep the friends you made in adolescence; their memories are too exact.

That September, trembling, I left my old firm and went out on my own: Rachel Y. Finn, PC, Residential and Commercial Interior Design. In October, Miriam gave birth to the dear and wonderful little girl we named Tamar. I coached her delivery and saw the baby come out before Miri did, whose eyes were closed in the passionate work of pushing. Yes, a girl, and how alive she was, arms and legs working, as though she were running to catch up: World, world, wait for me!

Doing the coaching, watching as the baby forced her way through Miri, I had been sitting at Miri's head, alert, cheering her on, but more often quiet, my hand on her shoulder, and I saw in the glare of light focused between her spread legs an immense wheel of light that rose toward me, its edge facing me. The wheel began a very slow revolution and the sound of it turning was Miri grinding her teeth. It was the wheel of the generations that was turning, and I with it. I don't know how that vision helped me to continue my healing from Niall's death, but it did, and it was one more thing that bound me to Miri and then to Tamar.

It's begun to snow and I assume that will be no problem for the search team in the cave because caves have a separate weather, temperature, and climate. I learned that much from having gone with Val and Tamar. Not all caves are cold and damp. Some are hot—day and night—or dry, or windy, with winds that change from morning to afternoon, like a giant breathing in and out. I want to ask what kind of cave this is, but I'm sensitive about being here. Miri doesn't know enough to ask such a question. I see people begin to put up little tents to cover the equipment, and someone comes and takes the heater away. Without a word, someone else motions for us to get up, because they're moving the piles of ropes and boxes we're sitting on.

The camp is now full of activity. We're told to go and warm ourselves in one of the trucks until the tents are set up. The snow is beginning to fall more insistently.

Escobar comes and tells us that someone inside the cave has found supplies. We gape at him, not understanding.

"Inside the cave," he says, "they've found clothing and equipment and food. It means they planned to come back and rest there. That means they're close by. The rescue's taken so long because the cave's got tunnels that the cavers didn't notice and didn't mark, but with this find, they're sure the two are straight ahead. The chief's called for an ambulance to go on standby and he'll come soon and tell me to drive back down to the first turnoff to lead it in. You can go to that tent"—he waves—"over there."

We see it sporadically when the snow curtain is whisked away for a moment. We'll find blankets and sleeping bags there, he tells us, and some foam mattresses. Tired rescuers will be coming in now and then for an hour or so of sleep. Someone will come and tell us of any developments.

We make for the tent and find the pile of foam pads there. Fully dressed, we get into the musty-smelling sleeping bags and I go back into the drowse-wake search for what happened to us all.

18

Miri was pale and seemed too fragile to start in mothering, and the baby, Tamar, was tiny, too, and too small, much too small, to be taken away from the safety of hospital care, I thought.

"Don't be fooled," Miri told me; "the hospital's full of sick people and all kinds of iatrogenic bacteria, hospital-grown. We're well out of this."

But her mood changed soon enough. I remember us going slowly up the walk from the car to the house. We were alone, painfully, terrifyingly alone. The old community of helpful, if feckless, squatters had been displaced and the sudden new community of houses (two styles, three colors) wasn't yet ready for its occupants, who would, in any case, be strangers, not inclined to care about an unwed mother in what they saw as an eyesore and a ruin.

There was road grit in all the rooms, the gray-tan of the local earth, fine enough to find between the roofboards and under the closed windows and the sagging door. Our steps left prints on the gritty floors. We could open the windows and get relief from the mustiness, but the fall air was too cold for the tiny girl. I asked Miri if she didn't want to come down to Denver and stay with me.

"No—I want to be here. All her little things are here."

"At least let me sweep up. Go into the kitchen; it's less gritty."

So they rested and I tried to get the layer of dirt and sand cleared away.

Then, we took Tamar into the small room we had prepared a long time before, put her down in the new crib, whose mattress

111

and sheets we had to shake out, and all of us fell asleep. We were awakened by her cry. I had taken the week off, intending to stay with Miri. Why hadn't she asked Ada to help? I was as inexperienced as Miri. Why didn't we call Ada? Ada would have come with all her cheerful competence, babied the baby, babied Miri, taught us what to do—

"I didn't want that look."

"She's not like that."

"Oh, you think not? That 'where is that no-good you slept with?' look, that 'why aren't you still married to Jacob and living a decent Jewish life?' look."

"Ada wouldn't—"

"Don't tell me she wouldn't. Even if she didn't want to, even if she swore to herself not to, it's on her eyelashes, in her freckles, in the way she folds clothes. It's in her smile and in the wrinkles of her face."

So we endured. There was panic when Tamar couldn't nurse, and Miri had no milk, and we finally did what Americans do— looked in the phone book and found a group that addressed itself to what we needed to know. Today, there'd be a hundred Web sites, and our lives would be lived on-line.

Nursing, diapers, washing, rashes, bathing the baby. Was Miri bleeding too much? Miri developed a stitch abscess. Miri's breasts were sore. I stayed at the house until her milk did come in and she had established some rhythm of nursing. In that time, Tamar had changed from a tiny, frightening homuncula into a tiny, beautiful infant, black-haired, with eyes the color of lapis lazuli, which were soon to darken. She had long black lashes and a gaze that didn't wander, but focused almost from the start.

Along with my residential work, I had been designing office space for small industries in and around Denver. Motion-study experts of a previous generation had made economy of movement their prime directive, and their rules and procedures had produced an army of carpal-tunnel patients and chronic work-related arthritics. My designs brought back some of the bend-and-stretch, less efficient, not-too-wasteful movement, and with enough variation in work to keep even the computer-bound from freezing up. Industrial work kept me from getting stale and bored with residential projects, and of course the money was better. Time off for grief and time off looking after Miri had made me nervous about money for the first time.

I was also soliciting invitations to speak at business conventions and architectural-design workshops. I found my talks creating interest, and larger contracts began to come my way. The awards Henrik and I had won helped some, but I hadn't found another garden genius to complete the indoor-outdoor relationship I wanted. The gamble, taking time to put myself forward as a speaker, was paying off, but I was still surprised when more business clients than residential ones began to come. My work schedule filled up. I hired a secretary.

At the time I was sharing Miri's and Tamar's lives and using my love for them to heal my anguish at Niall's loss, I was also beginning to set the arc of my professional life. As I comb all the events of those days, trying for the thread that leads here, I'm astonished at how much other work I did. I remember dozens of meetings and projects. I was functioning on one level intellectually and emotionally on another.

Tamar was eating solid foods; Tamar had a tooth. Tamar was standing up and speaking simple words. These were the milestones I cherished, the news I delighted in. I got Miri a good camera and kept her supplied with film. Before and after every business trip or convention, I drove to Boulder, where I dropped all my professional manners, my busyness, my arguments with rigid cost accountants, fussy clients, and reluctant office managers, to kneel, eye-to-eye with Tamar, and watch her open her arms to me, cooing-babble, hide the thumb, peek-a-boo.

She was a wide-open soul, fearless from the start. Chairs enchanted her. Climbing up, sitting high delighted her. She sat and then stood, lifted as high as Miri, crowing with pleasure. Tastes for her to experience, smells, things to touch—these sent me to stores and catalogs, hunting pleasures for her. At his High Holiday sermon, Rabbi Bender quoted Avot: "'Who is wise? One who learns from all men.' Yes," he exulted, "that's true. Even from a baby." He couldn't wait to rhapsodize on his own favorite subject. "Yes, even from my little grandchild. We learn from babies to be active, to learn to accept the world as it is."

I thought, To chew our toes, and began to giggle so hard, I had to stop my mouth with my fist.

Miri saw that activity, that world acceptance, in siege terms. She showed her maternal care in ways I thought were often endearing, sometimes useless, and occasionally all but fanatic. She conducted a blistering war against sugar, processed foods, white bread, ordinary milk, tap water, fried foods, concentrated juices, and anything pasteurized. "This child won't be obese," she declared, "or have carious teeth and bad skin." I believed it. The food regimen struck me as extreme, but I noted that my junk-fed nieces and nephews—Shirah's children—were over-weight and phlegmatic. Some of them were teenagers by then, and had grown into monosyllabic and passive starers at video games and head-wagging zombies plugged into their Walkmen, lost in the bark and scream of their idea of music.

Miri was still pumping Chinese into Tamar, which I thought endearing, if useless, and denying her vaccination, which I hoped wasn't dangerous.

"You know how many people die in this country from incompetently prepared vaccines?" Miri demanded.

"Miri, there are diseases out there—viruses—you know that better than I do."

"She's not around other kids yet; I'll wait until she's older, and then I'll begin to research what the drug companies are doing."

How would Miri trust Tamar with a baby-sitter?

"I've been taking her to the lab with me. There's a storage room I use, and with the door open, I can see her all the time."

"How does that go over with your coworkers?"

"They love it. It humanizes the place."

"It sounds ideal, but isn't it against some law or other?"

"I'm sure it is, but no one's turned us in yet. Why should they, when it's what should happen everywhere? Women are working in offices and labs and stores all over the country. Why shouldn't there be children in all those places?"

"Why not, but aren't there some people who resent it?"

"Yes, one or two . . ."

"Aren't you afraid they'll turn you in?"

"They know it would get back to the rest of us."

People helped her because they loved her. There was Ada, of course, and the teachers in our high school. I'd helped her with her homework since first grade. Henrik had been there to fix her house and ground and give her a child. Did traffic lights turn from red to green when she approached? Did snowstorms wait until her key was in the lock before splitting their seams? Was I jealous, ever? Now? Maybe. Maybe, except that I felt included in the magic; I always had been, enjoying the gracious light that Miri exuded and that brought out the smiles and acceptance of all the world. Celebrities have to act or play football, run, swim, be wealthy, own hotels. Miri needed none of these gifts. Her celebrity was herself. Of course the lab people wouldn't object to Tamar's staying there. Hadn't Miri needed it?

"The secretaries in my old office had little kids," I told her. "I can see a nursery and preschool there, but would the clients accept it?"

"If babies and small children were allowed in every office, the staff would get used to it. Kids in offices would be part of life."

"The secret," she told me later, "is Tamar. She seldom cries— she never has to. She's always picked up and comforted. She's a lovely, happy baby because all her needs are met."

Miri's needs were obvious; her solution made sense. I had very little experience with babies and children, and I mistook the good luck that made Tamar docile and contented for the work- ings of Miri's philosophy, and her lab mates' enchantment for a social master plan. Was it there, where the trouble began, in that enchantment?

I was at the lab to give Miri the playpen I had bought for Tamar. We set it up in a little ell where a cabinet for case records had been placed. The cabinet blocked the view of the playpen, so we moved the cabinet again. A pathologist named Darby Graham was head of the Pathology Department. He wasn't the homely,

115

avuncular man the name suggested to me. He reminded me of a mole, touchy and detail-mad.

"I'd better head him off," Miri said softly. "He's one of those people who needs to be in charge. All the ideas have to be his."

"I'll go, then."

"No, stay and play with Tamar."

I watched Miri as she went into the little glass-enclosed office off the lab. Graham had been seated, but he stood when she came in. A smile, a nod, yes, yes. She began to speak, her hands making metaphor. Their faces were three-quarters turned to me and I saw the twitch, every now and then, nose leading, mouth following. Miri began to glow at him. I couldn't hear the words, but her gestures and body language and a word read here and there on her lips helped to construct the line she was taking: "I love this work, and you appreciate my performance in it." She was radiating at him, her eyes claiming his face, then looking down, sparing him the pain she had put into some word. Her hands came up—"Can't you see a way? The job doesn't pay enough for Tamar"—I saw the name Tamar on her lips, difficult though it was to lip-read, but clear because of the special space that framed it—"for Tamar and me to live on. Is there no way? How? Oh, easily—she'll have her little playpen over there,"—a slight wave of the hand indicated it—"she'll have her play things there and never bother anyone, and I can care for her and nurse her in that little place, and that will allow me to work and stay here, and because of that, all my interest, all my dedication . . . " Her hands were held toward him, palms up—only give me this—and there was that radiance, growing in intensity to warm him, to melt him.

I saw the melting. I saw him succumb: Yes, but. . .well, yes.

It didn't take long, and I thought she would need to renew the enchantment from time to time. The force of it would have to be there whenever he looked at her. I realized then that I'd never seen her glow at Jacob, and that was what had alerted Ada, sitting at these Sabbath tables all those years ago, when they were courting. I'd seen it work on Henrik, and I'd been afraid of seeing it with Niall, the world she made warm and holding everything possible. She came out of the office. There was no smile of triumph on her face, no wink that said, Look what I can do. Instead, there was something modest in the little nod: This is what should happen and did. It happened because it was the right thing, a justice belonging to this place at this time. Her sureness about her wishes brought some of that glow to us, where we stood like the viewers of a comet or the floats in the Rose Bowl parade. If Miri had been smug, I would have hated her, but her face and gestures and the power had an openness and simplicity that were pure joy at the possibilities of a good and rational world.

19

The lab people hid and protected Tamar, who spent her infancy and early childhood there. At nine months, she appeared at a seminar in Dallas, where she lay playing with toys in her carrier while Miri made a presentation. The lab people must have used considerable time and energy in furthering Miri's plan and protecting her secret. Miri praised the arrangement. "Tamar sees lots of people every day, and every week I take her up to Pediatrics to play with the kids there. She has a mask on and I wash her hands before and after. She gets a social life any kid would envy, and all the stimulation she needs."

And Tamar—when I saw her on Sundays—was full of high spirits, seldom crying or sulky. She ate the diet Miri demanded with a good appetite, bubbled and blew into language with astonishing ease. She was a little darling of pleasant ways. Even the terrible twos seemed to be less terrible for her in the glow of love that surrounded her.

By that time, there were thirty-six houses to the south of Miri's old farmstead, built on the land she had sold to the developers. Streets now wound through the area, garages gaped with cars, shrubbery appeared, people barbecued in backyards and, in spite of watering restrictions, sodded the front yards to an iridescent green never seen on this land since the Cretaceous.

A full street of eight houses now faced Miri's, and into one of them the Yow family had moved. Miri went over with a tray of organic cookies and learned that the elder Yows did indeed speak Chinese and that they were teaching it to their children. "And it's not Cantonese; it's Mandarin, a better kind of Chinese," she told me.

"You can get some real Chinese speakers for Tamar instead of those silly tapes."

"Why not? Now is the time for language acquisition, and why shouldn't Tamar take advantage of these years? Why not give her two languages, three? By the time she's fourteen, she could be ready for college—other kids do it—languages early, the sciences, math..."

"Have you forgotten Jacob, how sheltered he was, how it hurt him, until he broke away and came out here?"

"It's not the same thing at all. Jacob was coddled by a whole community, stood up on every occasion to perform, to quote pages of Talmud that he barely understood."

Some time later, I asked her how Tamar's Chinese was coming.

"She's still using the tapes. We say sentences to each other."

"What about the Yows?"

"I tried to make that work," Miri said, "but it won't. They won't help me."

"I thought they spoke good Chinese."

"The language wasn't the problem. They speak it and, yes, they're teaching their kids, too, but they're not the right kind of people."

"Do they lie and steal?" I suggested blandly.

"Of course not, but they give their kids candy. They give Tamar candy, too, ice cream, and greasy snacks. You know how easy it is to addict a child to chocolate and sugar. Of course I want Tamar to learn languages, and maybe you're right about the tapes being artificial. Even the Yows, whom you would expect to have some traditional knowledge, look at me as though I am a zealot. Pizza! Pizza—and they let their teenagers watch their smaller kids."

"I suppose you've kept her sugar-free and don't want to spoil it. As for the teenagers—maybe you could bring them over to your house."

"They won't come."

"Why not?"

"We don't have television. They have Chinese tapes and shows they watch on cable—that's how they planned to teach her. I won't have television in the house. It teaches violence."

"Tamar's almost three now. What will happen when she's four or five and needs a wider world?"

"We'll meet that problem when we come to it. She does fine the way things are. She's learned all her colors and shapes, and some of the alphabet. She's learned where in the lab she can go and where she can't. The techs all love her and help her learn. You come, and I play with her, and when we go up to the pediatric ward, she plays very well with the children there, the ones who don't always have their faces plastered to the TV set."

"Is she still wearing a mask there?"

"Of course."

I couldn't see anything wrong with what Miri was saying, but I felt there was. The fault wasn't in the plan, or in the words, but there was something between the words, in the intensity of Miri's emotion. She was out to prove something and prove it through Tamar. A buzzer went off, the first of a series of warning buzzers, but since I couldn't put the warning into the proper words, I had to let it sound for me alone.

The lab closed for all national holidays; Rachel Y. Finn, P.C., didn't, but during Gay Pride Week we were out for a day on the AIDS Memorial Walk. I went up to Miri's lab.

The success of Miri's theory had emboldened her.

"I want Tamar to be better, healthier, smarter than we were. She won't have to unlearn things and make four bad decisions for every good one."

"And TV's at fault?"

"TV is virulent."

"Hold on," I said, disbelief replacing defensiveness. Miri's girlhood had been amazingly privileged and her way eased to cream. Her life had been a glide. I'd been there; I'd seen it. I said, "Be serious. You who engineered most of the escapes we made, who shaded the truth and connived for trips and tried and ate all the forbidden candy you could get your hands on."

"That was different."

"Are you telling me that our summer days at Elitch's and Lakeside were bad, or that sneaking off to movies or buddying around with Art and Abner and experiencing ordinary life was

120

wrong? You know how cramped we felt by the neighborhood, growing up with all the restrictions. You're only doing it again, but without the religious part. Was the junk food so bad? Was your mom's streudel ruinous?"

All of a sudden, I found myself angrier than the situation warranted and we were facing each other with tight jaws and hard eyes.

"I have to protect her," Miri said. "I'm the one she depends on to keep her safe and well."

"All right," I said, "all right."

There are moments in the best of friendships when it's possible to destroy years of happiness and shared experience with a word. There are also moments when the slow, long gathering of disbelief and disagreement can no longer be put aside, when the words not said, light as a curl of sluts' wool under a bed, make a mass, a cause. We were there, at that place. I retreated.

20

Tamar turned three and then four. She had a precise and specialized vocabulary with a knowledge of laboratory words and processes that amazed and delighted me. Miri discouraged her playing with dolls, but I kept her supplied with stuffed animals and a family of bears. At one time or another, they all had leukemia, hepatitis, and strep, but even though she took blood, sputum, stool, and urine samples from all of them, squeezing their stomachs, pinching their arms, she wasn't morbid or excessively frightened by the idea of disease. She once told me that my cough was probably "viral" and that she couldn't talk too long on the phone because her cereal was "precipitating" in the milk.

My firm had grown. That year, I hired a draftsman associate, and later, I took on another designer. Miri was also doing well. She and Graham convinced the hospital administration that expanding the staff in Pathology was essential as the hospital itself expanded. I'd left the condo Niall and I had shared and moved to one between Denver and Boulder, very chichi. He would have hated it. By then, I was getting work in both places.

I began to design for bigger commercial clients. That spring, Miri leased her back acreage to some wealthy Boulder horse owners and Tamar began to clamor for time to visit the horses and learn to ride. I marveled at her fearlessness, her wide-open acceptance of the world, all of which she thought had been designed for her pleasure. She could also nag and wheedle with the best of them, twisting the screws until Miri gave consent and found the daughter of one of the lab people to teach her to ride. The lessons went through the snowy and unsettled month of April and into May. In the summer, Tamar began to learn in a class in which she was the youngest rider. I have a picture of her on a pony, obviously proud of herself. She's sitting majestically upright and with her heels ostentatiously down, delighted with her high perch and perfect seat. There was talk of getting her a horse of her own, and we all enjoyed looking out the kitchen window or sitting on the back porch on nice afternoons to watch the horses in the big field. She often went out with apples for them.

Late in July, Tamar developed a slight fever and a sore throat. The illness was the first real one she'd had, but Miri wasn't alarmed. With the diet Tamar had and the right amount of sleep and exercise, she could shake off ailments that in other children became serious. Tamar didn't improve during the next few days, which surprised Miri, who was hesitant to take a culture, preferring to stay home and watch as Tamar dozed and woke.

The signs and symptoms worsened. The fever rose and Tamar became nauseated and began shivering. Miri was sure it was flu and tried to force liquids, but Tamar threw up everything she was given. On the fourth day—I was calling every morning for news—a crowing, labored, and almost strangled breathing drove them to the emergency room.

"He was new—a man I didn't know, who didn't know who I was," Miri cried angrily to me over the phone. "He was rude, insufferable. He said, 'Good God, woman, what kept you?' He started to look at Tamar's throat, stopped suddenly, and sent me out of the room. Later, they took a culture. That damn ER doc looked at the results and shrugged. Then, he said, 'I knew this yesterday. I saw it in Haiti. It's diphtheria.' He looked at me then, like I was a coconut fallen out of a tree. 'Didn't you have this child immunized?' I started to explain about the dangers of immunization, and he said, 'Okay, this isn't the time to lose our focus.' I could have wrung his neck, the self-satisfied bastard. I told him, 'We don't see diphtheria here in Boulder. Where could she have picked this up? She's as carefully watched as any child anywhere could be.' He gave me a look and said, 'We may not see diphtheria in Boulder, but we're seeing it here and we're seeing it now.'"

I put on my clothes and drove there.

They had Tamar in an isolation room and the hospital personnel came and went like ghosts, masked, gloved, and swathed. People came from the health department and the Centers for Disease Control. They questioned and probed and took samples. Men and women in uniforms from agencies I didn't know existed moved in on us with clipboards full of surveys. They told us they would close the streets around Miri's area and test the ground and the water. Neighbors' yards would be invaded.

"You don't understand," Miri protested. "She doesn't go out of our yard."

"She got this somewhere."

In the heave of Tamar 's crowing sounds, we waited through the night together and into the next day. I brought some work and was able to do a little now and then while Miri dozed. She went down to the lab twice for an hour at a time for whatever she was able to accomplish there. Some of the floor nurses told us we could wait where we were; others said that we'd have to move to the general waiting area at the far end of the ward. Miri pulled whatever strings she could, getting this doctor instead of that, this nurse instead of that, levering her rank and calling in markers all over the hospital. If I hadn't been frantic with worry myself, I would have been impressed at her reach.

There's a rhythm in waiting of that duration and intensity. Our energies picked up and then we talked. Confidences came, truths that challenged the feeling of removal, unreality, and the deadness that pervades those hours. We wove hope into a rope of talk. Time dropped on us as we sat on the institutional chairs or the harder benches. Someone got us coffee and the ready-made sandwiches, always with cheese and mayonnaise and some kind of pressed meat. I ate, waiting; we talked some more. Now and then, I felt a need to get up and pace. From time to time, Miri went someplace, the lab, something to check on. Our energy faded and a slow hopeless anguish built in us. We looked without interest at the others waiting. Our talk went still; we seemed to become patients ourselves, passive and hopeless. Then something exciting would happen: a nurse leaving, a doctor arriving,

124

someone wheeling equipment into the room. Our sluggish spirits remembered; the cycle began again.

I brought coffee up; we drank. Later, Miri went away and came again with a packaged bun for me.

"What are you going to eat?"

"I'll get something later."

The doctor came. The fear-hope ran up the ladders of our bodies. I felt my pulse beating hard. She stood over us. "We need to find out if she's allergic to the antitoxin. We don't think so, but we've had to run tests, and it all takes time."

"Is that allergy likely?" Miri asked.

"It's statistically significant," she said. "We'll want to be treating this aggressively."

That word touched off a fuse of hysteria in me. I got the picture of doctors and nurses rushing into Tamar's room, pulling her from the bed, yelling at the disease all the while, and I had to fight the urge to giggle. The hysteria was the product of exhaustion and fear.

More equipment was moved in. I began to doze, only to be electrified by another doctor standing in front of us.

"We've started the antitoxin, and we'll need to follow her condition closely," she said.

The door to Tamar's room was open and we could hear that fearful crowing of her struggle to breathe. How long could she keep pulling like that? The doctor noticed and said, "She is getting oxygen and we'll put her on a respirator if we have to, but not just yet."

When she left, I said, "How long has it been that she's been struggling?"

Miri gave me a piercing look. "What do you mean by that? I brought her here as soon as I knew how serious this was."

"Don't you think that maybe you waited those few extra hours because you work here and didn't want people to think you hadn't been taking care of her? I understand that, a single mother with a sick kid . . . "

I wasn't prepared for the rage that followed. She went white at the lips. "Don't ever say I'm not taking care of Tamar. She's the most cared-for child in the world. Her health, her education, her recreation—all . . . "

"But Miri, you didn't have her immunized." I spoke my thoughts, not conscious of speaking.

"That's what fries you, isn't it?"

"I think you should have done it."

A nurse was standing between us. Sensing that she would soon get more than she bargained for, she put up her hands and backed away.

"You're not her mother; what do you know? Do you know anything about immunology? Do you know there are risks, some of them unacceptable, brain damage, for example? Paralysis, even death?"

"I'm not her mother, no."

"Then stop trying to make decisions about her."

"Decisions—good God, Miriam, decisions? I wish I had that power. I wish I were her mother. She's a dear, sweet kid and you won't let her have any of her own experiences or be with anyone who eats candy. What the hell kind of life is that?" I felt my sinuses open, something that was blocked releasing. "Why did we run away, Miri? Why did we fight so hard to be out of the ghetto? You're only making another ghetto with just the two of you."

"My job is to keep her safe. Those inoculations could—"

"How safe is she now?"

"Who could have figured a thing like this, diphtheria?"

We weren't shouting; we were whispering, our anger not erupting, but seething, and it was uglier than plain rage. Face-to-face, we weren't a foot from each other. The intensity of what we were saying had drawn us up like dancers. If we had touched, we would have fallen on each other, biting and kicking.

A doctor—I saw his coat as he stood behind Miri. The nurse had fled. I looked beyond Miri to see his face, measuring it for bad news. "Mrs. Marigold?" She didn't hear him. He repeated her name. "Miri," I said, and stood back. She turned. He looked at the two of us, his expression not as cold as it had been before. "Go on home, please. It's going to be a long process, and we'll call you if there's any change. I'll do that personally."

So Miri went back to her house and I drove to Denver and fell asleep with my clothes on. Two hours later, she called me.

"'Chelle, I need you here."

I had never heard Miri apologize to anyone for anything in all the years I had known her. This was as good as it would get. I'd been hurt. I knew well enough that I wasn't Tamar's mother. Niall's death had made me needier than I should have been. I loved Miri. I loved Tamar. "I know," I said. "I'll be there as soon as I can."

⠂⠆ ⠂⠆ ⠂⠆

They've found something important in the cave—where they fell, I think. A man ducks in to the tent to tell us. The snow is heavy on his coat and hood, and he tells us there's an ugly wind aloft. The ambulance has been given its orders to move in, because there are no choppers flying, and I murmur a curse at that. It'll take hours to get Tamar and Val to a hospital if they need one, when a chopper could have done it in minutes.

We've been doze-waiting, I, reliving past years, in and out of a half dream. I've been thinking about the weeks of Tamar's diphtheria, making magic with the memory—surely she hadn't been saved from that to be killed here. Jews are not supposed to believe in amulets; mine are all invisible. Tamar's first illness had occasioned our first fight, called off by me.

We wrestle ourselves up in our sleeping bags. Miri is blurred in the light of the man's lantern.

"You've found them?"

"No, but we've found where they are. It's a hole. The rescue people got to a hole, with a shelf broken off, which they think gave way. That's all they know."

"Can't anyone look down there and tell?"

"No, Ma'am, but as soon as we get some more news . . . "

And he's gone.

I get up, freezing, and go to the tent flap, opening it as little as I can to see out. Snow is still falling, and its breath sound is all I can hear. The lights around the cave opening seem far away, a glow, not a light, in the veiling snow. I go back, find my shoes and a blanket, and go through to the outside, keeping my hand on the tent as much as I can so as not to lose myself. Avoiding the tent stakes, I move around to the back of the tent to squat on the rocky downhill edge of the camp and relieve myself, cleaning off with snow. I'm too lost to try to find the privy they have set up.

When I get back, men have arrived, three or four, taken the foam mattresses and sleeping bags from the pile, spread them out on the ground, and gone quickly away to sleep. This one mutters, that one has a long Cheyne-Stokes-like rhythm—deep, deeper,

128

deepest, and then nothing for what seems like forever, until he breathes at last and starts the routine over again. Now, I'm forcing myself back in time so I won't have to listen to that performance. I'm ashamed, too, embarrassed at all this work, all this effort being expended on us for Val's and Tamar's mistakes, and for ours.

21

Tamar was critical for days and slowly moved back, away from death. Now and then, nurses or doctors would pass where we sat and stare at us with a little widening of the eyes that said, Look at her, head of the path lab, this woman who doesn't believe in diphtheria, who tried to sneak her kid in where she works. Other waiting ones seemed to conclude that we were oddballs, lesbians, probably, from one of the squatter villages and shanty places up in the foothills outside of Boulder—commune, probably. Then, later, when the fact of Miri's employment as a pathologist in the hospital had fully circulated, the looks were more questioning. She hadn't broken the law, but even in Boulder, her decision was unconventional. Some people must have thought she felt superior, getting a free ride, safe because all the other parents had incurred the risks for her when they had had their children vaccinated.

There were also, in those early days, members of the staff coming through to see Tamar as a matter of curiosity, murmuring: "Diphtheria—you don't see diphtheria much these days."

"Why didn't they intubate?"

"Kostka says if they did, they would pull that tissue off and there would be heavy bleeding into the throat."

"Man, Third World stuff."

We were a curiosity, and the tourists to Tamar's room stared at us unabashedly.

But as she recovered and the grayish membrane, hallmark of her illness, eroded and was coughed up or swallowed, the curiosity diminished and things slowly returned to normal.

During this time, I was also fielding calls from my mother. "Do I have to be sick to hear from you?"

"Ma, it's Miri's daughter. Miri has no one to help her through this."

"She should have stayed married to Jacob Zimet; then none of this would have happened. Why don't you get married again? It's time you should stop waiting for Mr. Perfect. You could have your own children then, not hers."

"Please don't say any more—you're going to be mad if I hang up on you."

"I'm only saying what everybody says."

"They're not on the end of this phone line. You are."

"I'm only telling you—"

"Did you know that the elephant is the only mammal with four knees?"

"I'm only telling you."

I was happy enough that when Tamar moved slowly from under the wheel, I celebrated by having one of the pictures I had taken of her enlarged and framed. It's on the wall in my bedroom now, but I think I'll move it to a less central place, where it's not the first thing I see as I come into the room. I stand in front of it for too long—and wonder about too many things. Tamar sat up; then she got up, and walked. The doctors said there were dangers still to be overcome, diphtheria's many secondary ailments were still to be avoided, dangers of strain and overexertion. All of Tamar's systems had been weakened. When I went up to Boulder for my Sundays, I was greeted by a child who was almost transparent. Her skin had paled and thinned. She had lost all the ruddy chubbiness of her almost five years, and there was a wasted look to her face. Even then, she didn't whine or sulk, but occasionally she would weep silently from weakness.

Antibiotics have revolutionized our definitions of illness, so it was a shock when the doctors told Miri that Tamar would require a long convalescence, bed rest for days or weeks, perhaps even months. The medications with which they had flooded her system had dangerous side effects and there was the possibility of other medical problems arising from the diphtheria itself. In spite of Miri's dietary vigilance and care, some of these problems did arise. Blood work showed that the toxin was being eliminated, but Tamar's rapid heartbeat and fever weren't

131

diminishing. More tests showed myocarditis, an inflammation of the cardiac nerves. She might die of heart failure.

There followed weeks of low-level fear, worry about cardiac or kidney failure, or of simple sudden death; then, later, of life-long illness. Tamar was rehospitalized several times with the instability of her vital signs. Miri constantly campaigned for her release. "Rest? I can give her better rest than any hospital!" she shouted at me. "I've been taking her to the lab, where she's safe and warm and constantly monitored and is a minute and a half away from complete emergency services."

How she kept the secret of Tamar's all but living at the lab, I'll never know. When the two of them left the hospital, ostensibly to go home, they actually came back through another entrance and then went directly to the pathology lab, where they were greeted like returned hostages.

The ell in which Tamar lay had been screened off, and Miri continued to keep the secret of her presence in the lab. Although I understood there were rumors and whispers, as long as no one officially knew and forced an investigation, the game could go on. The only worry Miri spoke about was that someone in the lab would be sure to want the privilege of a baby or small child tended on-site and would press the matter because of Tamar and would bring an end to her special status there.

"Another kid recovering from diphtheria?" I asked. She winced.

One day when I visited the lab Tamar was sitting at a miniature desk lab, using her "microscope," a magnifying glass set up on a stand. There were report sheets in a pad, crayons and colored pencils, pictures to color and cut out, and a pillowed chair for naps. Off her little ell, the pressing work of the hospital pathology lab went on—the hum of voices, reports being made, the hum of lab machines. There was a buzz of special lights. It was an ideal setup, all but primitive in its closeness and immediacy, mother and child, community and child.

"What a delight she is," an older woman said. She was one of the techs waiting for Miri to initial a report. "She sang us one of the songs on her tape this morning. She already knows how to read."

Full recovery took almost a year, her heart being a little slow to heal. She emerged brighter than ever, and eager to catch up with her own running steps.

But more had happened to Miri than to Tamar. Miri had developed a chronic anxiety, which I was afraid would crystallize into an even deeper mistrust of the outside world.

"Miri, she needs other kids, friends, adventures."

"Other kids? Adventures? Where do you think she got the diphtheria from? Listen to her vocabulary. Hear what she *knows*. Listen to the rudeness and cheapness all around us. Do you want her to sound like the kids on TV, like the garbage mouths we go to movies to hear? There's language in the neighborhood and on the wards that would make your skin crawl. We're surrounded by ugliness and trashy values. Do you want her to drown in that filth?"

I was half-convinced, but I also remembered that it wasn't too long ago that the neighborhood where Miri lived had been a ragtag collection of shacks, that Miri herself had been part of a somewhat-social life among squatters who ran in and out of one another's trailers and tumbledown houses and had gone to Miri to get water and borrow food, and who shared the venison from hunting, and the trout from fishing, drank and fought within earshot of the farmhouse. The world Tamar was growing up in was geographically the same but culturally a universe apart.

Miri now had no contact with the neighbors or their children. Her relationships with people, except for me, seemed to be purely professional. Any men she had must have been fitted in like business appointments, although I couldn't tell where. I think Miri and Tamar went to the lab and went home. Her coworkers chatted over lunch about their children and domestic lives, but Miri attended none of the departmental picnics or parties because of her food restrictions and some little badge of superiority she wore. She knew her colleagues in the single context of the lab, and only lunchtime chat gave her the sense of being in an ordinary, everyday world. The group's single mothers were older women at that time, and they tended to mother Miri, even as she separated herself from them.

I was at Tamar's fifth birthday party, cake at the lab, only us at the house, when Miri announced that Tamar was to be home-schooled.

22

The year Tamar was five was the year of my great professional change. I was gone for almost half of it, a few weeks or a month at a time. I always saw the two of them before I left, and as soon as I came home, but my trips meant that some of the day-to-day immediacy of our relationship was lost. Friendships are tidal, moving in and out with mood or circumstance, all but unnoticed until there's a flood or a long withdrawal. Miri had hurt me by reminding me of my childlessness and had astonished me with her defenses against a world that had always been so strongly in her favor. My trips gave me a chance to get over my hurt and annoyance and to be refreshed by my affection for Miri and Tamar.

The home-school scheme Miri proposed depended on her complete control of her hours at the lab. She planned to teach Tamar early in the morning, be at the lab until lunch, then, get Tamar to the library to a children's reading program that ran from one to three, then back to the lab until it closed at 4:30. They would put in two extra hours, Miri at work, Tamar at homework, then have dinner and go to bed.

The whole ramshackle structure could fall to bits with discovery or sickness or any change in the hospital's procedures or the library's reading hours. What if someone in the lab protested? What if someone at the library wondered where Tamar spent the rest of her day, or called the authorities if Miri happened to pick her up late?

"Miri, where are there other kids?" I asked her once.

"There will be other kids, but the right ones, the ones who can help her development."

I had some sympathy for Miri's nightmares. God knows

135

there's lots of ugliness and cheapness in our time, and her work held metaphors for all the world's dangers. She peered at the universe in her microscope every day, counting the invisible cells of teeming harm multiplying in their broth.

I watched Tamar at her empty sixth birthday party—that one held at the lab, an event at which only two other children were present, and neither was Tamar's age. She seemed fine for all that. She received only gifts calculated to enrich creativity or stimulate the intellect, but she was used to such gifts and was more gracious than I would have been. I got her a princess costume, complete with wand, cape, and crown. Later, she crept up on my lap and hugged me; "It's the best present of all."

I know it was. She wore the gown to rags, until the "diamonds" in the crown were half gone and the "diamonds" in the wand had turned black. I remember the afternoon as seeing her completely recovered. She had come back from her illness to vibrant life, eating the cake Miri had made for her, a heavy organic item, sweetened with fruit juice, but which left a bitter aftertaste. The guest kids, used to sweeter, high-fat fare, picked listlessly at the offerings and later one wandered off outdoors. I waited for tears, but Tamar seemed as happy with adults as she was with children. I watched her work the room and thought that maybe Miri knew better than all the teachers and experts and psychologists, common wisdom, and even common sense. Tamar's charm wasn't overcute or precious. She seemed genuinely interested in what other people had to say and engaged in what was going on, all effortlessly. So what if she was more often with adults than she was with children? Childhood years are soon over, and childhood days, as I well remember, are often no great pleasure anyway. There was no wrangle in her life, no bitter mother or angry father, no financial worries, no sense of being left behind by poverty. Tamar didn't even seem trapped in Miri's web of restrictions and limitations of food, TV, associations, experience. Miri's plans were balsa and tissue paper, to be sure, but I thought she might just make them work for a year or two, and by then, something else would come along and another idea with firmer footing.

There was, for example, the Derek episode. A coworker

brought Derek over to Miri's house for an afternoon of play. Tamar had met him at the lab and liked him. I never met him, but I heard plenty about their playdate. He had a slingshot and taught her to use it, but her skill was nothing to his, and her eyes lit up when she modeled his walk for me. "It's like this, 'Chelle." The walk pictured the boy, a near swagger redeemed by graceful carriage. "And you can almost hear him say, 'Ha-ha' when he walks. And he has a hat with all the places he has been, pins that tell you, all around the hat."

"Is he a big kid?"

"He's bigger than I am—he's eight."

Things were going swimmingly, and then they weren't. When weeks had gone by without my hearing about him, I asked Tamar, who said shortly, "We had a fight, and now Mom says I can't play with him anymore."

"He was a savage," Miri said. "He punched her."

"In the face?"

"On her arm. She was black-and-blue."

"But she said she punched him first."

"Are you crazy? I won't have child abuse, even by another child. It was bullying!"

Then there was Maya, and apparently she was clothes-crazy. Then there was Mike, and the "language thing."

"Seven years old, that boy. I thought Michelle was raising him properly. The words that came out of his mouth!"

"But you said the kids got along well."

"They did, but 'shit on this' and 'fucking that'? No, none of that for Tamar."

"Fuckin', not fucking," I said. "It's the third word in any sentence."

"I told Michelle I didn't want that talk around Tamar and she shrugged and said she didn't like it, either, but what could she do? She said Mike had picked it up from kids at his school and it was impossible to make him stop. He may be a nice boy, but I can't have her hearing and using that kind of language."

"We heard all those words. Don't you think Tamar has the same built-in protection that we did? Lies we told—don't shake your head—we did lie. The bad things we heard had an effect on

137

us, registered, but how badly were we scarred by them?"

"You don't understand. The whole world has gone toxic since then. Look around you. Listen to the music, hear the talk."

"Don't you remember what we heard?"

"It's gotten worse. It's all gotten worse."

By then, I was traveling for World Wide. World Wide was an international resort chain with locations in picturesque spots in six countries. Their headquarters were in Mérida, on Mexico's Yucatan peninsula. A man had called at the beginning of the year and asked if I would be interested in working for the company. I had gotten up a portfolio, cleared some time, and flown there for the interview.

The headquarters were impressive, a white walled mini-village within the city, Mayan in look, the workings were hidden behind turns in the streets, and some were underground, so that service, air conditioning, plumbing, and electricity were all inconspicuously there without a break in the mood of lofty serenity.

Their CEO had told me, "We don't build hotels, as you see. All our projects are enclaves, small communities, self-enclosed. The model is based on a fine Japanese inn, or a Spanish parador, but expanded to include special tours and full resort services. The modern visitor to a country wants the flavor of that locality, not a generic hotel that might be anywhere. Yet, he doesn't want complete envelopment in what might be a perilous experience, dangerous people, a difficult foreign language, strange customs. He wants a comfortable bed and good sanitation. When he dines, he might want to sample the regional specialty, the octopus, the kava, but he might want to complete his meal with steak and a fine wine."

If World Wide and I were compatible, he said, I would visit each of their six locations. The company was planning to remodel in the classic style prevalent in each country, complete with modern convenience and luxury. I would be part of a team in each place, working with architects and formulating an interior plan for each remodeling. I would be compensated for the work I did during the trial period, and if things went well, I would need three or four years to complete the project. "You will be centered in Denver if you wish, but expect to be traveling for approximately half the year."

I stayed in Mérida for four days, meeting people and looking at plans. A month later, I was near Paphos, on Cyprus, in a villa over-looking the sea and with views of orange groves and olive orchards. I fell in love with the project.

For most of my career, I'd been spending my time weighing changes inside of houses mostly for staid people. In this work, I could indulge in some fantasy and fun. I felt a weight lift from me that I hadn't known was there. Part of that weight was the love and worry I had expended on Miri and Tamar and the intensity of my relationship with them. In the feeling of lightness and play, I experimented in the plans I drew. My joy communicated itself to the people on my project, and everyone became more interested, more creative. We were rewarded with ideas from the local stonemasons and carpenters. Our architects opened up to the new possibilities and began to integrate them into the overall design. We were, as my nephews, Shirah's sons, would say, "cooking."

The money was very good. It was good enough to let me hire people in Denver to run things while I was away. When the projects at World Wide ended, I would step back into my sensible Denver profession.

I was at Paphos for two months, back home for a month, then in Mérida, then in Zmiti, in Turkey, and Vila Real, Portugal. I spent a month away, a month at home. I saw Miri and Tamar often, but with a new dimension. They were part of my leisure, then my recuperation, after the intensity of the foreign resort sites and the increased pressure of the Denver office, where I still needed to keep things going. My Sundays with Miri and Tamar, now rarer, were less involved, so they gave me even more pleasure.

Tamar turned seven, and the home-schooling plan seemed to be working. She read voraciously, particularly in the natural sciences, no surprise to me, but because of my trips, she also began to take an interest in geography. I sent her lots of books, pictures, maps. The study of places would, I hoped, lead to an interest in their history, their people, and our people, which I hoped would lead her into an understanding of the Jewish part in all of it. By those means, softly, deftly, I hoped to lead her to an introduction to Judaism itself. Beautiful dreamer. I was very good at it in those days.

23

I'd just come back from Trinidad, where World Wide wanted an expansion. Things had been difficult there, and I was tired. It was summer, a Sunday afternoon, and the three of us lay supine on Miri's porch, drinking a fruit concoction, one of the few tolerable foods Miri prepared. With Henrik's departure, his inspired hand in the kitchen had left as well, and his teaching had dwindled to Miri's preparation of a dish or two, the least time-consuming and complex from his repertoire. We were half-dozing. Tamar was picking on the cut-down guitar I'd given her. She had begun to grow out of those stuffed bears. I'd seen the guitar in a shop in Mérida and hoped Miri would find someone "appropriate" to give Tamar lessons. We'd strung it up using instructions from a book I bought with it, and I liked the sounds of the tunes she was picking out. By then, I'd met Rafael Mendes in Mérida. He was part of the management at World Wide. He'd taken me around to shops and markets and told me I would have to learn to haggle over price, a participant sport in Mexico, and one that takes great skill and energy. I always started well enough, but soon lost heart in mid-game and watched the shopkeeper's face close a little as I agreed too easily to his price.

Some shuffling of associations broke into my dreaminess on Miri's porch and I sat up. "Listen—I go to Mexico in the fall. Why don't you both come along? You could see the city while I work. After my week there, we could all take off for the Yucatán and see the ruins—Uxmal, Tulum, Chichén Itzá, Cobá."

It was Tamar, of course, who burst apart, who jumped and cried out and took fire and wheedled and begged and all but turned inside out with eagerness to make the trip. Over the next weeks, Miri threw forward a dozen reasons not to go, and Tamar

141

and I took up the hobby of batting them down. My visits became contests, the house an arena. I'd pay for the trip; Tamar would be given a real sense of the land, the earth, distance, culture, and geography that no book or computer program could provide. What would they eat and drink? What about the language? Where would they stay? What about Montezuma's revenge? And on and on, until Miri's fight became pro forma and we were playing badminton with the words we had spoken many times.

As I argued, I couldn't help dragging out our past like attic rags. How had she become so cautious? What had taken the adventure, the spirit from her, the optimism that saw possibilities over there, over there, over there? She said it was because she had become a mother and had watched her child almost die and that I couldn't know what that was like. There it was again: Tamar was her child, not mine. I loved them both. I kept on arguing.

At last, more to please Tamar than to gratify me, Miri assented.

The planning took almost a year, by which time Miri had vacation days stored up, time that had been depleted by Tamar's illness. We went into active mode, working through one thing after another—passports, airline schedules, hotels. Wars are planned with less fuss.

All that time, I was showing Tamar pictures of the ruins, the magical power of the ancient and abandoned cities, once secret and covered in jungle vegetation and even now not completely revealed. "Do you see that man standing on the steps of the big pyramid? That shows how huge the temple really is." We read histories and bits by the great archaeologists who had unearthed the ruins. I bought Tamar a snorkel and we went to the local rec center's pool. "You can learn to swim before we go," I told her, "and then you can swim in the Gulf of Mexico or even the Caribbean." She was eager to learn and loved the idea of the snorkel, which allowed her to get over the beginner's fear of breathing in water. She was a quick learner, returning from the lessons babbling and bragging to Miri. "I want to be a swimmer! When you walk, you only use your legs, but in swimming, you move lying down and you use your whole body!"

So we began a routine of swimming at the center. Tamar didn't seem to want formal lessons, but was happy to learn what she could from me and we floated and dog-paddled and then did the strokes I knew, and we laughed a lot.

"Wouldn't you like to be as good as that woman over there?'

"No, no lessons. They're all working too hard. This is more fun."

She didn't want to race me, either, or compete with the other kids at the pool. She seemed to have no need to race, or to win. Now and then, Miri came with us. We showed off to her, splashing and kicking, inviting her in. She had once been quite a swimmer, but now she declared that swimming wasn't worth getting wet and that she was at the pool only to help Tamar. After a few times, she let us go alone and stayed home to catch up on office work.

One Sunday, after our swim, I suggested to Tamar that we play tourist. She would soon be a tourist for real and we should practice looking, feeling, making somewhat of a study of places, readying ourselves for the trip. Miri was doing a budget breakdown and had said we could stay out for the afternoon. She would be working and was happy enough with us out of the way.

"Where do you want to go?"

"Home," Tamar said.

I was disappointed. She persisted, so we drove back to the neighborhood.

"Stop here," she said, "and park." We were three blocks from their house.

The weather was mild; a light, warm breeze had brought people out to look at their post-winter gardens and wash their cars. A suburban domestication prevailed.

"Come on," Tamar cried, and began to pull me down the street.

The surprises started almost immediately. "First we go over to Spruce Lane," she declared. "It's where Phoebe lives, *Fee-bee*."

We all but ran. Tamar went confidently up to the house at the end of Spruce Lane where no spruce trees now stood, and knocked on the door. The woman who opened it seemed annoyed until she saw who it was and then she beamed at us. "Hello, Tamar dear, out walking?"

"This is my honorary aunt, Rachel," Tamar said, pulling me forward, "and we've come to see Phoebe."

"She's nursing right now," the woman said, but you can come in and watch, and when she's finished, you can help her with her appearance."

The two of them were chatting amicably and were obviously familiar and delighted with each other. Phoebe was the most obese cat I had ever seen and was obviously also a friend. After the nursing, we brushed her. The woman—Molly—gave us cookies and milk, and we left to go and check in at the Warrens', then the Bakers', the Van Dusens', and half a dozen other houses along the two streets closer to Miri's house. Everyone to whom I was introduced seemed to know Tamar well. Some knew her mother's prescripts about sugars and fats and offered us apples or grapes; others didn't know or knew and didn't care and came forward with candy, which we refused only after the fourth house. Closer streets yielded even more friends. Everyone had a greeting for Tamar, who knew all their names and the names of their pets and sometimes where the people worked and what their interests were. I was amazed. It was another world.

"How, when did you learn all these people?"

"Mom goes to sleep on Saturday afternoons and sometimes she lets me off at Spruce Lane so I can get exercise walking home, and I go out to play for an hour while she's fixing supper."

"Does she know about all this?"

Tamar's face changed, a kind of clouding, as she weighed the words. "Mom is very sensitive about some things. Mrs. Deetz is interested in Jesus. If Mom knew that I hear about Jesus from Mrs. Deetz, she would get upset, so I don't tell her." She looked up at me. "And there are the cookies, too, and I did watch Phoebe give birth. It's not exactly lying or keeping a secret. Mom sees the neighbors wave at me when we go past. She thinks they're too nosy."

"Are you nosy?"

Tamar jumped up and down and, still holding my hand, gave

a caper. "I'm a nosy-nose. I want to have a nose as long as Pinocchio's."

I'd thought that Miri forbade children's books and had kept them from Tamar. "Where did you hear about Pinocchio?"

"Kids tell me things. There are home-school kids at the library where I go, and they tell me lots of stuff."

When we came to the house and were at the door, Tamar stopped me as I was about to put my key in the lock, the key Henrik had used, and said, "It's not a secret, 'Chelle, only Mom would be upset."

"Yes, I think she would," I said.

And so, in that casual a way, on one late Sunday afternoon, we began our collusion.

Later, when I was leaving, I said to Miri, "Do you remember how we used to sneak out when we were kids and go to the movies?"

"Well . . ."

I knew she was trying to forget those days. "That took a lot of courage," I said. "Tamar has that kind of courage. I notice it in her swimming."

The secret, the collusion, was more problematic, and more ambiguous, and would submit its bill later on.

24

We flew to Mérida in April and I watched Miri gape and Tamar cry out in amazement and wonder at the buzzing heat, insect clatter, bird noise, city roar, the great trees, the parade of odors, aromas, stenches, the ripe rottenness, the fecundity of it all. I'd been to lush places before, but for Coloradoans, the eye, conditioned to the high, clear, semiarid, spare vistas of the Rockies, goes into a kind of sight shock at all the plenty. The ear, attuned to traffic sounds, vibrates with the unfamiliar cries of birds and buzz of insects. The nose is confounded. They stood on the street and went into sense trance. Rafael, with whom I was intimate by then, was our guide, warm and helpful. Miri's eyebrows lifted when she met him, and later I said, "Yes, he is."

"Married?"

"They live apart."

She was surprised, but I didn't take her surprise as insulting. I'd been surprised myself. Our relationship had started as we worked together on the remodeling of the Mérida headquarters. Because he was in the firm's management and I was a subcontracted professional, there was no sense of controlling power on his part or sycophancy on mine. He often arranged to spend time with me at the Turkish and Portuguese resorts, and we'd toured in northern Italy together for a week. On this trip, he took us to wonderful places and was entranced by Tamar and frankly admiring of Miri. He was a gallant man, gallant enough so that I felt a pang.

"They are beautiful," I said wistfully.

He laughed. "Yes, they are. I would not wish to disagree with the señora, though, who would make a splendid matriarch in this very patriarchal country of ours. We fool no one but ourselves here that women do not rule." He had been at some pains to find restaurants that promised food that was organic and pesticide-free. Miri was gullible enough to believe that only Americans did agribusiness and used chemicals on their crops.

I spent five days at work and heard about Tamar and Miri's adventures when we met for dinner. I was charmed and delighted at their first views of everything, the nights in which people strolled, ran, argued, sang, and shouted way past Boulder's bedtime, reluctant to relinquish the still-warm streets.

"Come here at two p.m.," Rafael told them, "and then the sun touches nothing that moves."

My office amazed them, and the tours Rafael arranged for them included everything that could please or amuse them both.

"I can't believe it, it's so *green!*" Tamar cried, "All these flowers and trees, all in one place. It's flower-tower-wower-power!" And we all began to use those words when we saw the spill of blossoming vines cascading over walls or climbing trellises.

On two or three evenings at dinner, Tamar fell asleep at the table, which delighted me. She was getting full value out of everything she saw and heard.

I'd put them up at World Wide's guesthouse, which I'd redesigned, and I could see that Miri was impressed, even though she wasn't one to take much note of her surroundings.

I worked around their plans. Then I was free and we took a tour bus to Chichén Itzá, where I had arranged our stay at a seaside resort that had bus service to the major ruins nearby. Our only problem was to choose what we wanted to see in the four days we had left.

The bus trip was my first—I'd always been taken to the Yucatán by private plane, flying over the green mat of rain forest, not the savannah. The slow speed and the immersion into the landscape gave us a chance to savor and wonder at the lushness, the all-but-overpowering growth, the trees that were dragged down by covering vines and, as they fell, it seemed, were sprouted upon by falling seeds. Everything scrambled to root itself instantly. To us, used to single trees standing well apart from one another, the savannah was an unbelievable sight. "You can hear the leaves," Tamar said. "You can hear them covering everything." She was enchanted by the ground-covering green, the bird racket that formed a background as steady as the ocean, flocks of vultures gathering at a death that I was grateful was hidden from us.

The people we saw fascinated her, too, appearing as they did in clothes somehow blinding white and clean, even as they walked muddy roadsides carrying loads on their backs or heads, or with tiny children in their arms or at their skirts.

We chose Chichén Itzá for our first sight of ruins, and spent the day walking in the dead city, marveling, and calling to Tamar, who flew up and down the huge pyramid with its hundred narrow steps. There was heat—the stones radiated it, the sky buzzed and watered with it—but it didn't seem to oppress us. I'd been here professionally, to study the style I had wanted for my Mérida remodeling, and I'd used many of the forms and spaces established by these ruins for my feeling of what the interiors should be. I had never approved of "decorator" surfaces applied to what was no more than a standard box of a room.

The day was perfect for us, a cloudless sky, a constant series of surprises. There was a troop of monkeys haranguing us from the encroaching jungle and flights of parrots and colorful birds moving across our line of sight as if on cue to delight and amaze us.

At the top of a pyramid, we stood on the platform and stared out at the huge ruined city and at the miles of jungle, a billowing green stretching in all directions, overwhelmed only by a still-vaster sky. We had climbed the pyramid very slowly and carefully, dreading the descent on those narrow stairs. Tamar was delighted that they seemed made for someone her size.

"Stay in sight," we told her. She came and went among the tourists, a mixed group, young and old, exclaiming in a bouquet of languages how big, how far, how long a vista, how blue a river, how wide a sky.

"Think of being a priest of this place," Miri said, "and standing here at midnight to count the stars. I used to do that in the horse field, but the city glare came, and now I'm lucky to catch the North Star and one or two of the brightest planets."

"I didn't know you could identify any of the stars."

"Henrik taught me." It was the first time I had heard her mention him in anything but a denigrating way and it pleased me to think that she was at last ready to see him more realistically. That meant she might be ready for someone new, someone more stable than Henrik had been. I smiled and said, "Here, there'd be an entirely new zodiac and no Greek pictures. What animals would these people see in their stars—jaguars, maybe, and plumed serpents?"

"Fearsome things, I think. Crocodiles and anacondas and condors."

A man next to us had been listening. He said, "Look at the ball courts and how wide the roads are. An army of people must have been needed to keep the outside away."

"It grows in a day," a woman said. "Did you see the toilet paper?" We looked at her. "We noticed it coming down," she said. "There are roads to houses or compounds off the main highway, roads no bigger than paths. The people mark where the path is with a roll of toilet paper on a stick. Maybe if they go out and work in the morning, the path is grown over by the time they come back at the end of the day."

Tamar, flushed and breathless, was doing the steps up and then down and up again. We saw her and gestured for her to slow down. The heat could be too dangerous. A man who seemed quite knowledgeable spoke about the orientation of the pyramid in relation to the city, and of the city itself. These ideas were a great part of my own work, and I began to question him. Miri, bored after the first two questions, wandered away. People were chatting, looking out in all four directions, and the very small space was becoming almost crowded. I laughed, looking over at the man beside me. "Not much room at the top here, is there?" As I spoke, my eye swept the steps. Tamar was gone. I went around the platform, looking down. She was on none of the steps.

The area wasn't crowded. I could see individuals and small groups strolling up and down the wide causeways of the city. Here and there people on guided tours collected in groups of bright colored vacation shorts, shirts, and dresses. I looked at each group carefully, thinking that Tamar might have latched onto one of them, listening to the Spanish-accented guides, whose voices rose to us as murmured sound devoid of meaning. I found Miri beginning to negotiate the very narrow stairs. "Where's Tamar?"

"Isn't she up there with you?"

We were annoyed at first. Sometimes all that enthusiasm Tamar radiated was hectic and wearing, and she certainly was all enthusiasm when she struck upon something she really wanted to do. We stood, helpless, at the top of the world, trying to locate her, and then we went down, hesitant about losing the advantage of height, calling, losing patience, and then calling again. Soon we were so anxious that our voices went shrill. We even lost each other walking rapidly up and down one street after another, calling her name. No one had seen her.

At first, I was sure she was with a group. I remembered how she had managed to conquer the neighborhood, a secret I was still keeping. Tamar was as dumb-friendly as a puppy. This was a country foreign to us, with attitudes and rules we didn't know, and some we couldn't even imagine. Might there be someone with the word *American* in his mind, American meaning rich and rich meaning ripe for ransom?

We searched for an hour, calling and calling, the panic rising in us. We walked here and there, later returning to the entrance, where there was an office for the park personnel who managed the ruins. They were polite but cold. Had we not looked for the child? Seven years of age—had we not told her to stay close to us? Responsibility for lost children was not a park responsibility, but a parental one, yes? The park would soon be closing, and then everyone would have to leave. It would certainly be better if the mother could find the child before their closing of the park, because an official search would be extremely costly and require both time and money, and one would expect the force to be compensated for its effort.

Then Miri lit the room, and once again I saw her gift not as a natural process, inherent, but as a studied art, one she brought to perfection. She bloomed in their presence, a magician transforming herself, a cherry tree in blossom. Surely they would understand the anguish of a mother. Oh, these children—look away for a moment and they've gone. Shouldn't their blessed searchers be recompensed for any effort they make? Two of the park guards rose like sleepwalkers and came with us.

We retraced our steps, sweating with panic and a mute despair. Our hearts were pounding with effort and terror. Our minds made dark stages on which awful possibilities were flashing. We saw Tamar being kidnapped, murdered, falling, an accident, and calling for us with the last of her strength. Two or three tourists responded sympathetically and went about calling for Tamar. The area began to close down for the day. Even now, people were moving toward the exit of the park, carrying picnic equipment and cameras, going toward the colorful tour buses and hotel vans that would carry them away. Finality was in the air.

We stood at the axis of the two main roads of the ancient city. No one. Nothing moved. With the sickness of nightmare, I turned slowly from one to the other. Miri and I stared at one another. Then, over her shoulder, I saw something, someone, then a woman, walking toward us purposefully. As she came closer, a bundle she was carrying shifted and a leg and shoeless foot fell free of it. Miri stood stunned, but I began to walk and then to run toward the woman, seeing Tamar's long black hair, freed from its barrette, tangled and muddy, the details becoming clearer with the woman's advance. The big woman, an older woman, a grandmother, we thought, began to smile at us. Tamar was alive.

Suddenly it was all noise and explanations and we stood in the center of the great roads of the dead city like a grand-opera septet, all singing forte. The guard who had reached us was gesticulating, joy and annoyance it seemed, in Spanish. I was thanking the grandmother profusely in English; she was answering profusely in Dutch, obviously explaining the details of finding this child. Tamar was crying; Miri was offering that incompatible outbreak of rage, impatience, love, and relief that erupts at such occasions. The other guard was beaming, congratulating us in Mayan-accented Spanish. The septet stopped abruptly when the guard left the stage. Then the Dutch lady made a polite turndown of my offer of dinner and left. Tamar stopped crying and we, too, began to walk toward the exit.

I said, "I thought Mexicans loved children," and Miri and I both burst into ungovernable laughter. Then Tamar said, "I went into the Magic Kingdom. I didn't have a light. If I had a light, I could have gone way way deep in the Magic Kingdom. There were magic birds there and special walls and special cool. If I had a light, I could see the magic things. I fell and then got scared, and for a minute I couldn't see where I was, but there was light from the roof. It was a small, small light. Then I got caught in the tree again, so I knew I was walking right, but I fell again and got wet and then I got scared again. Can we go back? Please, tomorrow, let me go back!"

25

I was stunned to hear Tamar say all this. A moment before, she had been weeping. She must have set up quite a howl for the Dutch woman to have gone even a little way into the darkness underground to retrieve her. Now, she was begging to go back into that place of darkness and cold. We were so relieved at her return that we didn't question her until we were back at the resort and she had been stripped of her muddy clothes and bathed, and her matted and filthy hair washed and combed. There were long scratches on her legs and bad bruises on her back and right hip.

"That's where I slid. The rock went down, and I couldn't see, but I fell and slid down where it was smooth and then rough." She mimed this, the sliding, "And then there were the birds."

Miri lost her temper in the letdown into relief. "What's this nonsense about magic? Where did you learn about magic kingdoms?" She gave me a hard stare. "Rachel, have you been talking nonsense about magic? I've worked hard to keep all that garbage away from her!"

I put my hands up, palms open. "Not guilty. No Oz, no Easter bunny, no Alice in Wonderland, no tooth fairy."

She went back to Tamar. "Well, you're safe, now, and that's what matters. You were overheated and excited. You were running up and down those steps too fast."

She wanted to cancel the rest of the tour. "We've had enough excitement already," but Tamar and I protested so loudly that she was forced to give in. I saw Tamar the next morning, stiff and pale, completely intent on showing no signs of pain as she sat and stood, ready for the day's excursion.

"I want to go back—with lights."

"It's obviously not a place visitors go," I said, "or there'd be lights there already."

"I want to go back, 'Chelle. Please convince Mim—Mom—to let me go, please."

Miri was adamant. "We go on, or we go home. You are not going into that place again, whatever it is."

So we went on to Cobá, where the essence was of an overwhelming dark grandeur. Chichén Itzá had been huge, but open, conveying a sense of wideness and air. Cobá was fighting against the encroaching jungle, and Tamar kept saying, "This is what it felt like. This is what the Magic Kingdom had—"

Miri was severe. "Never mind all that. I don't want you wandering off."

But the two of us found ourselves wandering off together, Tamar and I, and I began to ask her about the place she had gone in that disappearance.

"There were birds chirping, a funny kind of chirping."

"It was dark—you were underground."

"Yes, I was in a kind of tunnel, and then I was where the rocks were and some were very smooth and there was a net hanging down and some light was still there and I saw it was roots and I was underneath a *tree!*"

"That birds were there doesn't make any sense, unless they could have been bats."

"Then there was a wind there, a little blowy, but different than a regular breeze, and some things were shining on the wall, but the shine didn't make any light, and when I tried to touch them, they were very sharp and prickly. Mim doesn't want me to talk about it."

On the trip, Tamar had been calling her Mim.

"You gave us a big scare, Tamar, and no one likes to be scared that way."

"I did. I was scared, too, but I liked it."

"Tamar, listen to me. It's not right that you're keeping things from your mother and going off by yourself."

"I want the kingdom," she said. "I want the Magic Kingdom."

She wasn't hysterical then, not overtired or suffering from

heatstroke. She was speaking in full understanding of what she said.

"I'm sure that if you want to go into caves, she'll take you; just don't hide things from her."

"I'm not hiding about going. I need to hide about the magic."

I hadn't been comfortable as a keeper of Tamar's secrets ever since we'd worked the neighborhood for cookies and talk. The role of confidante was now verging on that of conspirator. Miri had left a tight religious community, where there had been certain kinds of miracle, and gone into a life in science, where cause and effect reigned supreme. She had preached that rationalism to Tamar—no magic, no fairy tales or Pinocchio, no miracles. Tamar knew more about biochemistry and virology at age five than I know now, but she had picked up magic some-where on the streets, blown between the houses on Spruce Lane, settled dustily in the shrubs of Aspen Way.

I understood some of Miri's anxieties. Boulder in the sixties and seventies was one of the drug capitals of the country. By the eighties, wealth was adding cynicism and privilege to the hippie and college scene. The nineties would give its share of goofiness: rumors of satanic cults and the recovered-memory slanders would hit the town hard. Those hysterias were more likely to reach out for a single mother in an eyesore house, than for a married one living eyes cast down. I didn't want Tamar to go on about magic in such times.

Our trip ended, Miri glad it was over, Tamar begging to stay for the cave, me feeling I had planted something but then finding something entirely different sprouting from the ground. We came back to Boulder and Tamar began to beg for visits to caves. At first, she seemed to gratify her excitement by going anywhere underground. We visited all the local mines now opened for tours. We went to some commercial caves, too. Miri went with us in the beginning, but we could both see she had no desire to leave the light, the geography of earth and sky, for the darkness and mystery of a mine, a tunnel, or a cave. For Tamar, even the terms *spelunking* and *speleology* were magic. I planned a trip to the Cave of the Winds in Manitou Springs, and thought about visiting Carlsbad Caverns. At least, Tamar's home education

155

allowed her to be free of the public school's rigid schedule.

I was also discovering the difference between sympathy and empathy. I found no excitement in cold, darkness, dankness, and labyrinthine trails that all looked the same to me but were as unique as faces to Tamar. I wanted her to find happiness even though it was not mine, and as much as I tried for enthusiasm, my joy was for her, not for the kingdom of her wishes.

The Grotto man is standing over us, and it's day. "We've gotten to them," he says, "but we don't know how they are. We think the little girl is moving. We're not sure about the man. Ordinarily, I would have waited until we knew more. The people down there have communication set up, but maybe because of the minerals or some magnetic effects in the cave, it's not working well and we only get very broken reception. We promised we would tell you as soon as we found anything. The cave is deep and its configurations are making the rescue very difficult. It's going to be hours, but we're doing a good, careful job, and as soon as we know more, I'll be back."

"Is there any way we can help?" I ask. I'm fully alive to the inconvenience we're causing by our presence here.

He looks at me and smiles. "That'll come later," he says, and leaves.

The snow is still being beaten sideways. People come into the tent, wet and exhausted, towel off, wiggle into the sleeping bags others have vacated, and, after a grunt of acknowledgment our way, fall away into their own deeps almost immediately. Even Miri doesn't have the heart to forestall their trips with questions.

We're on hospital time, every minute being sixty full pulse beats, fourteen breaths long, in and out. Sixty of those measured out one single hour. I go back again to find the day the blow fell on Miri.

26

The blow fell on Miri without warning. Someone had lodged a complaint that Tamar all but lived in her mother's lab, that Tamar had a cot there, had books and toys there, that she ate with the workers, and had a microscope. There had been flickers of trouble previously, but the techs had made a game of thwarting inquiry about a child's presence in the secluded section where the lab was located. The workers had always been warned of inspections and they had fended off all the questions and rumors. For two years, Miri had been working after the ordinary hours were over, continuing into the evening, well past the closing of the Pathology Department. The night security staff and anyone who needed to keep quiet had been bought off with her smile and Ada's occasional streudel. Suddenly, it was over.

Miri was called up to the administrative offices and told unequivocally that only authorized personnel were to be in the pathology lab. She argued, defended, objected. The powers were adamant.

"You've stalled them for eight years," I told her. "It's a mixed achievement. What will you do now?"

"I'll go in when the lab opens. I'll go back home at noon and work there for two hours, and I'll work two hours after the lab closes at four thirty. They get the extra coverage, and the extra time will be added up to give me a day off every six weeks."

"The plan means leaving Tamar at home for what seems like quite awhile each day." I had visions of all those families she cadged for cookies and companionship figuring out that she was alone in the big farmhouse and, being no friends of Miri, alerting

158

the authorities. That would be a fandango even Miri couldn't do and get away with.

But once again, she danced to the edge and the world opened a space for her. Once again, magically, the neighborhood sheltered the two of them and never made a peep. An unattended child of eight, taken notice of by the authorities, would ordinarily be cause for immediate charges of parental neglect. Nothing of the sort happened because of the kind of child Tamar was, and because the neighbors must surely have thought there was someone in the house with her. She was always well dressed and never asked for food or help. I'm sure she didn't always stay at home during those hours that Miri left her there with books and studies to do. She must have known in some instinctive way when to do her visiting and when to stay inside. Even at eight, Tamar was deft and tactful in her relationships with other people. She used a combination of self-protection and good sense. I know she waited for children to be dropped off the school bus. "I go home with them sometimes, and we play. We play video games."

"Do you like them?"

"After awhile they're boring, but I hear about regular school from them and, yow, 'Chelle, I'm glad I don't go. There are bullies there and some of the teachers are mean, and some of the kids, too, because they make friends with you and then they all get together and leave you out or leave some other kids out."

"I guess that sounds pretty bad," I said.

"You went to school, 'Chelle," Tamar said. She was playing with the ring on my right hand, a band of small rubies and tiny pearls Niall had given me. "Was it like that?"

"Yes, and no. Good parts, bad parts. I liked school."

"Mim tells me it's terrible."

"I know."

"Is it, though? Is it bad?"

"You know the kids you play with here." I was trying not to undercut Miri's view.

I know Tamar was disappointed when she took her cave pictures around to the other children, showed them the Magic Kingdom, tried out what bits of technical language she had learned and were her treasures, only to meet their passive disinterest.

"They don't understand," she told me, her voice high with incredulity. "I showed them the pictures in the book you gave me. I showed them the pictures from the Cave of the Winds, and how big it is underground, and how we aren't even finished exploring it, and all the different kinds of rooms and passages there are in it and how there are some places so small only I could get through, and some wide as a house."

"And they don't see how wonderful that is?"

"Some of them say 'cool,' but I can tell they would say that about anything someone showed them."

I was aware that she had said "we"—"we aren't finished exploring." She must have seen herself in each of the pictures—"only I could get through." This interest of hers was like none I had ever had in my childhood and it seemed to make her more focused and mature than I'd ever been as a kid.

"Are you disappointed?"

"They don't see how caves are any different from being anywhere else, in a desert or on a boat. If I went to school with those kids, I think it would make me shut up about the Magic Kingdom. I'd have to keep it secret."

"Maybe that's true," I said, and I told her that design excited me in that same way. My discoveries were about things other people weren't aware of. "It's when my design is good, and it works, that no one notices."

"Mim's Magic Kingdom is invisible, too, so small and secret it takes a microscope to find it."

"There are people whose Magic Kingdom is the planets and the stars, and those people talk about millions of miles and light-years."

Tamar began to clap her hands, and I thought, looking down at her, that her eyes could light a cave all by themselves.

By that time, we'd visited the Cave of the Winds and all the other commercial caves in the area. Size didn't seem to mean as much to Tamar as to others, and she called the guides braggers when they told how big or long a cave was. Complexity was what interested her, lifts and falls, water, the corkscrewing of folded stone, the howling of wind through the narrowed spaces.

"The cave is a giant breathing in and out," Tamar said. "Sometimes it breathes in the morning and out at night."

"And the giant snores?"

"And there are gasses there, so I guess the giant farts."

When we visited the caves, we wove around marvelous clusters of glowing minerals and crystal islands. We heard dripping and roaring. We walked through winds that sounded like subway trains, whistles and all. Tamar was always rapt and eager to hear every word regarding the exploration of the caves, always joyful, happy to go, happy to be underground; but in all the commercial caves, her joy seemed merely polite to me, not ecstatic as it had been when she was at Chichén Itzá, muddy and exhausted. Finally, I asked her about it.

"The caves are good, 'Chelle, but they're all lighted up, and someone walks us through and gives names to all the places in them, and people are supposed to see why those names are given, and that's supposed to tell everything about the cave, but it doesn't."

"Like naming a bluebird," I said.

I remembered when I'd seen the emptiness of that for myself, as though to name a thing said anything true about it. I'd asked my father years ago what the bluebird calls itself, having seen one suddenly there and gone in a breathtaking shock of beauty.

"Bird, that's what you call it," he said, "and in Yiddish, *feigel,* and in Hebrew, *tzippor.* Moses' wife, she was Tzipporah, a little bird."

"No, Papa, what does the *bird* thinks its name is?"

"Why are you bothering me? Go help your mother."

"We're not the first ones asking that question," I told Tamar. "I'll tell you the story of the labyrinth in Crete, and the Minotaur and Ariadne." When I had finished, Tamar decided she wanted to be called Ariadne, and there was something of a tussle between Miri and Tamar before Miri gave up and let Tamar take Ariadne as a middle name. I told Tamar I thought Tamar Ariadne Marigold was a bit too much. Tamar loved it.

All that time, over a year, I was traveling constantly, too. Thinking about it now, I'm amazed at how many places I saw.

There were two national conventions, and I was in Mérida for conferences. I went to our resort sites in Turkey, Trinidad, and Crete. I designed a questionnaire for the workers at the resorts to get an objective take on the success of what we were doing. I checked how many guests were revisiting each resort. As my work with World Wide tapered off, I took more local projects, and there was a bit of office upheaval over that, and a new assistant. Then World Wide acquired two new sites, and I began to campaign for sites in America, one near Chimayo, New Mexico, and one near Wenatchee, in Washington. That fall, I was in Mérida more than I was in Denver, and for a while, Rafael and I were seeing a great deal of each other. I even fantasized that if his wife died, we might marry. Probably not. He worked full-time with World Wide; my work there would end with the completion of the new projects, a matter of two or three more years. After that, I would be going to Mérida only to see him, unless he moved here, or I moved there, as his wife.

That winter, I was at the big convention in New York.

27

I'd been at many conventions when I was on my way up, needing them for contacts, but I hadn't been to a local one in quite some time. When they're large, the groups usually divide into subgroups. There are no new ideas, just the same old faces. I was standing at the big meeting board, trying to decide where I wanted to spend my conference time.

"Rachel?"

I turned. There he was, Art Kleinman, my old good friend from our foursome, and it was over twenty years later. I felt like Gerda in "The Snow Queen."

"I knew it was you from the back. You're Finn now?"

"Yes, I'm Rachel Yovel Finn."

"You married out—"

I wasn't ready for that—it was too close in, too soon, and it was tactless, but then I remembered that Art had always been tactless. The question proved he was still Art.

"Not so," I said. "I didn't marry out; he married in. He died in. A nice man, Art, and Jewish, too." And I suddenly missed Niall bitterly, my beloved, my dear, good synagogue vandal.

We brought each other up-to-date. I'd thought he was some kind of engineer. Where had I gotten that idea? He told me he had done industrial work and had switched to his new specialty five years back. He'd married a girl from the neighborhood, one of the Lasitch girls, who was much younger than I, and whom I didn't know. They had a child, Melissa. They had divorced and now shared Melissa's custody. He'd gone back to the Judaism of his childhood.

"Orthodox," I said.

"I don't like the term—say observant."

I told him a little about Niall, and he was sympathetic. I spared him the story of Niall's synagogue introduction to Judaism, but told him about our succah and Niall's conversion, about how excited we'd been about starting a family, about how happy I had been that Niall wasn't a street cop or a detective and so was out of danger. He asked about whether I was still close to Miri. Of course he'd heard about her divorce and all the scandal that surrounded it, her move to Boulder, and, surprisingly, her reputation. He said, after a little pause, "Sexually liberated." I can only guess what words had been used to describe that to him, or what words he was using in his mind.

"Who said that? What did they say?"

"She was always wild—willful."

"We were all willful for those times, in that neighborhood," I said. My good feeling was evaporating.

"I'm sorry," he said. "There were rumors; there still are."

"She's beautiful," I told him, "and a single mother, and she heads a lab, and she's ambitious. That's what the rumors are about."

My spirited defense was drawing looks from people standing close by, but I think Art was moved by it.

"Let's go to a nice kosher restaurant and talk it all over," he said, "someplace where the waiters tell you what to eat and yell if you leave anything on your plate."

We went to a place he had heard about and ate a hugely overpriced meal, and Art told me more about his marriage and divorce and his little girl, Melissa, about how shared custody was frustrating and enervating but at least allowed her in his life. Then, even though it was cold outside, we decided to walk. The meal had been heavy, both calorically and nostalgically. We went out to the active street. In Denver, the city closes down at eight or nine. New Yorkers don't notice the darkness. People were walking dogs, dating, strolling as though it were noon. We were way downtown, where there was a park, remodeled from the docks and wharves that Art wanted to see. That was closed, but we looked over the chain and saw the open space lined with shops and the wharf at the end. My idea of such a space would include lots of trees and flowers. My recollection is that no green

164

was there, but the very openness was a relief from the overwhelming canyons of the city. "They let in some sky anyway," I said. We wandered back up toward the hotel.

In adolescence, Art had been long and stringy, his face roughened by acne, and he'd been acutely, agonizingly in mute lust for Miri. His choice now was a modest, well-trimmed beard, and he had grown into his height, so that if not graceful, he wasn't clumsy, either.

"You're on your own—your badge said 'Arthur Kleinman, P.C.'"

"Yes," he said, "I started with Keller-Jackson, but I wanted to do something special, so I'm doing it. I design nursing homes."

I was interested and we talked about the special requirements, the need for beauty in such places, gardens and greenery available to the patients, places for dogs and cats, birds and fish.

"The need for medication diminishes in healthy environments," he said, "but it's difficult to convince bottom liners even when the research says it's so."

We talked about his ideas for a while and then he turned to me and asked what my work was like. I told him about interior design, and then about World Wide.

"Play preserves for the rich," he said.

I laughed. "Don't the rich also deserve beauty?"

"I've heard of consortiums like World Wide. They eat places. They devour the beauty spots of the world."

"Surely it's not as bad as that. There's lots of Mérida left, lots of Zmiti, lots of Vila Real we haven't used. Why should beauty be limited to the sick, aged, and dying?"

He said their need was greater; I said it wasn't. He repeated the bit about private resorts despoiling beautiful spots, eating the landscape. I found myself annoyed, and then angry. We'd been walking past unrelieved blocks of buildings.

"Why should all places be public places? People are willing to pay to enjoy uncrowded beaches and pristine landscapes. What's your problem with that? Would you prefer all those places to be special housing for the poor?"

"Why would you want to give your talents to make playgrounds?"

"Same reason as yours." I was beginning to get more of Art Kleinman than I wanted. His return to Orthodoxy seemed to have made him priggish and sanctimonious.

"Of course, the rich need beauty, too," he was saying. "It's the exclusivity that bothers me."

"Had someone called me to Mérida to design interiors in barrios, I would have gone," I said, but classless societies have playgrounds. Look at Russia, China, Cuba—Party members are the new privileged, aren't they?"

With thirty more blocks to go, we hailed a cab and went back to the hotel in silence. The next morning, he called my room and asked me to have breakfast. I wasn't sure I wanted any more of his judgments and pieties. Art had been a friend, a good friend, one of the long-timers in memory, and I didn't want to end the friendship with argument.

"I'm sorry about last night," he said. "I haven't been divorced long and I'm angry and bitter. When I get angry and bitter enough, I get stupid."

"All right," I said, "but no taking bites out of my job or my friends."

"You're on."

We had our breakfast and went our different ways to the presentations, meeting again for dinner. We didn't talk about old days—I think he was ashamed of them now—but we did talk about clients we had had and their expectations, and about challenges of the work, mending the rips he had made in my feeling for him. He seemed surprised and then interested in the fact that I had to gain the acceptance of the builders and tradesmen in the countries where I worked, many of whom had prejudices against women professionals and had to be convinced that a woman in a hard hat wasn't a ludicrous sight.

By the second dinner, I felt comfortable enough to tell him something about the years of my marriage to Niall, and about Miri's years with Jacob.

"How could he have been against her doing lab work?" He sounded incredulous. I was sure he'd been told stories about Miri that painted her a pure villainess.

"She was perfectly free to study in college," I told him, "as

166

long as she fulfilled a complete life as cook and hotel servant to Jacob's constantly visiting family and their friends, who were, of course, glatt kosher, and all the traditional meals, the helzel and kugel, the knishes and kishke." This wasn't strictly true. Without Ada, Miri on her own would have kept a much-reduced but still kosher kitchen, and maybe there would have been fewer visitors. I didn't say it; Miri was my friend. "And there was Jacob, too," I said, "not only a religious Jew but even though I liked him, he was . . . a little too dreamy and passive about his family. He had hang-ups that would have kept them even from eating where we went last night, or in a place certified by Hillel himself."

Then I had a thought. "If you're not too down on Miri, why not take your little Melissa to Boulder to see her and meet Tamar, her daughter. They're the same age, and Tamar's friendships are . . . limited in a way because of her being home-schooled."

"I've heard things. Is Miri really all right, not too . . . worldly?"

"'Worldly'? Whatever Miri is, it isn't worldly. I'll be there anyway. Miri's vocabulary is cleaner than yours. She doesn't allow Tamar to watch TV."

"But I heard . . ."

"Neighborhood cackle," I said.

Art smiled. The smile was the smile of my old friend, the boy I had met in junior high and hadn't seen in years. "I'd like to do that. The divorce threw Melissa into quite a tailspin, but even before that, she was a shy little girl." He looked at me with a look that said, "Here is my hostage. Don't hurt her."

Besides Tamar, I didn't know any children well. She was the model for my idea of childhood, and without being aware of it, I'd been spoiled by her exultant, arms-wide world dance. Without my exactly planning it, Miri and Tamar had taken up so much of my time, my interest, my energy, and my hope that I'd been left with very little for any other family, even my own. My nieces and nephews were nice enough, but I saw them only on formal occasions and we were stiff and not forthcoming with one another. They seemed lumpish compared to Tamar.

Art brought Melissa to meet us on the week after the convention, and I was immediately struck by the difference between the girls. Melissa seemed retarded by comparison, too big, too docile, too flat in manner. At eight, when Tamar was giving names to the individual granola shapes in her cereal bowl and painting faces on the bacteria in her mother's notebooks, Melissa had barely enough personality to elicit a preference for anything. At first, I thought that Tamar would be bored by her and wander away, but Tamar took one look and saw in Melissa a rescue project. She started in on that girl with the unquestioning enthusiasm of a climber on Everest. She allowed no shadow or hesitation to challenge her will.

"She *has* to learn to skate, 'Chelle, and she can't even use a microscope. We could go caving, too. When she goes into a cave, she'll like it, and we can be in it together. We're both small enough to go *anywhere* in a cave."

They did go skating the next week at a rink in Boulder, and Tamar actually did teach Melissa to skate a little, a skill Tamar must have learned from neighborhood kids, heaven knows when. She also took charge of Melissa's monosyllabic vocabulary, juggling words, dancing with them, presenting them the way magicians pull silk scarves and bouquets of roses out of the air to charm and enchant. Look what's here. Isn't it wonderful? Sometimes, the convincing sounded like badgering. Melissa took it all, I guess, as eagerly as Melissa ever did anything, with an unsmiling, dogged aim to please.

Arthur was grateful as only a single parent can be when his child is given attention by someone, is included and fussed over. We made a now-and-then foursome, Arthur, Melissa, Tamar, and I. People took us for a family. Occasionally, Miri joined us, and then we saw questioning on some faces, because Tamar and Miri were so obviously mother and daughter, both beautiful, both drawing the eye and the attention directly to themselves with no work and seemingly with no conscious need or effort.

When Miri did join us on our expeditions, Arthur altered in her presence, becoming quieter, more cautious. He was still worried about her reputation.

"I forgot how intense she is," he said after one of these excursions.

"She does come on a little strong sometimes," I admitted.

"Daunting."

"It's fireworks," I said, "not war."

"Yes, but the noise is the same, even when she's at rest and sitting or waiting. She seems to vibrate all the time and the feeling is like touching an exposed wire."

"I'll have to tell her you said that."

"I know how close you two are, and I'm fine with measured amounts of her. Did I like her better when we were kids?"

"You were mad about her."

"Hmm. Tamar—now there are fireworks for you, a crown of sparklers wherever she goes."

"I love that little girl."

"I can see that. She's got a quality I seemed to remember about Miri—a big glow. I think she might bring Melissa out a little."

It occurred to me that such a bringing out was what Miri had done for me all those years ago. I'd been illuminated by her; she had energized me. Without her, I would have been held in by the judgments of the neighborhood and all its pieties. I would have been like my mother, stifled everywhere but in her own home, and there, miserable and bitter and raging against the limitations that had been imposed by a thousand authorities, living and dead, and always by the most severe and judgmental.

Had I ever been as limp as Melissa, as passive? I wondered. Maybe beneath all that flaccidity urges moved, for which she had no names or pivot places.

All of Tamar's official friends had been of Miri's choosing. We didn't mention any of the friends she gained in the neighborhood, and it was comforting to watch the girls' heads together as they made plans. About one enthusiasm, Melissa remained resolutely blank. Her first visit to a cave gave her nightmares and she became increasingly phobic. Tamar explained, urged, pantomimed, propagandized, and all but threatened Melissa in her urge to convince her friend of the wonders of the Magic Kingdom, but to no avail. Of course caves were dark, but not if you brought a source of light. Yes, they might be cold, but not if you dressed well; bat-ridden, but not if you appreciated bats. None of it did the least good. Tamar had met with the first human intransigence in her experience and it had momentarily stymied her.

Noise wakes us and we shake our sleep-wrenched clothes into place and go out through the tent flap. We see that the snow has slowed and the wind eased a little. We look at each other as though our wish—doubled—could make the thing happen: the day clear, the sun putting in an appearance, the sky opening, the chopper that would take the rescued loved ones away in minutes announcing itself. People are going and coming from another tent higher on the slope and we move toward it. We—the rescue party—are camped well above and to the left of the cave opening on one of the few flat bits of terrain, so that any travel between the tents involves clambering up or down on the somewhat-unstable ground. The trucks are on a trailhead even farther up, and out of sight. Escobar has asked us to stay in one of them, but Miri, no charm at all this time, has bullied our way to the rescue site, and we're now climbing up and over a trail made only by wandering animals and by the rescuers coming and going to one or another of the tents.

We see a man come from one of the larger tents, holding a cup of what must be coffee, and we're immediately, terribly hungry. We make for the place.

Inside is the fug of wet clothes and sweaty feet, unrefrigerated food, sleep farts, heater fuel, and someone's cigar. A man looks at us as we duck through the flap. "Ma'am?"

"I'm the mother. This is my sister."

"Oh," the man says. "Well. Why don't you get you some coffee over there, and there're sandwiches and some sweet rolls. You can heat up the rolls on that skillet thing over there and I'd recommend you do that, because, they ain't very good cold."

"Do you have any news, anything about the rescue?"

"I don't know how much you've heard already. We got contact, but the evac has some complications. Eat first, and then Sam—that guy over there—he'll fill you in."

Another man has come in and is warming himself at the heater in the center of the tent.

171

"We've got coffee, lunch meat and processed cheese on bad bread, or a sugary coffee bun," I murmur to Miri, half-kidding, hoping to lighten the mood.

She shoots me a stare of disgust. "You can eat that," she said. "I'll wait."

I'm in no mood to argue over empty or full calories. I pour myself a cup of coffee and heat the sweet roll, eat it, and drink the bad coffee gratefully. Then Miri takes a sandwich, makes an expression Juliet must have worn contemplating the poison cup, takes a bite, and wolfs the thing down.

I think we both feel better. Our own smell is added to the atmosphere of the tent, the clothes we had slept in, the morning breath. We finish eating and see Sam with some other men, talking over something. Sam is giving outbound packages of rope from a big bag on the floor. He is obviously a leader, because he's giving them instructions, at which they nod.

Miri moves forward, but I hold her where she is. "Listen— we're here on sufferance. No one wants us here. Our best strategy is patience and keeping our mouths shut. They'll let us know."

She glances over at me, and if the glance isn't hate, it comes as close as I'll ever want. "Shut your own mouth, Rachel; she's not your child."

There it is again, the unanswerable reality, and worse than she knows, because I kept Tamar's secrets and I bought the rope Val needed. Escobar is in the tent. I see him standing to the side, waiting, as we are. When I catch his eye, he waits until I separate from Miri and then comes over and says, "I've got some reports to fill out. No doubt you've heard, so I don't want to bother the mom right now."

My heart enlarges, trying to pump blood that has suddenly stopped moving. My vision and hearing shut down for a second and then come back too bright, too loud. "Heard—heard what?"

"The little girl's alive," Escobar says, "hurt bad, but alive. The man didn't make it."

I'm stuck, standing, staring at Escobar with a bouquet of feelings so mixed and patched I know I'll never sort them out.

His hand comes up to steady me. "God, Miz Yovel; I thought someone had told you."

Miri says, "Tamar's alive? Hurt? How badly?"

"We don't know that yet, ma'am. Chopper can't run in this weather so the plan is for me to guide the ambulance in to wherever we can meet the chopper, or if the weather is this foggy, all the way in, then to Boulder or University Hospital, depending on what the paramedics think." He turns to me again. "Will you be okay to help with my report?"

I look over at Miri and she gestures dismissively, which Escobar takes as natural. Surely even the best of friends don't feel as much pain as the mother and lover would at the news, her child alive but her lover dead.

We sit on two supply trunks and Escobar pulls out a clipboard he's been holding inside his coat to keep it from the snow and dirt of this place. We go through the essentials, the who, what, where, and when, and then Escobar looks up at me and says, "Why would an experienced caver take a little girl on a trip like that?"

"Charm," I say.

"He wasn't . . ."

"God no. He had no desires of that kind."

"Why, then?"

"Tamar is—she could talk a fawn out of a lion's mouth. She was no first-timer in a cave, either. She knew a great deal about caving. She'd been studying for two and a half years, and working with Val for two."

"But even if Tamar was good, she was only a kid."

"Yes, and this was her find, her golden dream. As for Val, Val was in love, deeply, wholly, and not with Tamar, but with Miri."

"That woman is . . ."

"Beautiful."

"I wasn't going to say that." He writes something and then looks up. "He was in love with her; was she with him?"

"No, I don't think so."

Escobar writes some more, asks some more questions, and goes away. The ambulance is en route, he tells me; the rescue is going forward. With one, they will use consummate care; with

173

the other . . . the other will be wrapped, head to toe, and with equal care, will be raised to the road. If the body should bump against the wall of the cave on its way, the act will evoke a wince from the rescuers, and an indrawn breath.

28

Tamar's ninth birthday was coming closer and all I could think of for a gift was another caving book. I was idly thumbing through one of them, a big coffee-table affair loaded with pictures of famous caves. I'd presented it to her soon after we had been in the Yucatán, and she had disappeared into her cluttered room with it for days. How could I match such a triumph? I reached the end of the text and pictures, where there was an appendix, and there I found a listing of caving groups. Of course! There must be enthusiasts all over the country. I went on-line and found some local groups and the Web sites of dozens of cavers' organizations.

I ordered *Rocky Mountain Caving* and learned that there were meetings of Colorado cavers, called Grottos, one down-town in Denver, and one in the northern suburbs. My plan was to offer to take Tamar to six of the Denver meetings, which were being held at the small Friends Meeting House. The Grotto convened on the first Thursday of each month. We could go out for a quick meal, take in the meeting, and she could sleep over afterward. I would bring her home on the following day. With my trip schedule, we wouldn't be able to make every monthly meeting, but I thought six would be enough to get us known by the group. My own trips might be fitted into the plan.

I called the Grotto leader and found him welcoming and interested. He said that Tamar's age wasn't a problem, and that many people took to caving early in life. Trips to noncommercial caves were usually limited to age thirteen for horizontal caves, but Tamar might learn enough of beginning caving and good technique well before that age. I wrote up a little certificate and went to present it at the birthday party Miri was giving.

Art and Melissa were there and also the two children of a male lab associate. After the familiar grainy cake, the kids went out to play in the field, and we watched them through the back window as they argued and wrangled over the building of a snowman. We chatted with no great enjoyment. I knew what Art thought about my work with World Wide, and Miri's lab associate was obviously interested only in Miri.

We talked desultorily about raising children and I told Art and the associate about our Yucatán trip and how Tamar had disappeared in the ruins and how terrified we had been. I realized that the story would soon become one of those anecdotes old people store up for slow occasions, the recital of which gets longer and more intricate with each telling. So what, I thought, let them suffer.

I saved my envelope until everyone had gone. I had written out the certificate, and an explanation, which would take some time to read and understand. Tamar-like, she tore it open and her eyes kept skipping to the bottom as she read. "Go back. Read it aloud."

So she did, wriggling with impatience. The reading took awhile for her to understand and I had to explain the word *grotto*, but when what I had planned was finally clear to her, she gave a screech of delight and barreled into my arms. "Oh, 'Chelle—it's my best, best thing!"

"They only meet on the first Thursday of the month, so we have three weeks to wait, but if Mim can get you to Denver, I'll meet you at the office and we'll have dinner and go to the meeting."

"To the Grotto," she said.

She called every other day to make sure I was counting the days left and wouldn't miss or forget the date. That last week, the calls were to check on my health.

We arrived at the Friends Meeting House early and watched people come. They were mostly men, mostly young, but here and there we spotted women, who showed that tautness I associated with Olympic runners. People were bringing folding easels and poster-board displays and setting up equipment, all portable, rickety, here and gone. Chairs were being set up and displays and

176

pictures; sign-up sheets and announcements were appearing on the desks and tables. People were socializing and a sizable number were still outside smoking. I watched Tamar, who was all eyes, trying to see herself in place among these people, belonging, becoming one of the group, and, at the same time, recognizing a fuller, realer self. There were pictures of caves posted, and of rigging patterns for vertical caving, and Tamar stood spellbound before them. The other cavers were special people to her and she studied them with a peering intensity that in any other situation would have been seen as rude.

The meeting was called to order. There was mention of trips members had made, some of them illustrated with slides or videotapes. A man raised the problem of bad rope work in a place called Ponder Cave, and someone else made a presentation with a computer printout of the charting of Wild Horse Cave in Arizona. Apparently, the charting of caves was the cause of some controversy.

"That's why they need to name the areas they find," I whispered to Tamar, who nodded impatiently, not wanting to miss a thing. Any word from one of the Grotto members was gold to her. She didn't take her eyes from the speaker. There were also photographs of the insides of parts of some of the caves, the first few stopping places. One showed a faint wash of water flowing over a huge stone stomach outthrust into the cave area, then disappearing into a stone fold. Wind speed had been clocked, and wind direction. I saw Tamar shiver with pleasure. She was like the visitor to a cathedral, seeing its ranked priests as messengers from a deeper, richer world. These were people for whom her Magic Kingdom was a firm reality. They spoke of exalted experiences. The ropes and the lights they wore and carried were vestments, allowing them access to the mystery of sudden changes in the cave, falloffs and openings into great caverns, underground lakes and hidden rivers.

My interest in technique, and of what had happened or not happened on someone's last trip, soon flagged, and I began to study the cavers, who, I realized, would someday be Tamar's comrades. Aside from their obvious athleticism, I could find no other bond they shared. Some had the careful speech of scientists, some were rough and not well spoken, some displayed caving tattoos on bare, beefy arms. Most of the professionals I knew had long ago given up smoking. There were a number here who were still leaving the meeting periodically to stand around outside with cigarettes.

In the beginning, some of the members looked past Tamar at me. Enthralled and radiant as she was, she was only nine. Her long black hair was gathered in a kid's ponytail. Her long, thin arms and legs gave her a coltlike, paradoxically graceless beauty—but her obvious rapture caught their attention. She was radiant; I was detached. She was hearing golden instructions about deep mysteries, a whole kabbalah of literal steps toward the mystical truths of the Magic Kingdom. I shifted in my chair.

Yet, when we left, I saw that she had quieted and was withdrawn, answering me with monosyllables. "Tamar . . ."

"'Chelle, I saw."

"Saw what, sweetheart?"

"That in the end they wouldn't let me go. Remember how they were all getting in little groups, signing up for trips? I knew when I put my name down that they would erase it. I'm too young, and if I were going, it would have to be with you or Mim, or some grown-up who would be responsible for me, and even then it wouldn't work, because they'd have to know who that grown-up was. I'll never get to be in a cave, not for years and years." Her eyes were suddenly overwhelmed with tears and she began to sob.

I tried to comfort her. I told her that she now had a place to begin and that she would be coming back to the group again and would be studying all the books and material on technique that the groups produced, and accessing caving Web sites. I said that she could see all the videotapes on my TV set. By the time she was eleven or twelve, she might be able to go with one of the cavers on a trip, and later she would be ready and armed with all the knowledge she'd need to convince the leaders of her seriousness and application.

She cried for a while and then let me give her a Kleenex to blow her nose, and she let me talk, but I knew she was far from being consoled. Her charm and intelligence, her spirit and life with Miri, and her home schooling hadn't prepared her for disappointment or the delaying of any of her wishes. She had no experience of working toward a long, distant gratification. Except for Miri's lab people, whose chief was her mother, she had never been in groups. She had no idea of their power to make rules excluding her, even temporarily. Perhaps for the first time in my relationship with Tamar, I was impatient. Some of that unpleasant feeling might have been simple envy. Miri and I had been struggling with exclusion, and its rules, big and small, all our lives, Miri conquering by charm and I by patience, accommodation, and work. There was a pang there, over in a minute, that this fortunate star child was weeping because she had found her way and it wasn't immediately open to her.

Miri responded, as I knew she would, with impatience that Tamar hadn't been immediately accepted.

"But she is accepted. They want her in the Grotto. They welcomed her. She's sulking because they won't let her go on exploration trips until she's older."

"Make them know that she's different—smarter than other children, more focused."

"You could do that, if you went with her, maybe. I can't."

We went to the December meeting, and the January one. I noticed that the members showed none of the scorn I expected for commercial caves, even though these people might have done discovery work on their own for years. I pointed that out to Tamar. The meetings were full of reports that included all kinds of caving, anyplace in the world. Some of the members were avid conservationists; some were adventurers, some were scientists. There was a lack of snobbishness about discovery that impressed me. "These people aren't interested in fame," I told her. "I guess what they do isn't something like football, where there are stars." I knew that despite her expression of exasperation and her gestures, waving and pulling at her shirt, she was listening to me. "There are caves where you can go, tours of commercial caves you can go on until you are ready for the riskier trips."

"But 'Chelle, those caves are already—*over.*"

"Is that what experienced cavers are telling you?"

179

"No, but . . ."

"Listen to your rabbis," I said. Few kids would have gotten that metaphor. Tamar did. She nodded. I knew she was being thwarted for the very first time and that experience was a shock.

29

We missed the next meeting. I was helping to plan a tree-house resort on Mindanao. I began to think that after this project, I might quit World Wide. The thoughts weren't based on Art's hard judgment of what I was doing, but on my dawning discomfort with how things were being managed at the top levels. The company's expansion was beginning to scare me. It was overextending itself, a metastasis I had seen before in quick-success firms.

I'd been flying to Mérida to argue this view with World Wide's management. There were a few of us who feared the overgrowth and were attempting to make the administrators understand. Rafael agreed with us, but he counseled caution. "Don't speak out so directly. What you North Americans see as courage, we take for—your word, uh, brashness, arrogance. Something will come that will help us to show what we know. Until then, slowly, we go slowly." The work, the planning, the meetings took time and energy, and I was distracted during this time. I didn't want Art to be right—that World Wide was chewing up prime, unspoiled sites, only to abandon them when the fall came, leaving another stretch of headland ruined, another mountain crowned with wreckage. The rich are restless, but with superb upkeep we might keep them coming back to World Wide's places, or at least circulating among them. I argued this at the conferences I attended and addressed it often in e-mails as I worked on the details of my plans. I was taken up with matters being decided half a world away.

Miri and Tamar had learned that there was a Grotto in Boulder, a much smaller one than the Denver group, and Miri had promised to take Tamar to meetings there. I was happy enough then to let the remaining meetings I'd promised slide, making up the difference with a membership in Colorado Cavers and a subscription to *Rocky Mountain Caving*.

One day when I was home, I managed to take Tamar ice skating, and we went to a museum on another afternoon, and we were part of the fervor over Klondike and Snow, the two polar bears that had been born at the Denver zoo the previous fall. We watched the progress of the cubs that were being hand-raised at the zoo. "Sometimes bears live in caves," Tamar told me, "but they don't go far inside, not as far as I want to go."

I was away for a few weeks and when I got home again and saw Miri and Tamar their lives had changed.

Tamar flung open the door to me, holding one of the caving books I had given her. She was aglow. The last time I had seen her with that book, it had symbolized a dream thwarted, a desire put on hold. Now she all but danced. "Val says I have to learn all about this, knots and ropes and what shoes to wear. In caving, they use special shoes. Let me show you my old shoes and the new shoes I got to go caving with, and my hat, my special caving hat. You can't pee in caves, either, or poop. You have to go in special bags you take out of the caves. Val says real cavers do all those things."

"Well, hello," I said.

"I'm learning all this," and she ran to gather an armful of ropes to show me, a web of ropes and metal appliances like a rigging. "When I learn it all, I'll be able to try it out in a cave."

I looked up from her to Miri. "We met him at the Boulder Grotto," Miri said, "and he's eager to teach Tamar and take her on trips."

"I'll be a caving project," Tamar said.

His name was Mike Valentine—"Val"—and they had met him at the second meeting they had attended. "He's in Rocky Mountain Cavers, but he hates meetings, so it was just a lucky thing that he showed up," Tamar said.

"He likes Tamar's spunk and determination and he says there are lots of advantages to having a small person in a big cave." Miri was smiling also. "He's not prejudiced against Tamar because of her age. He seems willing to teach her."

182

"He likes caves as much as I do," Tamar said, "and I told him that he might even get Melissa to like them, but not as much as I do. He's taking me to a cave next month. It's a cave that's been explored but isn't commercial" (she said the word *commercial* the way a nun might say *apostate*). "It just has a ladder to get down, and some ropes where they're absolutely needed, but that's all."

There seems to be a magic in happy people that makes the rest of us want to keep them happy. I had no doubt that this Val, whoever he was, had seen Tamar shining and wanted to keep that glow alive in her. Their talk that day was full of his name and what he had said, and how he planned to make Tamar a caver.

Passover was coming and I responded viscerally, as I always do, to its appearance on the calendar. I cleaned, sorted, swept behind and under, working a room each evening, and by the Sunday before the holiday, I wanted to be ready for a quiet day by Miri's fireplace and a walk with Tamar. Shirah called to confirm my coming to her second day Seder. I said I'd bring my carrot soufflé. I was thinking about that and about my first day Seder at Reb Mordecai's. Could I get Miri and Tamar to go this time? I was about to call Miri, when she called me. "Come up tomorrow; we're having a party."

A party was just what I didn't want. I wanted quiet, a placid, flaccid day, barely stirring, with no need to be pleasant apart from what naturally arose in me. I had spent parts of Sundays at Miri's in a pleasant doze and yearned to do that again. "Miri—"

"Come on—we want you to meet Val."

I went, reluctantly. I wanted to see Miri and Tamar alone. I wanted to talk them into coming to the Mordecais' Seder. Miri had turned away from all of Judaism's traditions, and except for the times I took her to her grandparents' on visits, Tamar had had no chance to choose how she would house her spiritual life. I also felt Ada's and Rabbi Mordecai's yearnings. I'd been celebrating the first night of Passover with the Mordecais for years, and Miri, in a rather cruel turnabout, had rejected their celebrations, she said, because of the food.

That Sunday in Boulder, we had a buffet lunch. Some of the

food had been contributed by Miri's lab friends and that was edible. I brought a fruit pie and didn't apologize for the sugar. Those at the party fell on it and it had disappeared by the time I looked at the table again. Miri elected not to notice, and she had stocked the table with health desserts that only she and Tamar ate.

The forbidden food brought some spirit to the afternoon and I was reconciled to spending the afternoon there and I made the best of a conversation with one of the lab colleagues, a short man with a pleasant manner and a nervous left eye. When I heard the knock, I was closest to the door, so I nodded to him and went to open it.

My overwhelming impression was of his bigness. He was six-three or -four, broad and solid. He filled the door space without crowding it, and grinned down at me from a round, fleshy face, offering a hand like a catcher's mitt. Even in the chill of the afternoon, the gloveless hand was warm. "You're Val," I said.

He nodded. "The very man. You're 'Chelle."

"The very woman."

Some things take no figuring. If I wanted to climb that tree trunk of a body and be nestled like a small animal in those big-branch arms, warm and protected, what must Tamar feel, who had known no father? No wonder Miri, who judged all outsiders harshly, who was still raising an eyebrow at Art's tight-fistedness and Melissa's flatness, had allowed this man wholehearted entry into her daughter's sheltered life.

I was staring as I came to. "Oh! I'm sorry—come on in."

He walked in calling hello to Miri, who had seen him. Immediately, the walls of Miri's house moved closer, coziness without crowding, and people were looking up at him and smiling. He took two bottles of sparkling grape juice out of the big pockets of his coat and set them carefully on the table. When he opened the coat I saw the slight comfortable thickening of his waist, but no swell of a belly yet.

I wasn't love-struck with Val. I had a good, affectionate, cultivated, and considerate companion in Mexico. The friendship was a deep pleasure to me, but seeing Val reminded me what being in love was like and why Rafael and I wouldn't marry and why Art and I would be friends but nothing more. All these thoughts were working on me while I was bringing in the glasses for the juice and rummaging in the freezer for the ice. Tamar came through the rooms, bird-chirp happy.

"Soon I'll be talking cave talk, rope talk, and I'll be hanging from ropes, but I won't hang there like a dummy. No; I'll be on *belay*. My name is already Tamar Ariadne."

"I know."

"Tamar means palm tree, in Hebrew."

"I know that, too." We were glowing at each another.

She began to talk about a cave she and Val were planning to visit. "Why don't you come, too, 'Chelle, so you can see what it's really like and you'll be with Val and me so you won't fall or get lost or anything. It isn't creepy, it's exciting and you can tell Mim, who says she doesn't like caving, but really she's scared of it."

"Let me think about it."

Tamar went into the front room to work the party, but it was Val I watched. He wasn't onstage—there was no preening—but the afternoon radiated out from him. His palpable delight in being exactly where he was, and with whom, warmed the room. People responded by becoming wittier, livelier. Two of the children of the lab people began telling knock-knock jokes, and Tamar, to everyone's surprise but mine, brought out her own supply. I watched Miri to see if she wondered where these kid bits had come from. Maybe she thought Tamar had made them up. Some of them, in fact, Tamar *had* created: "Knock, knock." "Who's there?" "Flo." "Flo who?" "Flow Stone."

Only Val laughed. His delight came in a big-bellied baritone Santa Claus laugh, a gift from the heart of humor and good feeling.

"I'm going to change my name to Flo Stone," Tamar declared.

"Try it and I'll turn *you* into stone," I said. "This family has had enough name changes."

Miri came from the kitchen with herbal tea and cups on a tray and someone mentioned that coffee was also available. I was about to speak, when my eye moved past Miri to Val as he saw

185

her moving around the room. The moment seemed to go quiet, but the silence was in me. I was seeing the love, not hidden or even shy, that emanated from Val. It was a look as full of gratitude as of desire, the look of someone awed at the gift he had received, her simple existence.

I am watching these scenes unfold as we wait for the rescue, studying them for where things had gone so wrong, but the student mediates the study, and affects the outcome. I stand wearing a rescue blanket, reliving the day when I was in my own silence yearning for someone who would want me as much as Val wanted Miri. At that moment, standing in a sunlit afternoon, I saw dry years, decades of them, after Niall, and I found myself close to weeping.

30

I still don't know why I let Tamar talk me into going caving with them. I'd seen the look Val gave Miri, and I admit I was attracted to him, too. I wanted him to know me and to like me, even though Miri and Tamar filled his world rim to rim. It wasn't a matter of competition; he drew me to himself in the wordless way the sun pulls the faces of flowers to it: I'm here. This is who I am.

We got to know each other when I went up to Miri's house on the Sundays I could go there. I was always glad to see him. Niall and I, Henrik and Miri had made a good foursome. We were another kind of foursome now. Val's happiness encompassed me and Tamar, opening out into the complete acceptance that allowed both of us in as the friends he had always wished for. We seemed valuable to him on our own, independent of Miri, whom he loved. I had never seen a man who could make that happen.

So it was natural to all of us that I was going on the caving trip and Miri was staying home.

Val had given me a list of the clothing and supplies I was to wear and bring with me, and when I saw how his truck was outfitted, I realized that caving was an enterprise calling for great adaptations by the people who engaged in it. Tamar capered between us. We looked like a family, long at ease and natural with one another.

Our trip to the cave was a two-hour drive on the highway, another half hour on unpaved rural roads. Val surprised us with collections of comic caving songs on two well-used audiotapes. The songs had a country-western style, but without the whining, and they all seemed to express a wonder, a disbelief at the fascination of caving. Why would anyone want to subject himself to darkness, wetness, icy cold or fetid heat, the dankness and danger of cave exploration? Why would anyone want not to know where he was, except by compass? What could explain that other people's punishments were what the caver most sought out? The hobby took up all the caver's spare time and brought in not a cent. The girls were few, the settings in no way conducive to romance.

"I wrote a song myself," Val admitted, then took a breath and began to sing it to us, a ballad about a man losing his beloved to a slicker caver who had all the latest equipment. The chorus went:

> Oh, the light in her eyes was a carbide blue
> But it didn't, no it didn't burn for me.

He sang in a pleasant baritone. I asked him what had sparked his interest in caving.

"I guess all the songs are right," he said. "You don't come in on this interest slowly; it's there or it's not. I grew up in Pennsylvania, in mining country. I got lost in mines as a kid, I've fallen into abandoned bootleg mines and strippin' holes. Once I nearly died. That time I'd taken my dog, Dodger. Did Dodger run home and alert my family? Nope. He went home and lay under the house in his dog spot and never missed a meal. I was five or six hours climbing out of that slippery hole. All that should have turned me off; it sure turned all my buddies off. But caves made me feel like a citizen of another world. Our girl, here"—and he hit Tamar's head playfully as she sat between us—"she's starting early. Most people get the bug later."

Then the two of them chatted ropes and gear until we came to what looked like an ordinary campground. Val showed us a sign with a long list of rules about litter and behavior in and out of the cave, and we signed a register, Tamar proudly writing her name in an elaborate style, with odd, spindly letters, jointed at the crossings.

"I'm writing my name in rope," she declared, "and these are knots."

"Rope yourself up the trail," Val said, "but before you go, everybody gets to use the john. There are no flush toilets in this cave and it's the maid's day off."

I had brought two flashlights and a jacket, stout shoes, gloves, and the hard hat I used on World Wide project sites. We went up a trail and after walking awhile came to the cave entrance. I don't know what I expected—a walk-in room, I suppose. Here was a hole that seemed to go straight down. Tamar was shivering with delight. A rope ladder led down the hole, and Val, to my amazement, went down it as quickly as a sailor, all his bigness compressed to energy and strength. Tamar followed, laughing.

"It's funny—it goes backward."

I didn't understand until I tried the ladder myself. It lay against the rock and the entrance itself was tilted, so that all my weight worked against me. I felt like a spider climbing the underside of its web. By the time my foot hit the cave floor, I was breathless from the exertion. Tamar was slapping at the cave wall in her impatience. She had been calling to me as I hung on the ladder and inched my way down.

"Keep your lights off for a second," Val said. "Come away from the ladder—over here."

We walked away from the shaft, which was so deep that only a wan light reached us. Twenty feet from the opening, the blackness was complete.

I had never known blackness like that. I guess I'd imagined the darkness would be like what I experienced in my bedroom at night, or on the walk up Miri's road before streetlights had come, with the trailers and houses shut in for the night. No darkness in the upper world was so utter. The lights of a city reflect against the sky and make a glow seen beyond the mountains miles away. Stars make a light that blues the snow. In our houses, oven clocks glow; timers for the VCR make a puny but lurid light that signals location. Location inspires direction. I go confidently to my kitchen in the wide-eyed dark for a glass of water without disturbing a dust mote or the secret dreams of a spider.

Here was nothing, not the light of an open eye. Val was instructing Tamar. "You gotta get this straight if you want to call yourself a caver. The cave's not yours; when you're in it, you're its servant."

"I know that," Tamar protested. "We've gone before. You told me last time and the time before that."

"I'm ready to tell you every time until you're an old lady with a long gray beard and web feet from caving. No smoking, spitting, or use of chewing tobacco. Are you using chewing tobacco?"

"No."

"Excellent. I thought you were."

How good he was at sweetening the rules for her.

"So, Miss Tamar, and you, too, Ms. Rachel, you do what the cave wants; you don't track dirt. You don't break off anything to take with you for a souvenir. You don't dig or change anything, and you don't act stupid to other cavers. There are three cavers on this trip; if one gets hurt, everyone goes back. If one gets tired, everyone goes back, or we all rest until the tired one's ready to go on. Get it?"

"But . . ." Tamar was all but dancing with impatience.

"But nothing. Cavers are careful of their trip mates. You want people on trips who know how to handle themselves. A caver is someone who respects the slowest person on the trip. She does not pound on the cave walls and insult her trip partner."

"I didn't insult her."

"She does not grind her teeth or roll her eyes or run in circles."

"When I grow up—when I learn how, I'm going to go by myself."

"What am I, then, decoration?" His voice rose and rang in the cave with his humor. "People can go to the movies alone or up in the mountains to see the sunrise. They can sneak potato chips from other people's lunches by themselves—yes, I saw you do it—but they do not go caving alone. Good cavers go caving in threes. That's for a reason, for three reasons, really, one for each caver. You see a caver going in alone, you see an idiot."

"I'm not an idiot," Tamar said.

"Look in the dictionary under *idiot*, and it says 'a caver going alone.'" She laughed. "I kid you not, sweet pea. You slip and fall.

191

You drop your light. Your other light goes out. Your pack has come off in the fall. How far have you fallen? Where's your light? Who knows? End of story."

"But—"

"No buts. Start walking."

31

We climbed, in, among, over, up, down. Direction lost meaning. Walls became floor; the ceiling echoed with water that was coursing somewhere over our heads, and beside us, on the other side of what was, temporarily only, a room. Val was agile and swift as a bear, always surprising in large people.

Five or six times in what I thought was less than an hour, I was forced to stop, breathless and exhausted by a climb over smooth flowstone or smooth rock or balancing myself as I let my body down hand over hand. Inside and outside changed like a Mobius strip or something Escher would have delighted in. Around my light, Val's and Tamar's lights, the realities of space, location, and direction seemed to lumber out of ordinariness and into fantasy. I was conscious of the totality of the darkness and the strangeness. If our lights should fail; if I should fall into one of the raw, open chasms or between rocks that might move . . . This wasn't my world; it wasn't any normal human being's world.

It was also stunning, beautiful, mysterious, the Magic Kingdom Tamar had found, and this I could perceive even as I slid and faltered and climbed and touched the water-glazed rock, whose shafts of marble looked like columns in the cathedral at Siena. We moved through rooms with glowing walls and closets of upward-slanting floors, a phantasm of changing dimensions, sudden lifts and falloffs, now fun house, now house of horror.

I might have panicked if not for Val, big and capable behind me. Now and then, he offered a hand up, but not often, and he did even less to help Tamar, who slipped and scampered and slid on the smooth water-burnished stone. His chiding was genial but pointed. "You in a race? Got a date somewhere?"

"'Chelle won't hurry up."

"'Chelle is going at the perfect speed. She's noting where she steps and appreciating the structures and features she sees. She stepped over that little pile of stones back a ways, when you walked right through it and scattered the stones and made it harder for the next caver."

"I didn't mean—"

"Of course you didn't. You just didn't look."

She took it all well, grinning in the beam of our lights, but I could see that she was all but spinning around with eagerness and impatience to be going on. Once, when she had pushed ahead, Val said, "I give her another half hour and she'll be on her knees."

"Do I have another half hour?"

"It's easier going back. It's twice as easy going back, and she'll be on the fade."

"Don't buy stock in that idea," I said.

But he was right about Tamar, almost to the minute. I turned a corner and there she was sitting on a thrust of rock, and Val and I watched her deflate.

"I'm tired."

"I'll bet. This is a good cave."

"Do we have to go back?"

"No, but if we stay here much longer, we'll get very cold and hungry. Let's rest awhile and then start back."

This time, Tamar offered no objection. I could see she was exhausted.

We made our way over what Val said were the same places, slowly, stopping often. He pointed out features for Tamar to recognize, but I could swear I had never seen any of them before.

"Remember this twisting part, and the little echo just here?"

"I remember the white rock."

"Good. These are markers and you need to collect them for the caves you visit. See this flowstone—and these metallic-looking outthrusts here? Do you remember them from when we came past?"

"I think so."

Val himself seemed tireless, but I was rubber-legged with exhaustion. At last, at long last, we found ourselves at the ladder, and after a climb even more difficult than the one going down, we reemerged into the world.

I was shocked. It was sundown. The light was now shadowless, the day all but over. I felt I had just awakened. Tamar was quiet as we descended the trail, came to the park place, signed out, and saw the van, alone now in the deserted campground. The ordinary sights and sounds seemed strange to me, otherworldly, unreal. Tamar scrambled into the van and instantly and completely died away into kid sleep, that total rag-doll giving over that allows relaxation in any position and in spite of hunger, tragedy, freezing cold, or burning heat.

Val and I talked a little; I was all but fighting sleep myself. He asked me about World Wide. I told him about the resorts and he seemed genuinely interested, so I went on and found myself describing the way I went about my work, and what I was working to produce. He asked intelligent questions and said he had worked construction on houses and a few larger projects and had often seen judgments that favored size over convenience and practicality. I asked him about his other jobs. Construction wasn't all he had done. He had also, he said, been a bartender, a horse handler, a farrier, and had begun training in three or four trades or professions that he had decided against in midcourse. "All physical stuff, all outdoors, which I like."

"Is caving outdoors or indoors?"

He laughed. "I hadn't thought of that, but it's just one more paradox in a bagful of them."

"What do you do now?" I asked.

"I'm on the night staff at a halfway house. Now, that's indoors."

"That can't be very pleasant work," I said.

I was trying to keep condescension from my tone, because I had been taken by surprise. The job changes reminded me strongly of Henrik. Did Miri attract these capable, shiftless job swingers by some mystical force? Even as I wondered about this, I saw differences between Val and Henrik, and they were all in

195

Val's favor. Still, the question persisted. Val was young, strong, intelligent, and, I thought, educated. Why did a man like that work at such a job? He sailed by my presuppositions without seeming to notice.

"Done badly," he said, "it's awful work; done well, it's useful, and it suits me. For one thing, it frees my day for caving. My food and lodging are free, and for the first time in many years, I'm on very good terms with the police."

"Drugs?"

"How did you guess?"

"I didn't think robbery or murder."

"Or sex offenses?"

"No, not that, either."

"Well, yes, on the chemistry. I practiced creative chemistry for a while and became my best customer."

"How did you manage to avoid the long sentences they hand out for that?"

"Who said I did?"

We were quiet, driving through the dark. Tamar had fallen under his arm and he was taking great care not to hit her with his elbow as he drove. I pulled her away and she tried to wiggle back.

"Let me pull over," he said. "There's room for her back there."

The back of the van was full of caving gear, ropes, and cartons of clothing and shoes, lights, boxes of batteries, harnesses, pulleys. There was also a foam mattress with two or three blankets. We cleared a space and laid the mattress down on it, covering Tamar, who moaned a protest, still asleep, and curled herself into the blankets.

"I don't like her back here unsecured," Val said. "I'd rope her in with some of this harness, but that would take quite awhile, and I want to get her home before too long. I'll go slow."

We were back on the highway again when I asked, "Why did you decide to help Tamar? She had signed up for trips and never was called. I didn't think any other cavers would take her at her age."

"I could say it was a theory I wanted to test," Val said, "about kids. I think kids could make the best cavers. I was always big, and being big is a huge drawback for a caver. The physical needs of cavers are as rigid as for any athletes, and lots of athletes start young. Psychologically, kids are very open-minded, new. They don't prejudge. Their memories are good, especially for details adults miss. They have their drawbacks, too, of course. You want someone mature, someone with strong self-control and an instinct for self-protection to do caving. Those qualities are not kid."

"How do you know all this about kids? Do you have any of your own?"

He was grinning. I didn't see it in the dark of the cab; I heard it in his voice. "I used to be a kid, and I kept at it longer than most people. She's a natural, that girl. Did you see her navigate that difficult traverse over those granite boulders?"

"Actually, no. I was floundering around trying to keep my own footing."

"Well, she was fine. I can tell you that. She has an instinct for caving, the way some people have for music or art. I started going underground when I was a boy, like I said, but that wasn't really caving—no technique. It takes years to learn all the skills good cavers need. If she starts now, think where she'll be when she's eighteen."

I was too exhausted to think anymore and I dozed until we were back in Boulder to deliver Tamar, filthy and happy, to Miri. Even barely awake as Val carried her into the house, she was murmuring, "When will we go again? When can we go again?"

32

A t first I smiled at the hopelessness of the project Tamar made of trying to convert and remake Melissa into a caving companion. Later, it seemed a little sad. I watched her talking, urging, showing Melissa rope patterns and picking up rocks to identify, telling her stories of great moments in caving, of exciting discoveries, and of the earth folding in on itself to form chambers inside of chambers, confusing, beguiling, mysterious. Melissa was passively, utterly blank, and soon even Tamar was forced to subside. She wanted to enlist me, too, and after an assault almost as strong as the one she had tried on Melissa, she retired, disappointed and incredulous. How could so obvious a source of wonder and joy fail to enchant us? I told her I was enchanted enough, or almost enough, but that the physical demands were beyond me.

"You could get stronger, 'Chelle, do exercises and get strong."

The other side of Tamar's charisma was a willfulness that needed to remake the world to suit her. The willfulness echoed Miri's so much, it seemed to me that the trait might be genetic.

Val often came with ropes and equipment. They climbed the outside of the house with it, they took trips to three or four commercial caves and obtained permission to go through some of the areas forbidden to ordinary tourists. Now and then, I went with them and enjoyed the park, taking a book and a picnic. When Miri found out that I wasn't in the caves with Val and Tamar, she sometimes came along, and the two of us would camp out while the two of them disappeared. I could see that Val's adoration for Miri was as strong as ever. Miri liked him; she enjoyed his company, trusted him with Tamar, and was aware of his strength, humor, kindness, and good sense. She seemed aware also of his love for her and maybe a little aware of my feeling for him, but I don't think she had anything like the affection for him that she had had for Henrik, who was nowhere near the man Val was. Jacob had come with a world Miri was rejecting and he had been too adored, too sheltered to be full-grown. Val didn't seem to judge, or label us, or if he did, the judgment went in our favor. Miri was a goddess; Tamar, all that a goddess's child should be. I was the goddess's friend. The world must surely love us as he did.

When bad weather closed our caving down the following winter, I made up for my dereliction as a caver by doing daylight activity with Tamar. I drilled her in geology and mineralogy and cave ecology. I was amazed at her grasp and range. Her memory was phenomenal, fully engaged for everything she was seeing or might see. The Magic Kingdom spoke to her in voices she was yearning to interpret. It had never occurred to me that caves were being formed constantly, by wind and water, by shifts in the earth, pocketing warm or cold air like the pockets sleepers make when they turn in their beds, by minerals leached out of rocks over centuries of time. I'd never given the science of speleology any thought, but what I had seen in the cave, pointed out by Val and being assimilated by Tamar, was, in fact, fascinating. I'd noticed the leached minerals, hardened, softened, washed away or calcified into stone. Now, I understood how pressure had caused this twisting and cracking, how water had worked hair-fine fingers on that braille rock, reading the face of what seemed to be solid granite, then finding its smallest unseen fracture, and insinuating itself, subtle as a whisper, to murmur the rock away. Tamar told me that gold flecks and tiny jewels often rode in the shining wash of water revealed in the caver's headlamp and under certain lights, phosphoresced into a dozen colors broken from the darkness.

I'd always had reservations about Tamar's being home-schooled. I thought it might be an effort on Miri's part to protect Tamar too much. Although Tamar had broken free on her own and found acquaintanceships in the neighborhood, I didn't see any of the give-and-take, the friends and enemies, the real social learning that ordinary school life provides.

At the same time, she truly had been saved from the crassness, the violence, the cheapness of the contemporary childhood scene. She'd been kept away from the fads and consumerism, the ugly fashions, the precocious sexual images young girls are presented with. I thought this remove to a simpler girlhood was what added to her charm and the spell she cast on the neighborhood.

Her education was certainly coming along well. Where Melissa, left to herself, would probably never have gone beyond the simplest lessons, Tamar was absorbing high school geology and mineralogy. I imagined that her studies would lead to other sciences, paleontology and then to the natural sciences, zoology and botany. Geography and ecology would lead to history and then to the social sciences, perhaps. I watched her burn her way through stratigraphy and mapping studies, vital to her needs, because in caving, height and depth are as important as location and direction.

She had begun to see the differences between herself and her neighbors, too. To the enthusiasms she radiated, there were no takers. The kids in the development were still open and friendly with her, but they didn't understand her. She made a little more with her mouth. "They don't know why I want to be a caver. I tell them we'll take them on trips, Val and I, and that they'll see how beautiful the Magic Kingdom is, and then they'll want to learn all about what makes cave pearls and stalactites."

Her generosity was moving. I thought that had I come upon some special calling or gained a corner on some arcane knowledge when I was her age, I would have wanted to keep it for myself.

Much of that spring, I was in Turkey, and my Mexico visits were longer than usual. World Wide was facing a crisis in its mission, and half of its management was thinking about expansion. The rest of us saw maintenance as its prime directive. I was being enlisted by the maintenance faction to keep on making my statements and presenting my views. Rafael, who had left World Wide by then, was trying to interest me in helping him to design a shopping mall in a rising part of the city. I came home to Denver to an offer I felt I couldn't refuse.

A Japanese industrialist had sent his emissary to the premier architectural firm in Denver. He had bought land in Aspen and wanted a mansion constructed there: ten thousand square feet— modest, as modern mansions go. They called me in to do the interiors. Could we meet with the client? No, the drawings and plans were to be passed through the emissary.

We followed the understated elegance of Katsura and the villas at Nara. The client was an elderly man; we put an elevator in the long, low two-story structure. There were to be fine woods, which we would have beautifully finished, and rooms of all sizes, intimate to grand (we had been told that the client intended to entertain). The kitchen was centrally located. The project would cost $3.2 million, and much of this cost would be spent on an indoor-outdoor bath with one wall of rock where hanging flowering vines would spill over a water ledge, and clefts where bonsai would grow. The tub was to be carved from a large rock, all but a pool in size, and would have recessed fixtures. The bathroom was planned like the half cave or almost cave that Tamar had introduced me to, lit from above but secret, intimate, and full of things to see and textures to feel. The internal planning and design took up parts of four months of my time.

Through it all, the emissary nodded, yes, yes. A central kitchen? Yes, serving food easily to all the rooms at the lower level. Views saved on all sides of the house? Yes, yes, maximum efficiency combined with maximum comfort and beauty. I loved the place. We presented our finished plans to the emissary.

The client rejected the plans outright and sent us a picture torn out of an Okinawan magazine. This was the idea that had been his original impetus to build. It was a six-story white cement snowman, with large black shoes and a black top hat. The hat revolved. There were windows all around the stomach and in the buttons running down the body. A pair of four-car garages were in each foot.

We told the emissary that the city planners of Aspen would never allow such a structure. Words were exchanged. We got fee for hours. I lost lots of money, time, and a vision of the elegant aesthetics of the older generation of Japanese translated to the mountains of the American West. Pffft. Gone.

I told this story to Val, Miri, and Tamar the weekend after that bust, when it was dark and I should have been on my way home. Val and Tamar had been rappelling off the side of the house and had come in filthy and happy. I seemed a little down, Tamar noted, and I gave them the story. Val erupted in laughter.

"I'm sorry, Rachel, it's just such a hoot of a picture. Was there supposed to be a searchlight in the hat, turning?"

"Very funny," I said, but a look at Val standing at the kitchen sink, his face still wet, made me laugh, too.

"It'll get funnier," Val said, "and when you're rich and famous and telling this one at a keynote speech, it will be hilarious."

Miri asked if we hadn't checked with the client. Had he wanted a Japanese house?

"We never saw the client, only the emissary, who seemed to have kept approving our plans. We got yessed to death."

"I'm going to have you design me a house, 'Chelle," Tamar said, "in a cave I discover. We'll put the lights on top and we'll have special ceilings so we can save the bats but not have all the guano."

"Stove?"

"Vented." I kept being surprised at Tamar's vocabulary. I suppose that was a lab word. "Lots of things will be vented, and there'll be the pipes sticking up, but not so high that people see them. And there'll be pools, some hot, some cold, but I'll take a shower first so I don't pollute the pools, and no peeing in them, either."

"The Japanese baths are that way," Miri said.

"Don't talk about anything Japanese for a while," I told them. I turned to Tamar. "If you live underground, your hair will get very fine, fine as spiderwebs, and your face will be white as a slug, and you'll grow little webs between your fingers and your toes, and your eyes will grow very, very big so you can see any of the light at all that comes through the little vents and skylights, and you'll turn into a *giant albino BAT woman!*"

Tamar screamed, but I think it was with pleasure.

"I'm being surrounded by dreams," I said, "by the mad dreams of dream-soaked people."

33

In November of that year, the first snows fell. Miri and I were alone, reading and dozing. Tamar and Val were off caving or training with ropes or studying whatever else they needed to perfect their technique. The Grotto people were still turning Tamar down, and she and Val were still trying to get outings. Val wasn't Tamar's parent or guardian, the Grotto leader said, so his sponsorship of her was denied. She raged. Val said he would keep putting their names in. I counseled patience. "Wait a year or two—get Tamar known. She'll get a trip eventually and then another, and by the time she's twelve or thirteen, people will be used to the idea that she knows her stuff."

"It's prejudice," Val said, "because there are kids who go caving with parents at early ages. I'll admit, I don't know any Tamar's age who do, but I'm sure there are some."

"Princes and princesses?" I asked. "Children of well-known cavers, kids all the local groups know?"

"Well, yes. We go to caves I know—established caves, but there's something about an unexplored cave . . ."

"I was working behind the counter in my father's store when I was seven," I told them. "For years, I thought it was a huge honor because no other kids had such privileges—only I got to touch the stock, dust, clean, polish the silver. Only I was allowed to open the glass doors of display cases where the more valuable things were kept. Believe me, I'm no stranger to the heady heights of rank and privilege."

Val laughed. "I guess so. I grew up traveling, and because of that I had lots of responsibility early."

"Army brat?"

"They were radical activists, my folks. They went to communes and organized groups in schools."

"Rank and privilege?"

"I guess so. I delivered messages from people in hiding, people who had to go underground—God, I never made the connection before," and we laughed.

Tamar got Miri to take up her cause. They wrote letters to the Grotto, looked up precedents for young people doing advanced cave exploration. None were as young as Tamar, and even they were always accompanied by one or both well-known parents.

I watched Miri get impatient, then annoyed, then insistent about getting the rules changed, and I watched her scratch at Val to get him to be more aggressive in promoting Tamar for trips. "Why shouldn't they amend the constitution of the Boulder Grotto?" she protested. "Anyone who can prove competence should be accepted at any age."

"I understand why there's an age limit," I said, the voice of moderation.

"Val knows people in all the Grottoes," Miri protested. "He could agitate to get the membership to make an exception in Tamar's case."

I'd seen Miri do years of ballet leaps, triple axels, and balance-beam somersaults over the rules, astonishing me and everyone around me. I had no reason to think that the Boulder Grotto rules wouldn't be danced over, leapt over, thrilling even those rule makers who had sworn that no exceptions were to be made and yet getting them to make the exception. This hadn't happened because Miri had been content to let Val and Tamar handle things. Now that she was turning her eye on the situation, miracles would be forthcoming.

But I was older now, smarter, more careful. Once, when we were alone and she started in again, I said, "Miri, I think you should be careful of what you ask Val to do. He worships you and adores Tamar, and that's dangerous. He'll do what you ask, even though it may violate his own ethic."

She waved the words away. "Yes, sure, he likes us. We're a kind of family for him. His parents were reformers who lived on lots of communes where people let them stay. They slept around and did drugs." I was about to remind her, with a look, that her own past held closets full of skeletons, when she said, "His parents were anarchists or something." Miri had never been interested in her own past, and I think that blunted her interest in other people's pasts, as well. "He did drugs himself when he was a teenager, and, I think, booze, too. I see how careful he is about drinking and drugs. He never even has a beer at dinner here. I doubt he takes aspirin."

"Miri, he loves you."

"He loves our independence and our ability to dodge stupid rules and the ideas that choke creativity."

"Okay," I said, "but be warned."

Thanksgiving came, and Christmas. My sister Shirah and her family celebrated Chanukah, the now elaborate Feast of Lights, pumped up from a minor holiday to assuage the jealousy of kids at the overwhelming Christmas tide. I took Tamar to a party Shirah had. We carried a bag of organic vegetables for Tamar, but she caused it to be mislaid, somewhere. I wondered if she would start proselytizing to the new group of kids about caving. I clamped my mouth shut on warnings, and we dived in.

The talk was all about computers, and Tamar, who had learned about them at the lab when she was five, was right at home.

I was wishing for kid games, gone years ago—Pin the Tail on the Donkey, or blindman's bluff, even for dreidel, the traditional Chanukah game. It was good, though, to see Tamar's pure girlish quality as she agreed and argued, giggled and was silly, then went serious in a minute, fully alive to the actions and words around her.

And, as if by magic, one of the older kids had seen a caving program on the Discovery Channel and Tamar was able to get in a little talk about it. To my surprise, when the conversation wandered on, she seemed content to follow it along, subject-hopping. Later, I mentioned her tact in that. She said, "I know they weren't serious. It's a different kind of talking than Val and I do."

"Did Miri teach you that?"

She gave me her penetrating look—"Oh, 'Chelle"—as though

I had said something ridiculous.

Later that week, I took her to the Mordecais', who celebrated the last sundown of the holiday with a few students' children. I had loved those celebrations when I was a girl. There were special songs, which, as on Passover, we sang at no other time.

I loved the Mordecais, too. I wanted Tamar to be their beloved, well-known granddaughter. Sometimes Miri came to these evenings, but most of the time, I acted as stand-in. Tamar fell upon the

Chanukah delicacies—challah and honey, potato pancakes, fried crisp in chicken fat and slathered with apple sauce, brisket, glazed carrots, honey cake, and the sweet, heavy wine that's traditional, and is on no gourmet's list of drinkable beverages. We left the evening sated, bloated, hoarse, talked out, sung out, and contented. Tamar held my hand as we walked to the car and said, a little wistfully, "It's fun to be normal, sometimes. It's nice."

"Did you like the kids, there?"

"Yes, I did, but I thought they were too big of caring about what's *in*. They read things just because everyone's reading them. They like certain games and certain music because it's what's popular. And of course,"—she sounded just like Miri, then—"none of them wanted to talk about caving."

"Caving isn't a popular sport."

"It's not a sport, I don't think, because sports are what people compete in. There's no caving Olympics or World Cup in caving."

"True," I said. "I can see you being competitive, but not Val."

"Val?" And Tamar laughed Miri's delicious two-octave-range laugh. "Val won't even walk faster than he has to. He won't *ever* hurry in a cave."

In the months when they didn't go out caving, Val and Tamar spent time assembling belay patterns and doing rope work, making knots. I found a training film for cavers, which the four of us watched on the TV in my living room one afternoon with varying degrees of interest. Miri stayed with us for a few minutes and then slipped away into my bedroom to do some catch-up work for the lab. She came out and ate a little. Val brought out a battered guitar. He strummed a few chords and played a pleasant running tune.

"Back in my parents' day, you were no activist unless you knew a bagful of protest songs," he said, and began to sing in his rich baritone to Miri. I had heard him before, but the full, pleasant sound, even as it flatted out on the high notes, delighted us. Tamar kept time by pounding on his leg until Miri told her to stop. "Val's leg isn't a drum." He sang thirties protest songs about unionizing, forties songs about world government, fifties songs about radiation, sixties anti-bomb songs, seventies—Vietnam, of course—eighties about environmentalism. "Then," he said, "I discovered caving," and he sang one of the songs on the tape he had played for us on our day up at the cave.

Tamar had fallen asleep on my living room floor, and while he was singing, I looked around and saw the place as through his eyes, a comfortable, unexceptional room that made no statement and had no individuality. It wasn't a room I was interested in. It served my purposes, but I could leave it at any time, never return, and have no pang at the loss. I was suddenly aware of how travel and my friendships with Miri, Tamar, and now with Val had lessened my need for a home. I had two offices—one in Denver, one in Mérida. I had a place at Miri's cluttered, messy house and at the villa I stayed in with Rafael, small, calm, elegant, but not truly mine, either.

Val must have seen me looking, and understood what I was seeing. "You didn't live here when you were married, did you?" He was asking this with interest, not criticism.

I shook my head. "This place illustrates the case of the barefoot shoemaker and the threadbare tailor. The rooms I want to live in are all in my mind."

"I think people take too much trouble with what they use and how they live," he said, and I remembered that he had a room at a halfway house, and was "homeless" in that way also. Then, he realized that he was speaking against my profession, and laughed. "I didn't mean . . ."

"When I design a room, it's so the people coming into it won't have to think too much about the room itself and what it imposes on them unless they're into the room's style. There shouldn't be a statement unless the person living there wants to make one. I think spaces should be convenient, but not interchangeable. When they're here in America, people should know it's America, and when they're in urban Mexico or rural Turkey, they should know that, too, by something in the rooms they stay in."

"The opposite is true of caves," he said. "The cave isn't home and it isn't convenient—its own world, not ours. In a way, we're perpetual guests." He smiled at me. "I never thought of that before, about being a guest. A guy at the halfway house did drugs, he said, to put himself in a sacred place. The drugs swallowed him up, like they did me, but the gape, that awe, that wow is what the drugs do at first, what they promise, and what caves deliver. Sacred places. My folks hated religion because it took energy from the cause. It made people feel satisfied and at peace. They weren't much for awe, either." He looked over at Tamar, folded in her cat-drowse on the floor. "She knows. She's always known, that one." Then he turned toward Miri, and there was that love again, open and guileless, in his face. "This one sees it in the swimming things she studies." He looked at me appraisingly, warmly, too, because his world was warm with love and some of it would radiate from him naturally. Rocks stay warm hours after the sun has set. "We, you and I, we love things, but we don't shine like they do. I swear that girl is a carbide lamp."

You might not light a cave, I thought, but you could warm it.

"Oh, yeah," he said, "I forgot to tell you two. We were practicing last weekend and someone from the *Camera* took Tamar's picture. I guess he saw that glow."

209

34

Here, here is where it began. I've just seen the moment in the Icarus story, when the first feather, light as the air it floated in, began its soft way down. Now, as then, no one noticed. There was no wind taking the feather to me, or to Val, or to Miri, to make us ask where it had come from, or what it signified.

Val had been taking Tamar to the Flatirons to do rope work at the base. Every summer, people climbed the huge, leaning slabs of rock and now and then had accidents, some fatal, but Val and Tamar were there to lay rope patterns and practice belay techniques to train for caving. When the snow retreated from the bases of the rocks, climbers and cavers might be seen practicing for summer climbs. The photographer must have recognized Tamar's photogenic qualities, and that gift for joy she had, and singled her out to illustrate an article on Boulder's signature Flatirons background.

"That's exciting. When will the picture come out?"

"In a week, maybe. She really did look cute in her hard hat and caver's boots. She's so proud of those boots. The soles don't leave marks on the flowstone."

"I know. She must have told me five or six times."

"She must have waterproofed them eight times already."

The picture did appear on Sunday on the front of the second section of the *Camera*. It was lovely—Tamar in full radiance. I got six copies and sent one to the Mordecais, gave one to Miri for the scrapbook she was keeping about Tamar, mailed three to Miri's brothers. I sent one to Shifrah, and when we next met and I mentioned it, she nodded but said nothing. I'd been in Mexico when her eldest was Bar Mitzvah and it still rankled. The picture heralded the coming of spring, a meaningless announcement in the Rockies, since any day until June might be greeted by a six-inch snowfall or a blossom-killing frost.

The picture showed Tamar hanging from a rope no more than five feet from the ground, where Val stood, his back to the camera, but obviously instructing. She had turned away from the rock to look at him, and at his height they were eye-to-eye. She was smiling, grinning with the out-and-out triumph of her success. "Ready For Spring," the headline read. The following week, Miri and Tamar were called about an interview for the paper. Response to the picture, the editor said, had been exceptional. Would Miri consent to Tamar's being asked about her interest in caving, and her struggle to become recognized as a serious caver? Tamar must have given the photographer an earful. Apparently, Miri didn't mind, because the article appeared on the following Sunday: "Little Girl, Big Cave."

Tamar showed me the article jubilantly. "It was a lady interviewer. She came up on Saturday and asked me about caving and I told her how I was ready and how many caves Val and I had been to and how he let me go first so much because I was so good and steady on my feet and didn't rush—well, I try not to rush—and how we even charted a little bit of a cavelet no one had charted before, and how even after that, the people on the important trips didn't want me along."

I read the article, sighing at the usual flattened slant. The writer had decided that a stuffy, entrenched group of older cavers was denying the eager wishes of a bright and articulate eleven-year-old. The article reminded me of the newspaper treatment of young math whizzes who struggle to enter college at the age of ten or eleven. The same spin is put on all of them. The prodigy is really just a normal kid. Fussy and fusty bureaucrats want to deny his creativity. The pattern is laid out in the head of the writer before she leaves for the interview. All she has to do then is meet the child to satisfy the ethic and put the requisite words into his mouth. Such ventriloquist's-dummy performances had been used on me many times and in many forms over the years in interviews about my work or about World Wide and its aims. The familiar canned words leapt off the page at me. "Don't take this seriously," I told Miri and Tamar. "It doesn't really concern you or relate to your actual lives. You're probably upset because you may not have said any of the things that the writer says you did, or in the way you meant them at least. She may have led you to hang your words on her framework. You're not at war with the Grotto, and you don't have the power to force the membership to take you on trips."

"It isn't fair," Miri said. "The members want her membership money, but no one wants her in the caves."

"What's the rush?" I asked.

They stared at me. I suddenly felt I needed to defend my position. "Doesn't Val say that waiting will get you where you want to go sooner than beating the members over the head? Can't you and Val do lots of safe and interesting trips in mapped caves until you're thirteen or fourteen?"

"But 'Chelle, look at me, how small I am. I can wiggle in where nobody else can. I'm limber, too, and that means I can do moves grown-ups can't. Who knows, maybe I'll be big and fat when I'm thirteen and won't be able to do the things I can do now."

"That's unlikely, given your diet," I said, "but what would be so wrong with exploring the caves that are available to you now —the cave we three went to, for instance? We only got halfway through that one, Val told us."

"Oh, 'Chelle, Val and I have done that whole cave a dozen times and mapped it so much, I wouldn't even need a light."

Her hands were all but flying with gestures of righteous impatience. She was the home-schooled girl who got local kids to teach her to skate, to ride a bike, to explain Pinocchio to her, and all as softly and deftly as snow falling in deep woods.

Yes, I think our problems began here. I believe it was that article that gave Tamar a picture of herself as a crusader, a fighter for rights no one else demanded. People who conquer by the force of their personalities may not realize how much harder the way is for the rest of us, who don't have their gifts. Val didn't see what could happen. He couldn't help but be moved by both of them, by their energy and charm and, above all, by the certainty, the absolute sureness, they had that the path they had picked out for themselves was the right one. It seemed that for Tamar and Miri, there would be no doubling back, none of the false starts and dead ends by which caving teaches caution to its acolytes. Failure teaches caution also, and neither Miri nor Tamar had failed as often as most of us do. I remember looking at both of them for a moment, my best friend and my beloved godchild, marveling at their dedication, their strength, their will never to compromise or give in to something less than they were. The two of them lived lives well above the mental poverty line that defined the rest of us. Their paths cut straight as a bullet through the perilous world.

35

Letters began to come to the paper about the article and Tamar and Miri collected them and took turns reading them to me. Some writers were hooked on the home-schooling angle and praised that choice. Others saw it as elitist, depending on the writer's prejudices. A few cavers defended the Grotto decision, and there was a balanced and rational letter from the president of the Boulder Grotto, stating that children as young as six had been on designated trips to commercial caves, accompanied by an adult. For other off-trail exploration, the usual rule allowed children age thirteen and over, also accompanied. "We welcome young cavers," the letter concluded, "and look forward to their increasing interest as they mature."

I went to Mérida again. Events taking place in cities around the world, economic and political, were beginning to determine what World Wide would do, whether my faction would win or lose. As I threw myself into the argument, I felt tuned in to international harmonics: the weakening or strengthening of economies in distant nations, political changes, the upheavals of drug wars, the accession of new leaders, military coups and rebellions. These made me see the world as a vast organism, changing and flowing and half-poised against itself.

At home, that perception faded and my sights went small to encompass the people I loved. I told this to Val one mellow afternoon in March as he and I sat on Miri's back porch and watched the horses in their winter coats as they nosed the brown grasses under snow patches in her field. The day was warm, one of the deceptively mild days that opened everyone's windows and left us vulnerable to the next big snow. Miri was inside with Tamar, having a small argument. Now and then we could hear

214

their voices, rising and falling, paradoxically a comforting sound. Val had asked me how my work at World Wide was going, and I'd found myself telling him in detail about the excitement of planning with the Turkish architects on the expansion at Izmir, of the thrilling skill of their stone masons, who carried out the work with a joyful pride, and of the party we had when the workers finished. I talked about my worries concerning overbuilding and about possible takeovers of two of our resorts. "You might have to teach us all caving, so our staffs can find places to hide."

"Why not? Name a place and it's probably got caves nearby."

"I never thought about visiting any of them, not even when they were famous," I said.

Val laughed. "Not all caves are Tamar's Magic Kingdom, and not all cavers are like us. There's a whole other category of caving whose adherents use caves to hide drugs in, to decorate with spray paint, to take girls to and get stoned in. Would it shock you to know that I did some of that myself?"

"Frankly, yes, it would."

"It makes me cringe when I remember it, but in those growing-up days, long protracted in my case, when I set out to get screwed, stewed, and tattooed, my drinking buddies and I did deface some very nice underground real estate."

"What changed you?"

"Time, and I got interested in the caves themselves, and then I met some of the more serious caving people, the scientists, and saw what they were doing, and I slowly began to realize that I could use it all, my body, fully, my mind and spirit up to the brim, everything I had. It took quite awhile, but I think the discipline of caving helped me get off drugs. It wasn't like what happened to Miri and Tamar. Miri looked into a microscope and saw a whole world in there that made her go 'Ah' and Tamar saw the Magic Kingdom."

"Do you think you and Miri will get married?"

"I want to; she doesn't."

"I know you love her."

"Yeah." He suddenly looked like an uncertain boy. "She knows it. I told her."

Val was easy to talk to. I found myself opening up to him about Rafael, the joy and challenge of our working together, and the simultaneous feeling of reserve because of all our cultural differences, and then we were content to be silent for a while and look out at the horses. We heard Miri and Tamar in the background, still arguing.

"Willful, both of them," he said, and his voice was full of love. After awhile, he said, "I'm okay with the way things are for now, but I don't have a lot of time, five, maybe six years. Tamar'll be sixteen or seventeen by then, and I don't want to fall in love with her in any other way than the way I love her now. I'm twenty-five years older than she is, and I'm father, brother, and friend. As soon as I get lover signals, I'll have to bow out, if Miri won't have me."

"You seem to have thought quite a bit about that."

"It's occurred to me."

"Can you rein her in a little?"

"You don't rein in Niagara Falls," he said. "All you can do is try to channel it a little."

"Something's happening, isn't it?" I said.

He nodded. "I know. They're both getting tighter, winding themselves up too much. It's almost like something has to be proved. I keep telling Tamar she's not in a contest; there's nothing to be won here except the satisfaction of having done a very tough thing."

"Miri sees life as a win-lose proposition; she always has. We grew up in a small, tight, enclosed community. She broke out and took me with her. Look how far she's come."

"How far you've both come. Now that you're here, though, isn't it time to ease up a little?"

They came out then and we had to finesse the topic. "Nice footwork in that cave," I murmured to Val as he was leaving.

"Yeah, and in heavy boots, too," and he winked at me.

The Denver paper picked up on the Boulder story as a human-interest piece. Here were two extremely photogenic people. Here was a cause; here was a single mother with a home-schooled daughter (how does she do it?) and a prestigious job. The paper

216

sent a reporter and a photographer out to the house, where I was forced to get into the act. The thrust of the article, when it appeared in the "Life and Leisure" Sunday section, was that this beautiful, radiant girl was one of the nation's youngest cavers, competent enough to break the barriers that the caving establishment had constructed to thwart her. Her mother and "aunt" supported her totally. She was accompanied by a competent spelunker and had mastered all the techniques necessary. My comments to the reporter had been frank. Tamar had never been denied experience in a number of established cave trips. She was still a child, and both her endurance and strength were limited. She was well known in the Boulder Grotto and trip leaders had the right to determine the participants of the trip. None of those comments appeared in the article, only my praise of Tamar's dream and my hope for her to accomplish it.

This time, the news broke on the Denver relatives as the Boulder article hadn't. My mother called, Shirah called, and the Mordecais called me after they had spoken to Miri. Was Tamar safe? Was this caving business done by people who knew what they were doing? Were there lights in the caves? Was she in some kind of harness? Was she caving on Shabbat? Why wasn't Miriam going with her? Two friends from high school called. Was Miri going to sue the Grotto? Was this a woman's issue? Was Tamar really being protected from the perils of modern life, TV, the Internet, movies, the virulent influences they themselves were working unsuccessfully to shield their children from? Did Miri know how lucky she was not to have a passive child in whom enthusiasm had to be stirred every day? How had she arranged Tamar's life?

"When will this die down?" Val asked. We were sitting in his van, waiting for Miri and Tamar to come out. They were going to a concert; I would go home. "I never understood this celebrity stuff," Val said. He sounded incredulous and annoyed. "People are calling me, guys I haven't seen since two jobs back, an old girlfriend. What's the interest people have in someone's being in the news?"

"You're amazed?"

"Am I suddenly important?"

"Maybe it's just bringing you to mind," I said, but I wasn't being honest with him. "Open the paper and here we are."

"I've been here all along, 'Chelle, and anyone from my bad old days could have gotten hold of me and heard all about what I've been into."

"I can't say I was happy with the article, but that's nothing new. Luckily, most of my media exposure has been in the Mexican press."

"Olé!" he said. "Do you have a scrapbook?"

I nodded, and he saw that I was blushing and laughed. "Hey," he said, "it's good to remember what and when."

"After it's all over and when I'm in one of Arthur Kleinman's nursing homes."

"He's okay—maybe a little bit one-way."

"He wasn't always like that, unless I've forgotten how it was when we were kids. We sneaked out of the neighborhood, the four of us, and went to Elitch's and Lakeside, and we went to movies and ate forbidden food. Later we smoked, did lots of things."

"Big sins." Val was smiling. "But I can't see Arthur doing any of them. Who was the fourth?"

"Ab—Abner. He died in an accident when we were eighteen. How shocked I was at the possibility that such a thing could happen to kids like us. That might have helped drive Arthur toward the place he is now."

"Yeah. I notice you're calling him Arthur, not Art or Artie."

"I used to call him Art, but not lately. It's Arthur now."

"That says something."

He reached over and turned on the heat. "Do you think it would help if I converted—became a Jew?"

I was so unprepared for the question that I turned to face him to see if he was joking. He wasn't. "I don't think so. We were raised Orthodox, neighbored all around by people just like us. What felt like a warm coat to them felt like a straitjacket to us. Miri's Orthodoxy is outside the faith."

"What's it like, being Jewish?"

"Well," I said, "action trumps belief or wishing. Heaven and hell aren't religious matters; charity and compassion are. And the state of the world is a shared project between us and God. Life isn't a game, but laughter is somehow sacred. We were intentionally created. There it is, basically, Rachel Finn's version of Jewish theology."

"I could live with that," Val said.

"But I don't think it would get you much closer to Miri, and that's what you want."

"I guess so. You all have a link to something bigger than you are, a source."

I saw that Val had thought Miri was religious, even though he had never seen her off to the synagogue or shared any holidays with her. People mistake physical beauty for all kinds of other things, virtue, wisdom, inner light. "It's a faith worth looking into," I said, "but it's a faith without guarantees."

He was quiet after that, and Miri and Tamar came down the walk. I jumped out and they climbed into the van.

At about eleven o'clock, the ambulance backs in on the narrow track we took yesterday in the police car. I'm awed by the driver's skill. He and a partner get out and survey the scene. Visibility has improved, but that's only true on the ground. Twenty feet or so above us, a thick mat of frost-wet fog covers the mountain and the chopper's possible landing spot is lost in it.

The fog mat has done something to the sound, muffling and dis-torting it. The sound of the ambulance's tires and engine is amplified. The tread of people walking and the equipment boxes being dragged are annoyingly loud, but voices sound hollow and deadened, like conversations held underwater. The personnel are two EMT's and a paramedic: two men and a woman. The print on the side of the ambulance reads CLEAR CREEK RESCUE. "Aren't we in Boulder County?" I ask them.

"No, Ma'am, we're ten miles or so into Clear Creek."

Why this should bother me, I don't know, but it adds to my feeling of dislocation and unreality. "East of the sun and west of the moon," I say to Miri.

Someone has alerted the Grotto team leader, who comes out of his tent. Escobar has also come down. "Nothing yet," the Grotto man says. "We're doing this very carefully and the area around the pit is unstable, but we've got them both harnessed in and halfway up. There are all kinds of rock outcroppings and ledges on the way."

"I heard you had one and one," the youngest of the Clear Creek people says. He doesn't realize who we are, or he might not have said that. "We can take 'em both. Coroner said for us to transport."

Miri snaps into awareness. "You can't do that," she says. "What if Tamar wakes up? She can't be allowed to see a body— God knows how it looks."

"We'd wrap up the body," the boy says. "She'd only see a blanket covering something."

Miri is in full flow. "You will not transport my daughter with a dead body."

I know that is true. Val has gone, and what remains is a corpse, but her response seems very cold to me. I look at Escobar. "Officer, isn't Val's van down the road? You'd have to have someone drive it out of here anyway. In the back, there's lots of space, a mattress or two, and blankets. Val could be secured in there, couldn't he, and be driven down to wherever the coroner wants?"

They agree, and I feel I have justified my presence up here. Escobar looks at me with sympathy and says, "Press is here, too. They came in with the ambulance: Channel Four, Channel Seven, and a cable newsperson, too."

Miri goes to stone. I start to cry.

I've been sane and responsible and admirable all this time, and suddenly it all gives in—frustration and anger, grief, tension, loss, loneliness, guilt, and the simple physical discomfort of cold, hunger, and night after night of broken sleep. They all stand around, embarrassed for me, and staring. Escobar moves close, takes me by the shoulders and turns me and guides me—we're like paired skaters as we go up the hill to his police car, and he puts me into the passenger seat and goes around to get in and sit beside me while I sob. The tears seem to go on forever and it's a while before they slow. "My husband was a cop," I tell him hoarsely, "Niall Finn, Denver P.D."

"I'm state," he says.

"I know."

He reaches across me to the glove compartment and pulls out a Kleenex packet. "Take 'em," he says, "live it up." And I give a forlorn little laugh.

The press—here they come. These are not part-time people from a small town paper. We rate the first-string: *Denver Post, Rocky,* three TV channels—and they descend on Miri.

"Let her do it," I tell Escobar. "Get me out of here before I throw up on The Public's Right To Know."

Escobar grins at me. "Woman's got a mouth on her."

I begin to quote Miri from our college days: "The human being is, above all else, adaptable. A new virus kills large numbers

221

of people before the forces that resist it can be marshaled. The new virus is raging. The organism will not die out; it will build the forces of resistance."

"New virus?"

"Celebrity."

"I wish we had some plum wine," Escobar says. "My mother makes it from wild plums. They're San Luis Valley people, my folks, wind-dried and sandblasted. Wine's as hard as booze. If I had some, I'd give you a shot of it now."

We sit together and watch the press go at Miri.

36

They made their find late in March, a new cave, unexplored, they said. Tamar was so excited she called on her new cell phone from someplace on the way back. She was kid-loud on the phone. "We found our cave! We were looking upslope on a trail Val knew, and then *I* said we should go up and look downslope, and we did and I saw it—I didn't exactly *see* it, 'Chelle; it was like I felt it, something that wasn't normal, the way the hill was going, right? Do you get it? And there were rocks sticking out and it was all rocky in front of it. We had to clear two or three away to get past the big rocks and then we thought it wasn't a cave, but just a hiccup in the side of the hill, you know, a cavelet, maybe, but that was because it turned around and its back was to us—its back is to you when you go in." She was heaping her own enthusiasm, stoking its fire. "Val warned me. Most caves are hiccups, or cavelets. They go in a few feet and then they stop. Maybe the mountain fell in on them, or maybe the hiccup is just a little bit eroded away or something years ago pulled off or melted minerals inside it and it's only fifteen feet in and that's all."

"Take a breath, Tamar, or you'll faint."

"He gave me the speech he gives before every trip about when real cavers get disappointed, how they act and how they don't take it out on where they are, kicking at the rocks, or knocking things over or littering to get even—you know."

"What happened when you got behind the rocks?"

"We went up, not down, and where I didn't think the cave would go." She was kicking at the words for failing to express her wonder-joy. "All of a sudden, there was a kind of balcony we

223

were on, and Val made us go back and mark things and do mapping."

"So you had quite a day."

Later, when they were home, she hadn't calmed down. Val had let her off at Miri's and gone on to his job at the halfway house. She pounded on the door—she was too short to reach the doorbell Henrik had put in. She bulleted into the house, ricocheting off the furniture, eating, talking, sitting, standing, running, hugging Miri and me.

"It's going to be so cool, 'Chelle. All summer we can go and we'll do a perfect job and we'll get to name all the places in the cave, but I don't want any of those fancy names like Silent Splendor, or Neptune's Ballroom. The Magic Kingdom is a secret thing; when you talk about it, you should be whispering."

"Are you going next week?"

"I don't think so, and it makes me mad. Val wants to buy new rope and upgrade all his equipment, and he doesn't have the money to do it."

"How much money are we talking about?" I asked.

"I don't know, but it's not too much."

"Then couldn't you wait?"

"Oh, 'Chelle!" Her voice rang with her impatience. "It would be wasting the whole summer."

"Tamar, the April snows haven't come, yet. You'll have to keep the lid on for a while anyway."

"I want to start. We have to start before someone else goes there and finds it."

Her voice had risen to the top of the scale, shrill with hurt at the world's unfairness. I tried for a sympathetic tone. "The cave is there. It's been there for centuries and centuries. It'll wait for you."

"That's what Val says, but—"

"But you're not getting any younger, are you? Six months or a year and you'll be too old to go caving."

"'Chelle, you're being mean."

"I am, yes, and I'm sorry. You're too impatient, and Val says that's not good caving."

"I know—he says don't try to eat the cave or it will eat you—

but you don't understand. We found our cave. What if somebody else finds it and goes in and discovers all of it while we're trying to get the ropes and things we need?"

"Val says most of the caves in the world—"

"I know, that they're unexplored, but this one is *our* cave and I'm even afraid to think about it because maybe someone will catch what I'm thinking and go where it is, and be the one who—"

"Tamar . . ."

She had begun to cry. Hope and desire were exhausting her and I couldn't dampen her ardor too much. I'd been an eleven-year-old crying with thwarted desire just as strong as Tamar's at being denied any of a dozen immediate, instant wants. Tamar's hunger, although childishly expressed, was more permanent and worthy than what I had wept for at ten or eleven. I remember that I yearned to celebrate the forbidden Halloween that was talked up in school and derided at home. Tamar's yearnings might supply a lifetime's satisfaction and develop into a life work, perhaps in geology or hydrology or any of a dozen sciences. I wanted to believe it would. I wanted to help them.

I hate special pleading, the cry "Forgive, forgive me. I didn't realize; I didn't know. Erase the mistake. I meant well; give me extra points for altruism." I called Val and asked him how much money he would need to buy good rope and whatever other equipment they might use. Val said he wanted to renew all his line, not knowing how much vertical work they would be doing.

"I'm a little short right now, saving up for the trips," he said.

"I'd like to help."

There it was. I was glad he didn't shuffle and demur. "I think two hundred would do it," he said. "I've got the vertical hardware and most of it's in good shape. It's the new rope I need."

I'd thought he would give a figure in the thousands. I don't remember what else I thought, but I was surprised and relieved. "Tamar doesn't want to waste the spring," I said.

Val laughed the warm, welcome laugh, which was a part of his great charm. "Tamar's hot to trot. Too hot. We are going to do this cave well, map it, and later register it. We'll be taking photos and a videotape, I think, but that'll be later. First, we'll do a rough sketch-map and follow it up trip by trip, all carefully. Later, she'll hate me for teaching her good mapping technique, because those folks who do it well often get stuck with the job on the big expeditions, but a little stop and draw, a little look around'll cure some of that overeager cave eating she does. She may not be the youngest caver in America, but I'll bet she's the youngest trip leader."

Val must have said the same thing to Miri, because a few days later we were sitting on the porch, still wearing jackets and hats but relishing the late sun. She said, "The reporter's coming, later. I told her Tamar and Val had discovered a cave, and that Tamar was leading the trip."

"Miri . . ."

"It means she'll have the leverage she needs to get into their Grotto's upper levels, and get on their lists. She'll start ahead of the game and not have to crack her way in or go for years before someone gives her a chance. Did I tell you she's going on TV also? Channel Four is doing an interview."

"What does Tamar say to this? Isn't she adamant about keeping the cave a secret until it's been investigated?"

"She won't tell where it is, but tomorrow, I'm staying home and she and Val will do the interview. We got her a Web site after the second article came out—she has interest from kids all over the world. She already has kids sending her e-mail every day, and because of the Web site she has a fan club now. One of her fans said she should have a T-shirt, so one of the secretaries in the office is designing it. Of course, it needs a logo. We want a variation of a logo I saw in a caver's book. I wouldn't be surprised if they got her on *Good Morning America*."

"How do you know about *Good Morning America*? You don't even own a TV set."

"We're getting one. I can keep it in one of the rooms upstairs. We'll only use it when Tamar has her interviews—so we can see them later, when they air."

I sat in the sun and heard Miri speaking words I couldn't believe were hers. This was the Miri who wouldn't have television in her house because of its evil influence, who wouldn't let her daughter read children's books or go to school with other kids for fear of the baleful pull of modern life, whose monitoring of food, real and intellectual, was pervasive and constant—all to ensure that Tamar would be protected from the pollution of the youth culture and common childhood.

"Miri . . ."

"They get head starts, these kids. Look at the girl gymnasts and skaters who get to the Olympics at seventeen and eighteen. Didn't they start at six and seven? If you begin as young as Tamar is, by the time you're a teenager, your way will be made for you. People give more respect to a serious, motivated child. Doors will be open for her, not only in caving but everywhere. Do you think Jodie Foster or Michelle Kwan or any of those people who were famous as kids have the same experiences that you did, the same adolescence that I did? They have all kinds of support and recognition."

I was amazed. Had Miri ever felt herself poor or neglected or underappreciated? "You were Reb Mordecai's daughter," I said. "I saw you go to the head of the line at the bakery when we went, because of who you were, and because you were pretty, and because people liked to see you get your way. Wasn't I at your wedding? Didn't I see the presents that overflowed the house? What about the house itself? How many young people start their married life with a house like that?"

"I didn't know you were jealous, 'Chelle," Miri said. "My house, my lovely house, if you remember, had to be open for guests, always had to be ready for Shabbat visits that lasted for days, and dinners for eight."

"Your mother—"

"The marriage was her idea, and that's why she owed me. She promised that if I married Jacob, I wouldn't be the loser, but I was. I had to lie to him. Tamar won't have to marry anybody or lie to anybody or rig structures to hang her life from."

What could I say to that? Miri was rewriting her life in darker colors so that Tamar's might show all the brighter and more dramatically against a grimness I had never seen in it.

"I'm not jealous, Miri; I never was. I'm only confused."

"Freedom, 'Chelle, it's about freedom."

37

Spring in Colorado is a misnomer. The air is light and iridescent, the ground littered with the dried pine needles a windy March has combed from the trees; the pasqueflowers, tender as whispers, pull blue-gray heads from ground that was empty the day before. All is ready: Act 1: Springtime. The actors have only just come onstage when winter closes the show again. Snow after snow falls in deep, wet dumpings, beautiful for an hour only as they cover the sins and mistakes of previous months, but taking back the earth. The native leafy trees, the aspen and wild maple, a shrub, here, put out no leaves until the summer. The transplants, trees and people, are always fooled. The lilac, the cottonwood, and Russian olive, the few leaved shrubs and trees that survive here, bend and break with their too-early flowering, deceived by the mildness that seduces between the loading snows.

Growing up here, I had taken the springtime treacheries as universal law and was astonished at the openheartedness of spring in other places. My trips to Turkey and Greece came to my Colorado eyes as revelations. The long, sweet Norwegian springs made me weepy.

This spring, I was home most of the time, and back at Miri's most Sunday afternoons to sit on her porch, even though it meant huddling in quilts, watching the winter bury us again. In those afternoons, Miri's new tension eased a little; the tightness in her face made her look less drawn and more elegant, but there was still a pull about her mouth and eyes, which Val and I might have called intensity and her coworkers, drivenness.

Things were happening at the lab; I wasn't sure what they were, but they were making Miri tense and angry, and our

Sunday afternoons together were more necessary than ever—to help relax her, in the slow releasing of inner knots that prayer provides, a quieting of the spirit.

Miri's tension should have been eased, because the stress of her keeping Tamar at the lab had been removed. Miri had found another home-schooler family whose dietary and societal worries mirrored her own, and who was willing to include Tamar in the studies at its house. Again, Miri's charm, and Tamar's, opened the doors to what their wills decreed.

The Mordecais and I celebrated another Passover in snow. Tamar didn't come this time, because I didn't have time to pick her up.

"And I don't have the shopping done—no food she can eat."

"Oh, Miri, don't you remember how much we resented not being able to eat at schoolmates' houses when we were kids. The party at the Thunstrums in sixth grade is still on my list of hurts, even after all these years."

"It's cancer and immune deficiencies I'm against," Miri said. "Our systems are very delicately balanced by now."

"Let them have their granddaughter."

"I don't like their rigidity, I don't like what they tell her, and I don't want her to hear that I'm not doing the right things to raise her."

"They never say that."

"Their *lives* say that, 'Chelle. What they do and where they go. Tamar's life is rational, scientific, and healthy. I mean to keep it that way."

There were children at the Mordecais' seder who asked the four questions. The Rabbi had always invited two or three poor families to his table, but the grandchildren weren't his. Noah and his family were in New York, Dan and his in Israel. Elias had left the family and the neighborhood and Judaism too and was now Ellis. When Ada's eyes met mine across the table, hers filled suddenly and she looked away.

I hadn't raised the issue strongly in the past. Now Miri's attitude was hardening just as Tamar was getting older, seeing other children, hearing about grandparents who celebrated Christmas, Chanukah, Tet, Kwanza. They had B'nai Mitzvot and *quinceañeras* and Tamar's natural curiosity would someday cause her to wonder where her place was and who her people were.

On the second day of Passover, I went to Shirah's, where my mother was enjoying her own grandchildren as they asked the four questions. She'd given up on me as a supplier of that pleasure, and I enjoyed the freedom to look at my four nieces and nephews: two sated, stolid materialists and two nice kids— nice, but with none of Tamar's strength and liveliness.

We don't choose our memories; they choose us. Many times in my life, I've set myself to the conscious act: "I want to keep this day, this sight, this experience, to seal in my head. I want the beauty of this scene, the richness of these people met on trips, the first sights of islands I've visited, cities, all the moments of revelation, happiness, gratification, fulfillment. I want an album of mental photography—life stopped at height."

It doesn't work that way. What I remember most about the day Rafael took me to the gorgeous botanical gardens in Oaxaca is an argument we had. On the day I first saw the ancient city of Izmir, I wanted to remember the beauty of the white houses, the mosques that seemed to hang from the sky, not rise from the ground. What I remember best is the beggar who followed us all day, even after I had given him alms, and given them again. At Chichén Itzá, I wanted to savor the height of the pyramid, the vast sky. I get Tamar lost. In my memory Miri isn't standing under the wedding canopy as a bride, but sitting on the floor of the coatroom in her spread-out white gown, listening to me sob. Niall—I have many, many pictures of Niall to give myself, but none of the ones I want, the special moments for which I had prepared my spirit like a hostess opening the door to a long-awaited guest. He had been given a full police funeral, a thrilling ceremony, of which I remember not a thing, but he's in here now, pointing a butter knife at me, saying, "Madame, you're a fruitcake."

I went to Miri's on the Sunday after the Seder still harboring a little annoyance. We'd been sulking from our argument and I decided to hold off speaking until I had eaten the last of the treats Ada, all but weeping, had sent home with me. There was haroset—her special recipe with dates and coconut. There were matzo balls, chicken soup, flanken in raisin wine sauce, carrot tzimmes—carrots stewed in honey to a luscious, thick stew—spinach soufflé.

Someone was sitting in my rocker on Miri's porch, bundled against the cold. Boulder is a windy city, blown against the base of the mountains, but the day was cool and still. Who was it?

The door opened and a man came out on the porch and stood rubbing his hands. The person in the rocker was female.

"Miri, your luck holds," I muttered. I couldn't yell at her for missing her parents' seder while these people were around, and by the time they left, I would be thinking that of course she was her own woman with her own life and that she had already done great and necessary work and that her work might even have saved lives while we were singing "Dayenu" and eating the bitter herbs.

I went up to the porch steps and recognized the reporter who had interviewed me about Tamar's caving. The woman was dark and pretty, but less naturally so than Miri and more made-up, showier. I thought I remembered the name—Gomez. The man was introduced to me as another photographer. They were doing a longer, deeper interview for a national news outlet, she told me. Tamar had indeed been invited to appear on *Good Morning America* and would go to New York for the show. Miri appeared, glowing. She saw my raised eyebrow. Anyone else would have dithered or been defensive. With complete self-possession, she told me that she and Tamar were planning for the trip to New York. They would spend three days in the city. The planning had kept her from going to the Seder, and she would make up to the family for the loss. When the Mordecais saw their granddaughter on TV and heard her tell the story of her discovery of a cave and her scientific work on it—the mapping, geology, hydrology—they would realize how special, how important her raising had been, and there would be a refutation of everything the family and the world said about how single mothers might not provide the best environment for their children, of what pundits said about today's young people, and of what older cavers said about children on their expeditions.

"So she's really going on TV?" I asked.

"She sure is—national. Tamar will be representing all young girls who have more going on in their heads than people think kids can have. Tamar has been studying—not dancing or skating or doing gymnastics, but involved in deep study, learning geology, when most little girls are collecting fad things and demanding fad clothes."

As I couldn't argue about the seder, I couldn't argue about Tamar as a showpiece, not with the reporter there.

"This is real achievement," Gomez was saying. "I know she doesn't want to disclose the location of the cave, but on the other hand, what proof can she give that there *is* a cave?"

"Oh, they're taking pictures; they have maps, lots of evidence," Miri told her.

"I'm not saying the pictures are a hoax"—the photographer was syrup-voiced—"but I've been fooled a couple of times. You go to a remote site and they show you footprints and say they've got proof of Bigfoot and they show you a blurred picture of something hairy on the run. Fixed footprints, fixed pix. Another one, guy a hundred and twenty years old, pumping iron. Great stuff."

"She's not doing this on her own," I said, "Val's with her. They do measurements of all kinds. There's a book, an album, and when they're ready, they'll register the cave—they said they would."

"Have you seen the cave? Were you in it yourself?"

"No; I've been caving with them, but not recently. This cave has just been discovered."

"Then how do you know it's real?"

"What would be the point of making it up? Tamar loves caving, not faking. Faking would take time from the authentic experience."

"Mrs.—uh—Finn, what kid wouldn't want to be on TV, to be a celebrity, even for a very short time?"

"Well then, take Val, her caving partner," I said. "He won't be getting any publicity. The light'll all be shining on Tamar. Why would he want to cheat?"

"People have lots of reasons for scamming."

I shot a glance at Miri, who seemed to miss what my look was trying to convey. "Tamar's the real thing," I said. "I know that. It wouldn't make sense to her to fake a cave, TV or no TV."

"But she's got the logo and the T-shirts. She's got a Web site and a fan club. What separates her from any other kid with a shtick?"

I was surprised to hear the Yiddish word from Ms. Gomez. The word hurt, too. I wanted to boot her in the butt and send her flying. Tamar was no publicity-hungry faker. Why had Miri let this happen? I bit down on my anger. Years dealing with media had made me sure that any real emotion would come back to sting me, to sting Tamar.

"Listen to Tamar," I said. "Hear what she says and how, weigh it, measure it, turn it upside down. What you see is what's there—all the way through."

38

We sat out on the pleasantly chilly porch, the reporter—Alicia Gomez, the photographer, Miri, and I, enjoying the brisk day, well bundled. I brought chairs out for myself and the photographer. We waited for Val and Tamar to return from their day of exploring. Val needed to be back for his job at the halfway house by nine. As we waited, we chatted about one thing and another, desultorily returning to the subject of Tamar's home schooling, or how she had pursued her caving interest, or how much geology she actually knew. When it got too dark and cold for the porch, we went into the house. Gomez asked to see Tamar's room. It was a mess, like the rest of the house, clothing here and there, some clean, some dirty. Piles of possessions were heaped on the floor. The sheets had been pulled up, but the bed wasn't made. Here was a shoe, there a sneaker, papers, a model.

Tamar's extra caving equipment reflected none of the messiness of her room. It was all in a footlocker at the end of her bed, and when we opened it, we saw rope neatly coiled; a carbide lamp that had been taken apart, its fittings clean, its extra felts and cleaning tools with it; two light sticks in their packing; flagging tape; plastic containers carefully packaged; and, in a box, maps and a journal. She had taken most of her equipment with her, but even looking at the spare items, we saw a care and order that Tamar demanded in no other part of her life. We stood looking at the open footlocker, saying nothing.

At 7:30, Miri decided we should eat, and I went out for the makings after some discussion. The natural-food market was closed by this time, and I had to promise to get only produce from the organic section of the supermarket. I knew what brands of crackers and packaged food Miri would eat. I remember no anxiety about why Tamar and Val hadn't returned. Enthusiasm would keep them at the cave site. Caves are dark and have none of the hour-ordering information that the outer world gives subliminally. Hadn't I emerged from a cave stunned that the sun had disappeared and the day gone without my knowing it? I was wondering but still not worried when I got back to the house and saw that Val's truck wasn't there yet.

The sun had set, but we would have half an hour at least of rosy afterglow. I looked around and felt the beauty of the late day easing itself over the snowfields behind Miri's house. The horses boarding in her field were all at its far end, gathered in the afterglow. I looked at the line of cottonwoods and poplars Henrik had planted as a windbreak and about which some of the neighbors had complained, saying that the roots were invading their septic systems and the cotton from their seeds was a nuisance in their yards. The trees had grown quickly and had attained a height of fifteen feet or so. I had met Niall, married, thought about a family, become a widow; Henrik was gone. All our lives had changed. I can remember watching the light that evening, how it seemed to alter the size of the field and slowly render the horses invisible. I remember the snow—a luminous blue.

We unpacked the bags I had brought and made dinner. I was enjoying the company. The photographer was a witty man who had been to Mérida and to other World Wide sites, including an island it was planning to use for a resort. The room was bright and warm. Even Ms. Gomez let down a little, and Miri was in a mood to charm. She showed them the medical books that Tamar had "illustrated" when she was six or seven—organs with little hats they were tipping: Larry Liver, Sammy Spleen, with a tennis racquet in his single hand, two big eyes and a simper.

Only when it was eight o'clock did we begin to grow anxious, checking the time, speaking casually, but without paying much attention to what we said. Val had a phone number at the halfway house and a cell phone number. When Miri called, the people at the house said he hadn't contacted them. The cell phone Val was carrying was dead, Miri said, after punching in the number. I remember studying the shadows cast by a light we turned on outside. A wind had come up, one that made us feel the drafts in the house a little more. The comfortable warmth we had been enjoying drew away. Night was here, dark and cold. At nine, Miri called the sheriff's office, and he called someone from the Boulder Grotto, who then called us. At eleven, the photographer left, but Alicia Gomez stayed with us, hoping, I thought, for a display of Miri's fireworks when Tamar returned at last. Underneath Alicia's concern hummed the hunger for something dramatic. She must have seen a hint of the zealot in Miri, the need to prove her point at all costs.

The Grotto man told us not to panic. "We know the cave is within two hours of here," he said, "and we can pretty well eliminate everything to the east of where you are. They won't be impossible to find, if, on the off chance, something has happened to them. My guess is that they got held up somehow and will be in contact with you soon. Does she have a journal, maps, something that might help?"

Miri said she did, and said he sounded cheered by that. He told us he would be in touch with the cave rescue group just in case.

So we waited through the night. Alicia went home at 1:00 a.m.; the sheriff called at 1:15 to see if there had been any developments. After that I went into Tamar's room and to that neatly arranged footlocker and hunted through the notebook and set of papers for a clue to where they might be. I wanted to find instructions, a location. I heard Miri pacing downstairs. She had never thought enough about the house to lay carpet or even rugs to deaden the noise, and I could follow her steps in the pattern they made, kitchen, hall, parlor, side room, forward toward the front of the house, back, and then forward again. The part of me that was a friend ached for her; the part that was a co-conspirator in this caving venture felt guilty and fearful; the architectural designer thought again how old-fashioned and inconvenient this house was, with its spaces and priorities designed for public show and a private life separated from it, and the relegation of the womenfolk to the back of the house. There she went again, up and back.

At about 3:00 A.M. we were blurry in each other's vision, and we lay down. We couldn't go upstairs to bed; it was too far from the phone. I stretched out on the floor, Miri on the couch in the parlor. I drowsed on and off and must have fallen deeply asleep sometime before daylight, because Miri woke me at nine and I called my office.

She was drawn and haunted-looking. I told her about a meeting I had later in the morning but said that I could cancel the remainder of my work for the day and would be back as soon as I could. As I left, she was on the phone with the people from the Boulder Grotto. They were sending someone to the house to look at Tamar's journal. Had she mentioned any difficulties getting into the cave? Was there climbing with equipment involved? I left the house grainy-eyed, went home, showered, and went to my meeting, half-attentive.

39

By the afternoon, we knew it wasn't a highway accident, something happening in the daylight world of police radios and official contact. We've all had twenty-four-hour-a-day coverage now, newspapers, radio, and TV.

Alicia Gomez was back at the house that afternoon and people from the Boulder Grotto and the Colorado Cavers Rescue group were sitting in the front room because the weather had changed to a damp chill, threatening snow. The Grotto man had Tamar's journal, and when I came in, they all looked up at me as though I might have the clue they needed.

"We've got a general idea of where they are," the Grotto man said, "but it would help if you could remember something, any scrap of talk that would give us a hint as to direction or location. Did they climb—did they go down or up inside the cave—was the sun shining in? Anything we might put together with what we already know?"

"Up," I said, not knowing how I knew this. "The cave went up, and there was another way in, another hole, because the light came in, and they hadn't known that at first." I was remembering Tamar's ecstatic chatter.

Grotto looked interested and made a note. "Were there bats in the cave, did she say?"

"I don't think so. She would have mentioned it. Val said something about dust, their kicking up a lot of dust." I pulled at my memory, trying to get at what shreds there were of talk between them, the excited bursts from Tamar, joyous talk of discovery I had barely listened to and now desperately sought. "They wanted to keep the discovery a secret," I said, "until they had it all mapped and claimed, or whatever you do to make a cave yours."

Rescue asked, "Anything about the drive—dirt roads that got the truck dusty, or were they on private land, someone's ranch, something like that?"

I shook my head. "Val's truck was always dusty—wait—wait—" I was struggling with something Tamar had said. "There's a view from the deck, an overhang, but it can't be seen from the road—you go in from the top, not a climb up, a climb down, and then inside you go up, and that's the secret. Why it's a secret is that if you come at it from the front, you'd have a tough climb, with ropes, but from the side—I think there's a trail that's hidden from the road by rocks. Does that make any sense?"

They were at the maps again, and the question again, "What's the least time they ever took to go and come back?" They were asking Miri and me, and we looked helplessly at each other. We counted and figured and cursed our careless inattention.

"There was the time Val was late. He got here—was it eleven-thirty or noon?"

"Minutes could be important," Grotto said, "to narrow the search area. Were they always back before dark?"

"They were always back after sundown but before dark. They were eager for the days to get longer so they could get more caving in. Val had to be back for work."

Grotto turned to a silent colleague and began to whisper, and they took out a map, on which they had drawn a rough circle.

"You've ridden with him—is he a speed demon or slow and careful?" the sheriff's man asked.

"About average," I said. "He—they, they like to sing. They like caving songs and they make up new words for them, and that takes a certain concentration. The roads we traveled, the times I went with them, were difficult roads, winding and steep, and it took skill to drive them."

Another whispered conference followed, and a new map. This time Grotto took out a compass and made what looked like a dauntingly large circle. My heart began to race and I felt my eyes fill. The rescue man said, "Did you ever notice the van as it left the house here? Did it turn north or south?" Again we tried to

239

visualize something that might have been created by our own urgent need. Had we been on the porch on any of the days we saw them off? Oh God, the trees, the cottonwoods that Henrik had planted, stood in the way, and even bare, their trunks closed off that edge bit of view of the turnoff onto the main road. I told them that.

"One more thing," the sheriff's man said. "When the van left, was it over on the far right or was it more in the middle of the road, like it was getting ready for a left turn?"

Straws, wood chips in a river, those clues. How I tried for the remembered detail that would send the search arrow-true to where Val and Tamar were. Gomez was writing away. When she looked up, she saw Miri, whose face had gone hard, and she rose and left.

"I don't remember any of that," I said, "I wish I did."

"A long shot," the sheriff's man said, trying to make us feel better. "Don't sweat it."

I knew they were glad, all of them, that neither of us had broken down, gone into hysterics, screamed. We were both too stunned and miserable to draw the necessary breath. I thought, When Tamar comes home, Miri's iron face will break apart and shatter and the old, soft Miri will be underneath. What I was thinking came out in such an inappropriate way that heads turned to me. "Mir, do you remember the day at Elitch's when the four of us took pictures in that photo booth? I wonder where those pictures went." Into their stares, I said, "We should have pictures of Tamar—maybe someone saw them climbing or on a trail or walking along the road."

Miri remembered the album she was making for Tamar and took it to Grotto and showed him the work Tamar had done, pictures and early accounts of caves she had visited, and lists of the books she had read and studies she had done. I could see the men's former view of Tamar altering gradually as they read. She and Val were no longer self-advertising ignoramuses whose recklessness had caused this headache, but serious cavers needing rescue. I could see respect where there had been something of exasperation mingled with the sympathy they had shown.

"Makes the problem tougher," Grotto murmured to Rescue.

"Experienced cavers can get into worse trouble than duffers."
They were hoping Miri wouldn't hear. She went to the ringing
phone and brought it back to Grotto. "Yeah, that's what I think,"
he said to the caller. "Anywhere around there. Listen—I've got
some sketches and some of the preliminary scouting they did
before they found it. . . . Yeah. I'll put everything out and maybe
somebody will respond."

Then they all rose, stretched, thanked Miri, said a reassuring
word, and left. It was almost midnight. We sat alone.

"I want to *do* something," Miri said, "to be moving. I can't go
for a run—I need to stay by the phone. What should I do? I can't
just sit here."

"People will be coming," I said. "Let's clean."

We started in the attic where there were boxes and crates of
things Miri had never unpacked after leaving Jacob, things she
had taken with her unsorted. All the furnishings of the house had
stayed with it, but there were monogrammed towels with her
name, a quilt with her name, and things from the Mordecai house
that were to furnish her more private rooms—a desk she had
used, a bookcase, boxes of clothes and books she had taken
when she had left Denver all those years ago.

We swept and dusted, unpacked, repacked, trying for full
involvement in the task. We worked our way down to the second
floor, and I was amazed at how little living had been done in
those upper rooms. They were messy, but Miri's mess was
uncaring, her bedroom impeded by furniture she had salvaged
from lab throwaways—a bookcase standing in the middle of the
room, unused, a collection of trash cans, and two metal stools.
We manhandled the bookcase up to the attic and brought the
stools up and stacked the trash cans. We picked up, dusted, and
ran the sweeper, and I found Miri's box of pictures and took it
downstairs for later perusal. Tamar's messy room we left as it
was. The disarray there was the result of intensity. Tamar was
living too quickly to put things away, and the effect here was
subtly but pervasively different from the dusty disinterest shown
in Miri's living spaces. We did the bathroom. We went at it the
way an underdog nation goes to war.

We worked through the night, fuddled and clumsy from

241

exhaustion, and by the time we were finished, all we could do was to struggle downstairs and fall asleep on the couches in the still uncleaned living room, wanting to think of ourselves as merely napping, rather than going to bed.

Two or three hours later, I crawled to work, did what I had to do, and went back to Boulder.

The sleeplessness and sick fear reminded me of the diphtheria watch in Tamar's early childhood. It had the same hung-in-the-present quality; can't go, don't want to stay. When I did take the trip to the office, I was so fogged and unfocused that it would have been better for me to keep away, and I finished the day at Miri's. Now and then, a rescue person or sheriff's man would come by.

The next day was the same. We sat and waited. We answered questions, we cleaned; we saved some of Tamar's shirts and underwear out of the loads of wash we ran—providentially, it turned out, because on the following morning the sheriff's man came for the pieces of Tamar's clothing. They would be searching with dogs. I imagined the eager hounds, straining forward on our behalf, gifted with senses that anguish had dulled in us.

Miri's rooms were now clean and uncluttered. After our mammoth washes and foldings, I hoped the house would look like her neighbors' houses—normal, ordered, sane. When the rescue had been accomplished and the reporters came to see Tamar and get her story, that normality, lie though it was, would testify on her behalf. The energy generated by our worry had been sublimated into order. It helped that our hands were busy, because our minds ran endlessly. Where were they? Why weren't they being found? Were they hurt? Were they dead? And over and over again.

Tamar's disappearance had been in the morning papers and on the six and ten o'clock TV news. New York had been calling also, because she had been tagged for a slot on *Good Morning America* and another show, whose name I have forgotten. T-shirts, caps, and gloves with Tamar's caving logo were selling with increasing vigor at her Web site. Now I was glad Miri had contracted out for the distribution. I had complained to her about the cost of it all. The T-shirts had The Magic Kingdom printed on them, plus the caving logo they had designed, and pictures of Tamar in what I called 'pediatric caving gear' were also available. Miri said she had done the PR with Tamar's approval to promote the cause of speleology as a sport, a science, a way of life. I had been unaware of most of the publicity, the gear. The announcement of her appearance on *Good Morning America* had shocked me. Miri and Tamar had known how much I disapproved of all of it and they had worked around me to create it. A secret—another secret.

That morning, the Mordecais called. Why hadn't we told them? What had happened? How could we have let Tamar be exposed to such danger? Who was this Val person? Call them right away if anything changed. My mother called, as hysterical as if Tamar were her granddaughter. How could I have let the child get into such a situation? Wasn't I a friend?

Then the parade of neighbors began, the people who loved her and waited for her visits. There's a list of them somewhere. They came with Tupperware containers of soup and the comfort food of childhood—potato salad and chocolate pudding, fried chicken and biscuits, chocolate cake and brownies. Phoebe the cat's owner came and Mrs. Warren and the Bakers, all of them, and the Van Dusen twins, Mrs. Deetz, who talked about Jesus, and her daughters-in-law, and neighborhood people in a steady stream to feed and console us.

"She's such a darling little girl. I know they'll be all right." "We're all praying for her. I've organized a prayer rota at church and it's going to go on every day until she's found." "I know Jesus won't let her suffer, such a darling girl."

We repacked the food for the sheriff and told him to send it on to the searchers and the deputies. After Miri answered the door for the nth time to a woman who was a stranger to her, she looked at me without any dawning of understanding. "Who are these people?"

I was moved, but I kept my face expressionless and my voice bland. "Neighbors—just the neighborly thing in time of trouble."

"But I don't know them," she persisted.

I shrugged and said something about a Colorado custom. I planned to tell her later all about it, when Tamar and Val were

243

found and everything was fine. Then I would shake her up. Then I would tell Tamar to stop protecting her.

40

On the fifth day I had to spend the morning at work, dull with sleep denied. I was supposed to be planning for a trip. World Wide was negotiating for an island near Tristan da Cunha, to create another resort. There would be shops, and a harbor, a fishery to supply the resort, a farm, a ranch for the resort. This was to be World Wide's most ambitious project and, I thought, my last with them. I had planned to have been at meetings with all the environmentalists, naturalists, foresters, fishing experts, government officials, et cetera, who were involved in the project. Now I was subsisting on e-mails that could only suggest what was going on in Mérida. The outline of a pine tree carries no birds and wafts no scent, but I couldn't go and I told them so. I wanted to be present for Miri as she had been for me when Niall died and I was stuck in that confusion of loss before sorrow comes, a miasma that takes over the early times of tragedy, through which we can barely see. Miri had guided me through those days. If necessary, I wanted to guide her through these. Friend wouldn't have done. I told them Miri was my sister.

She had closed around her wound, her face tight, her eyes huge with sleeplessness. But for me, she would have been catatonic. I made us work, eat; I made her go to the lab that morning while I was at the office and delegate work. Miri wasn't loved by everyone there, but she was still capable of eliciting great loyalty in some of the staff, and a lost child arouses empathy in everyone. As always, the lab covered for her. She went and got reported to and signed whatever was necessary. Then I met her and we shopped, after which we went home and scoured pots, did windows, stared into the black cave of the filthy oven and cleaned it.

I had brought over a little TV set for news, and its chatter seemed to relax us as we worked. We listened to the 10:00 p.m. report, and then I went home. Tamar's situation had been on the 10:00 p.m. news the second day of her absence: little Boulder girl lost in a cave she had been exploring. Some of what the reporter said was inaccurate and Miri had fumed and wanted to call in to the station.

"It won't do any good," I'd insisted. "The details are beyond them anyway. They make things up and don't correct their assumptions easily."

"They're assuming Val is a kid, maybe a little older, but just another kid, and that I would let that happen."

"Miri, they have a story. They don't care much about what it says." The phone had rung.

After that first TV spot, I began my steady job at Miri's, fielding her calls and monitoring her messages and mail. A wave of inchoate human feeling swept on and over us, drawing from a place deeper than reason. Love, sympathy, rage, hate, people's obsessions rang in my ears. Of course, they assumed I was Miri. How could I have left my child alone in the dark? Why did I have children if I was going to neglect them? Who did I think I was? Some callers hoped Tamar would die in the cave.

"And that will teach her a lesson?" I said to one man.

"Yes, and the next time . . ." Only then did the caller realize where his rage had taken him, and hung up.

More women called than men. The women railed; the men threatened. I was glad to have them assume I was Tamar's mother. I felt I was performing a task I was born to do, loving Tamar, loving and protecting Miri. The mail, too, produced a heavy packet every day, less emotional than the calls, but more disturbing. Psychics and visionaries hurried to our aid with their hands out. Grief counselors sent their cards. Lawyers shot off e-mails. Clairvoyants and mystics claimed to have had messages from Tamar. A person sent a wand that, held out in front of us, would lead us to her.

Already, we had a routine, and we found ourselves clinging to

246

it as we drowned in fear and fantasy, our own and other people's. We drew fantasy to ourselves as water draws lightning. Our routine was our only defense against the fear and the mental pictures that now and then broke through all our careful walls and drugged sleep. Even Miri broke her health rules and brought home a rainbow collection of pills from the hospital—sedatives, mood elevators, tranquilizers. By that evening, we were working doped to the eyes.

The rescuers had been through Tamar's notes—the childish writing in her ruled tablets. She had named the cave but not given an exact location. The Grotto man who met with us this time was named Fred. He knew the local geology very well and began to use the clues we had given him to eliminate everything to the north of us and then due west in that daunting circle the other man had drawn. He knew Val and seemed to like him, but he was obviously puzzled about the situation.

"Most good exploration is carried out with a minimum of three cavers," he said. "I wonder why there were only two of them."

Miri was in the other room, just then, so I was free to say, "That would be Tamar. She would have wanted the cave to be hers, I think."

Fred gave me a quizzical look. He had known Tamar from Grotto meetings, an eleven-year-old, eager, intelligent, but who let an eleven-year-old have her way in such things? He left soon after, telling us that we had been helpful and that they were narrowing the area of inquiry and should soon find the cave. And it was morning and it was evening, day five.

Art Kleinman called. Why had we allowed Tamar to go on such an outing? Miri was headstrong and had spoiled Tamar by denying her the understanding that there were rules that forbade the danger and uselessness of going somewhere simply out of curiosity. Why had I not— I hung up on him, wishing I had left him back in my girlhood, laughing with us in the forbidden movie houses, eating the forbidden foods. Shirah called, offering sympathy. By now, the Mordecais were on the phone three or four times a day for news and consolation. Ada tried valiantly to keep from panic and hysteria, from blaming Miri, from howling into the phone, from coming up to Boulder with pans of noodle kugel, which she knew Miri would throw out anyway. People sent rosaries, amulets, prayer cloths. Rafael called from Mexico, gentle and quietly sympathetic. Someone on the staff had seen the news.

"They've been away so long," and for the first time since Tamar's disappearance I blew into sobbing.

He waited, saying nothing, and when I stopped, he said, "From what you told me, they were not careless. You have not given up hope. . . ."

"No, not yet."

"My dear, take care of yourself also, as well as you will of Miriam. Sleep, if you can, at home, some of the time. . . ."

I said I would.

On that fifth day, there had been an article by Alicia Gomez' in the *Boulder Camera*.

When we got home from shopping, we had unpacked our groceries in Miri's newly orderly kitchen and opened the paper on the counter, sitting side by side to read. Miri turned the pages. A picture. Was it? . . . Yes, it was Val, but it was a police picture, front view, side view. Headline: She trusted her daughter to him. The "story" followed.

Val had told us some things about his childhood in activist communes, and of his living in Boulder when the underground press called it "Crystal City." Colorado had had few drug laws then. I'd heard that the activists scorned the drug users, but Val told me that some of the kids in the movement sold drugs for the money their parents scorned. Old news, I thought, decades old. Why didn't they look at Val now, who he was, what he stood for, *now?* Easy: no story there. Much more fun to rake up the file of a man who had put a criminal past behind him. How young he looked in those pictures. He had no beard. His look was, I'd say, resolute. He was nerving himself up to serve his time. What had jail been like? He'd never spoken of that. Now here he was, set in the minds of thousands of readers who didn't know him— front view, side view. I was shaking with impotent rage.

The paper published his record: He had finished his youth in foster care; at sixteen, he was supporting his own habit by dealing at his school, and was arrested for the first time while making a sale to an undercover agent. His youth and the lighter sentences of those days freed him in a year. After some time in high school—he hadn't graduated—he'd lied his way into the navy and been sent to Korea, where he also dealt drugs. Caught and convicted, he spent a year in the brig and received a dishonorable discharge.

The tenor of the article was that Val had been, and probably still was, a criminal, a misfit and, for all anyone knew, a child molester, a predator. Miri had trusted her child to him. No newer deeds were studied, no other questions asked.

I wanted to call the paper, to tell Gomez or whoever would listen that there was a Val I knew, a Val Miri and Tamar knew, a Val lots of cavers knew and respected, a Val respected by the people in his halfway house. He loved Miri and Tamar, and he liked me. I knew about his prior addiction and his selling drugs. He was open about it all. By now, I was talking out loud to the paper. "You're the great ones for turnaround lives, for big human-interest Triumph Over This, That, and The Other stories. Why not now? This one's the Dark-Dyed Villain Story. Drag the river for it and up comes the mud." I knew that Tamar had enchanted him; her wanting, her insistence had charmed him away from what he felt and knew to be right. He was deeply in love with Miri, who charmed. I, too, in my own way, had been giving validity to all the dreams, a solid presence. I had cheered Tamar on; I had paid for the rope. We had all pushed him beyond where he would ordinarily have gone. I turned the page and read on.

After Val's navy service and imprisonment, he had worked at a series of low-level jobs, including tending bar in a saloon where there was so much trouble, it was put on the local precinct's frequent-call list. He'd married and left three women in rapid succession, gone to a rehab program, and then another. He'd found a job with the second program and had been taking college courses for an eventual degree in social work. "He plans to work in corrections, about which he already knows a good deal." Gomez must have been proud of that bit.

The rhetorical newsprint nanny then made her presence

known. Was this the kind of man a sane and loving mother would entrust her daughter's safety to in a situation that left them alone together for hours at a time? Even as the article was being written, weren't the two of them lost in a cave, the location of which he had kept a secret?

"It was Tamar who demanded that!" I cried uselessly to the print. "Val told us that as soon as they had done the preliminary mapping, they would register the cave. I heard him; Alicia heard him. This isn't fair!"

We were crying then, sobbing. All the tight, steely-eyed control we had kept for days disappeared in tears.

The article clothed Val in a monster's mask and cape: dishonorably discharged, a dropout, a drug dealer, a felon, an ex-con, and, even now, a fringe dweller living in a halfway house for ex-cons and the mentally ill. And a caver. What did he do in those caves, and with whom?

But there was more. Tamar's mother was his lover, a divorced single mother, a careless slattern who had allowed her daughter to contract diphtheria rather than take the trouble to have her vaccinated, thus also risking the lives of other children. She had allowed the convict full access to her child. The woman's "close friend" was in constant attendance.

We had stilled the phone's ringer and had muted the message machine, but I could hear them clicking constantly. Miri's e-mail address had also been put on someone's Web site and was measuring hate by the megabyte. "Looks like Gomez saw this house before we cleaned it up," I said, trying for a lighter note. Miri was sitting on her counter stool and her face had frozen into hard lines, her body tense as a runner's. The cords in her neck stood out as she gritted her teeth. I was about to speak, when the doorbell rang. We were both afraid to go and answer it, but after a back-and-forth of yelling through it, which I did, while Miri sat pulling at her shoulders with her crossed arms, I went, opening it to a sheriff's deputy. They had found the cave.

41

I want to go there," Miri said.

"Miri . . ."

"You have to take me," Miri told the deputy.

He looked at her quizzically. "I'm on duty here," he said, and left.

Miri began to seethe. "Fred; get Fred."

"The Grotto man?"

"Yes, the Grotto man. Tell him to take us up there."

"Miri, they obviously want us to stay and wait. If we go up there, we'll be in the way. Someone will have to be taken off the rescue to be with us. Necessary food and equipment and time will have to be diverted—things that should be going to the rescue. This is a bad idea."

She looked at me as though she had never seen me before. "What kind of a friend are you, Rachel?"

"I'm your friend, Miriam, and I have been your friend. I hate the whole idea of Tamar as the 'world's youngest caver.'"

I knew she was vibrating with tension, tight, besieged, stringy with sleeplessness and patched eating, but I was in no better shape than she was and I felt my anger rising from a depth I hadn't known was there. "What are you proving?"

"Call the Grotto man—Fred," Miri demanded. "Get Fred to take us up there."

"No, Miri, I won't. They've found the cave, but how long will it be before they find Tamar and Val? There might be any number of bad situations that will require a long time for the rescue. There are fissures in caves, rockfalls."

"Those people are supposed to be experts."

"If you had taken the time to find out what caving is about,

251

where they went, what they were doing, the rescue might have been made days ago."

"What are you saying? Are you blaming me?"

"Tamar is not a bargaining chip. You're up to your eyes in justification and you can't see past it."

The anger was moving. Soon I wouldn't be able to hold it. "You used Val; you all but made him a baby-sitter for Tamar's needs. Maybe you can't help it, but you use people all the time."

"Everyone uses people—for lovers, for employees, as teachers, as doctors, as pathologists."

"You use us without gratitude. I know that better than anyone, how you shed light and how people are drawn to you. They want to be in that light, but you never realize—"

Then I was being pulled by the anger, all but jerked off my feet. "Everything works for you, Miri—you come to the intersection and the light changes; you dive off the diving board and the pool fills on your way down. It takes a village to raise a child? It did, and you weren't even aware of it. Then, God, what sleazy crap was that about the country's youngest caver? Why didn't you stop it, all the garbage you said you couldn't stand? If you hadn't promoted that and the T-shirts, and the Web site, and *Good Morning America,* Val wouldn't have broken his own codes of safety in caves, and I wouldn't have ended up as an accomplice."

"Here you are again, trying to raise my child. You're the taker, and you're jealous, selfish and jealous!"

I hit her. I slapped that beautiful face, hard, and watched, fascinated, at how her head flew back and her big eyes opened wide and how her still-magnificent hair came forward and then fluttered back. For half a second, she was off balance, and then equilibrium returned. We were in the kitchen. She saw the plate on the table and picked it up clumsily and threw it at me. Close as we were, it missed, and I heard it shatter on the wall behind me. Then we both broke loose. I was past red rage and into white. I threw a pan at her, rejoicing when it hit her. The food we had been preparing was in the air. When she was close enough, I kicked her. She threw a serving plate, which grazed my head and crashed. We cursed and threw things, we hit and were hit, we looked for things to throw, and we screamed years of things, and all of it true, or half true, or partly true: my envy, her selfishness, my greed, her fanaticism.

From the welter of screaming, the red of blood behind our eyes, the shattering of thrown things, a steady hammering intruded and we came up out of the rage into the evening and someone was banging at the kitchen door. I went. It was the sheriff. He looked at me, took a breath, blanked his expression.

"I've been at the front door for some time," he said laconically, "and after I realized you were involved here, I came around back."

My face went hot and must have been very red. There was something in my hair. I put my hand up to check. Lettuce, yes. I took it out of the tangle and looked at it.

He had a little smile—embarrassment, I thought. "It's been a tough time," he said.

He came in and sat quietly while we cleaned up the mess and washed up a little. Miri had a cut on her forehead and I had a salad in my hair. Luckily, my hair-do is short; a quick shake and a few minutes at the kitchen sink fixed it. The sheriff sat on a kitchen chair hiding tactfully behind a spring-skiing issue of *Ski Colorado*. When she was cleaned up, Miri faced him.

"I want to go up there," she said.

"Where?"

"Where do you think?"

"Mistake," the sheriff said. He told her everything I had told her. She wasted no charm on him. She was pure will.

"If you don't see to my going, I'll call that damned Alicia Gomez and the Denver papers and I'll tell them I've been kept from my daughter by a bunch of jealous cavers with no authority and by local bullies with badges."

The sheriff didn't respond with anger. He wasn't even defensive. "I've advised against it," he said, " but there's no law forbidding it. I'm not going up until sometime tomorrow, if they haven't completed the rescue before that. Escobar's going up. Let me see if he'll take you. He's a state trooper and they want him on-scene at the trail-head."

"Call him," Miri said.

253

The sheriff took out a cell phone and made the call. "I'm here with the mom," he said. "She's strong on going up there with you. . . . Yes, I know; I told her all that. . . . Okay." He looked at me. "Are you going, too?"

"Should I?"

"You're family?"

"Friend," I said.

He suppressed a smile. He looked at Miri.

"Okay," Miri said, "she goes, too."

The sheriff signed off. "Ms. . ."

"Finn," I said. "Sheriff, are you married?"

"Divorced," he said.

"She's an idiot," I said.

42

ere they come. The sudden movement in the camp alerts us. Radios buzz. We've been sitting on the storage boxes in our tent, staring out at the distant hill, dreaming, painting dark pictures, feeling disembodied in the blur of unreality in a situation that is all too real. All at once, people are here and we're told to move. The tents are coming down.

"The bodies are coming."

"Bodies?"

"No—sorry; one survivor and one body."

We get to our feet, stiff with waiting, and move quickly, clumsily, outside into the drizzly cold and up the hill to where the ambulance is parked.

The cave is below us, the trail maybe two hundred feet up. A Grotto man climbs to the group that is on the way down the rocks to help with the litters. They have ropes and harnesses and are deploying them from here. The setup looks very complicated.

"Conversation!" the Rescue man says in a voice meant to carry. "Watch your conversation, people. The little girl's conscious." He goes on giving instructions we don't understand, but there are lines of rope all around us now, cables. I hope they'll remember what I said about not transporting Tamar and Val in the ambulance together, but will take Val to his van and drive him to the place he needs to be.

I see them moving. The cave opening is much farther down than I thought. The rescuers and the rigs look small and shaky and Miri is grinding her teeth with impatience beside me, trembling with it.

The climb is turtle-slow and they stop often. Tamar has been packaged like a mummy in the large railed litter, roped, as are the men and women guiding the litter. They struggle slowly up the slope. Their hard hats hide their faces, but I see that now and then pebbles are dislodged by the movements of their feet and fall in a scatter from the upper tilt of the litter. Now and then the ropes are causing falls of earth and pebbles from above and the person at Tamar's side—a woman, I think—leans over Tamar, protecting her. Up, up.

We're standing by the ambulance now, and as the rescue goes on, we begin to shiver. The rescue path and the mountainside are below the fog, but everything above us is covered and we are all trapped in the imprisoned cold of its blanket. Last night's snow hasn't stuck to the rocks the crew is scaling; the slope is too severe, but every flat surface is hooded with it, and hand and footholds are risky. The ambulance drivers are sitting in their cab to keep warm. Escobar motions us over, but Miri and I are too intent on the rescue. After a while, he gets out of the car and comes over.

"You ladies will be icicles by the time they get here. I figure they'll be half an hour or more getting up." But we're hanging from the ropes ourselves, and Escobar goes back to the police car and lights up, waiting.

And now, at last. It's noon and Tamar is up over the lip of the cliff and the woman who has been at her side says loudly enough for us to hear, "Your mom and your aunt are here and here's the ambulance. You'll get to take a ride."

Miri goes right to the litter and pushes aside the men who are unhooking it from its supporting ropes.

Tamar says, "Is 'Chelle here?"

The rescuers look stunned. Their conventional assumptions take over. The girl is hurt. She was unconscious when they first got to her and then she came to and was in and out during the time of packing her up, restraining and moving her. Head-injury victims are often totally irrational, but demanding all the same. They come out of it later and don't remember what they had demanded so vehemently, or why. I move closer. Miri's position has blocked Tamar's view of me and she says again, "'Chelle—"

"Your mom's here. You're safe and we're going to get you to—" the woman rescuer is saying.

Tamar goes rigid, adamant. "I want 'Chelle too!"

One of the rescue men moves toward me. I see he's wearing a paramedic patch on his jacket. "Ma'am—"

"Yes, I'm 'Chelle."

"I think you'd better go along with her—"

I go to the basket, where she looks all but lost in the blankets and wrapping. "Tamar, here I am. We're all going to the hospital. I'll be close, but you'll want Mim to stay with you while you ride down."

She looks terribly pale. There are bruises on her face and a large lump on her forehead. Her leg has been splinted. I can't tell what other injuries there are. Behind me, I hear one of the rescuers murmuring, "I wish we could get the chopper—fifteen minutes and she'd be there. This ride will be hours."

"What's holding things up?" another asks.

"Tamar."

She begins to scream. So does Miri. The woman rescuer moves in and touches the paramedic on his arm and together they escort us to the back of the ambulance and motion us to the bench on the right. We watch as Tamar's cot is slid in beside us and secured.

I move in close. "We're here, Tamar." She opens her eyes and I say, "We'll ride with you."

Before the two doors close, I feel the need to turn and look back at the Grotto people and thank them. Miri hasn't done it or said anything to them all the time we've been here. "You guys did a great job," I say. "We're all so grateful."

Then I see them turn, and just before the doors close, up comes another basket. Val. They're doing it gently, as gently as they have raised Tamar, and for a moment I'm overcome with gratitude I hadn't expected on his behalf. I guess I took for granted that they'd think it didn't matter, that nothing could hurt him now, but Fred has seen me looking.

"Thank you, Fred. Thank everyone for us—it means so much."

"Take care," he says. The doors close.

In her seat, the paramedic is asking Tamar questions. Tamar answers vaguely and doesn't move much when the paramedic frees her arm and puts the IV needle in.

The ambulance has started and is very slow, bumping its way down the rutted trail up which we came. I can't see where we are or know any more than that the direction changes several times, now smooth, now bumpy, and at last we are on paved road and are able to go a little faster.

Then Tamar is awake. I see her eyes open. "Hi," I say. Tamar says she's thirsty, and the paramedic lets her suck some water out of a gauze pad.

"Val's dead," she says.

"I know," I say.

"It's my fault. I wanted . . ."

"Don't talk," Miri says. "Stop talking. Save your strength."

She's quiet for a while, resting. Then: "I said goodbye to him. You're supposed to have three cavers, you know. We should have."

"I know." I want Tamar to free herself. The small expense of energy seems worth it to me. She wants to tell us what happened.

"We didn't know it was a ledge . . . . Piece broke off."

Beside me I could feel Miri shift with impatience.

Tamar is breathing hard. "The paper lady told me I could make people care about caving and there was being on TV."

Little dots of blood are coming out of Tamar's mouth when she exhales.

"Don't talk any more," Miri says. "You need to rest."

Tamar takes a huge gulp of air. "I'm okay."

"Please, Tamar," I say.

"It wasn't fair to Val."

"Honey, you've had a bad fall and some terrible experiences. Please wait."

"It wasn't fair, Mim—"

"Tamar, not now, please—" I'm pleading. She's dead pale and I can see veins in her temple and the throb of desperate heartbeats in her neck.

She shakes her head strongly and then regrets it and is almost overwhelmed by nausea. The paramedic increases the flow on the IV.

"'Chelle, I need to say how it was. Val landed first and I

landed on him, then all the rocks." Hearing it from her, in her high, clear voice makes me shiver. "We were there for a long time before he died."

"I know, sweetheart."

"'Chelle, I have a secret and I need to tell it to you."

I look at Miri. She is seething.

"Are you sure?"

"Yes. You swear you won't get mad?"

"How can I know that, if I don't know what the secret is?"

Her voice is now so faint that we are leaning in to hear her. Miri gives me a murderous look and straightens.

"'Chelle, the secret is . . ." I lean so close that the seat belt I'm wearing strains against my neck, and I flip it open. The paramedic begins to say something. I shoot her a look and she shrugs and sits back. "I peed in the cave."

43

We ride on in a fog that makes it impossible to know where we are. I see that Tamar has gone into a sleep-nonsleep that almost seems rhythmic and from which she comes weaker each time. Now she's awake again, abruptly.

"Val."

"You were telling us about Val." She wrestles with the words, with trying to compass the feelings.

"We were in the dark—"

"Could you move?"

". . . Val was talking and I thought he would get better, but said he would die. When he tried . . . he'd be screaming. He was bleeding and sweating, too, and something about how he was hurt . . . but he said he was glad he fell the way he did so I could fall on top of him . . . We had long talks."

"What did you talk about?"

"First it was about getting out . . . He started telling jokes."

"It's a man thing," I said. "There's even a word for it."

"What is it?"

"Gallantry."

"He was using his gallantry . . . he started to scream . . . turn it into cursing because of his gallantry, but he couldn't do it."

Miri looks at the paramedic and says, "Why don't you *do* something?"

The paramedic says, "I'm doing everything I can," but then she increases the flow of the oxygen Tamar is getting.

Tamar speaks again: "I was so scared that nobody would ever find me."

I so want to take her in my arms and murmur "poor girl" into her hair.

She's away for a few minutes. The blood spots stipple her face, and the paramedic wipes them away with a wet gauze pad. Then Tamar rouses and says, "My hands were shaking, but the poem helped. . . . climbing sideways . . ."

She sighs. Whatever drug the paramedic has given her, it seems to reach her and I feel a tide of hope, of confidence that we will arrive at the hospital in time. I will hand her over to the wizards who will cast their spells and restore her.

Miri's worry comes out in petulance. "Do we need all this cave talk now? Can't you see it's taking energy she needs to survive?"

The paramedic nods in agreement but says, "She seems to need to—" but Miri cuts her off.

"Haven't you done enough, Rachel, making Tamar your child?"

She's right, of course. I bought the rope. Tamar, beyond us, far beyond us, is still telling her story, now spiraling into smaller and smaller circles. I must strain to hear.

"Then there were the jitters and I got so tired. I stuck myself to the wall . . . I said the poem . . . the whole ramp was gone. The cave told me a lie. Not fair—gone so far, climbing up and up and had all my hoping . . . Val wasn't spotting for me."

She's fighting to stay with what she's saying. The paramedic begins to tell her to stop, but I put up a hand and miss some of the words as I whisper to Tamar. "Not now. You can tell us later." She isn't listening.

" . . . so good, 'Chelle, the sleep I had. There were worms. I ate them—tasted good."

She's breathing too fast. The paramedic pulls something up into a syringe and injects it into a place in the IV bag.

Miri has been stirring beside me. "Why are you letting her go on about this? Why do you want her to suffer it all over again?"

"She seems to need—"

"That's just the point. Explain to me? No. She hasn't addressed one word to me. It's you she wants to understand her while I sit here like a statue—"

Tamar is murmuring. "I fell—no reason . . . I landed on a rock—not Val's body—it hurt. Then . . . a bunch of lights. People were telling me things."

She drifts off and this time I think it might be into a gentle sleep because she's been sweating heavily. She's been short of breath, but the blood drops are bigger, and suddenly a gout of something dark and foul erupts from her mouth. She has a gray look, and she is shivering. For a while she has an awful restlessness, moving, shivering. Now she's still. I wait.

After a time, the paramedic reaches over the IV line and the line from the oxygen, and up over Tamar's body, and uses her stethoscope. She talks to the driver over the walkie-talkie. She faces me, and her look isn't medical at all, removed and objective, but womanly, a helpless look, with some horror in it.

"We're too far out," she says. "Even if they had choppered her in from the site, I don't think they could have saved her."

Miri erupts. "Why don't you do CPR? Why don't you ventilate her—or intubate her?"

I look at her, disbelieving. She takes my hand and puts it on Tamar's neck, down near her collarbone. Cold. Still.

I've never watched someone die before. All the activity, the motion, breath, beat of life, flow, flood, rise-and-fall, flutter of eyelid, response of eye, twitch, flicker, murmur, singularity, gone; away.

The paramedic says, "CPR would just produce more bleeding, I'm sure of it. With broken ribs—they'd be forced up, and she already has ruptured organs." A pause. Then: "I'm going to ask him to pull over." She looks hopelessly at the IV and stops it. She turns off the oxygen that had been giving Tamar what it could, and unhooks everything. She tells the driver. I feel us pulling to the side of the road. We stop.

What I see on Miri's face isn't shock or sorrow or anguish but rage. For shock, there would be the warming of my arms around her. For grief, the shoulder to cry on. For rage, there's no way of opening, nothing to be done. What procedures weren't performed? Why couldn't the chopper have come? Why weren't these people trained, people who knew their jobs?

Maybe rage is a hedge against sorrow, and I should understand, and be sympathetic again, but I'm tired and in grief myself. Miri rages on. Why hadn't Tamar been found earlier? Tamar had loved caving. Caving is dangerous, yes. She died doing what she loved. Why wasn't that enough for them? Who were these people, the letter writers, the phone callers, the e-mailers? Who were they to question any of it, to criticize her life style? What did they know about home schooling, or her decision to let Tamar grow up free, doing what she wanted to do?

I've slid further away on the bench to give her what privacy I can. I tell Miri that we've been through a lot and some of it was my fault. I think that later, when this is all past, we'll talk about loyalty and friendship and what those things really mean. "Now, please, can we stop for a minute? There've been two deaths here. A big, good, kind man died saving Tamar. He died thinking about you and Tamar. Let's at least cry for them both."

Miri waves me away. "Val doesn't matter," she says.

"What?"

"Val's dead," Miri says, "and we can't change that."

"I don't think Val's being dead is what made you say that." The ambulance starts up again and jolts back on the road and I feel suddenly jolted awake. Who has she grieved for? Why didn't I see? Was it only the people who didn't love her? Her father's heart is failing. Ada weeps into her Sabbath cooking. Jacob didn't matter. Val doesn't matter, and neither do I. There are only two people who can make her cry: Henrik and Tamar. It's a very exclusive club. Easy conquests? God, the rest of us were. I was the easiest.

"Miri, if I disappeared from your life tomorrow, would you miss me? I don't think you would. Tamar would—would have. Tamar grieved for Val for days."

Hard words, and they're out before I know it. Surely they shouldn't have been spoken in the hour of her grief, but they were, and I said them because I believed them and because I was too tired and sick to summon the energy to suppress them.

She looks at me and I see her wrath moving from its old target to its new one.

44

I haven't seen Miri since then. I went to the morgue and identified Val's body, officially. I called Rabbi Mordecai and Ada. I call Shirah and my mother. I called Val's halfway house and went over there and watch the hard, inchoate grief of people whose suffering didn't quite eclipse this new pain.

Miri has changed her name back to Zimet, and she has cut her hair, Ada tells me. Scheherazade is no more. Tamar was cremated—a final slap in the face to her parents' faith and tradition. There was no funeral, nothing for any of us. Amazing, the pain that can be caused by wielding the sword of charm.

Shirah calls. "Can you come over after work? Everyone will be away and we can be alone. I think we should talk."

"Shirah—I can't take any more blame. I've never been good at it, and I don't think I need any more of it, now."

"Funny, I didn't know I was going to do that."

Her house is in the new east Denver suburbs. I had thought it was too big when their family first moved there, a pretentious place, high ceilings, huge windows: the new signs of wealth. You could pay off the national debt with its air conditioning bill. The interior design is impressive and inconvenient. I realize that most of the houses I've been working on lately are even bigger than this one. I've been comparing Shirah's place to Miri's and to the house Niall and I had lived in. Times change; expectations rise.

Miriam's brother is in from California. He's come to move Ada and the rabbi to the assisted-living condos they just built near here, Shirah tells me.

"I didn't know."

"I want to comfort you, but before I can do that, I have to tell

264

you how far away you've been from me, from all of us, for years and years."

"Whose fault is that? Ma wanted grandkids I can't give her. Papa disapproved of Niall and made him know it. You were always criticizing me."

"You left us long before that. You were always at Miriam's house. Your love and attention always went to her. Shifrah's far away in New York. She and Sy seldom come back. We go there maybe once a year to see them. You're the only sister left. When I need help with Ma and Papa, you're busy with your other family."

I'm tired, and anguished. I'm grieving for Val and suffering for Tamar. What Shirah says is true, but it's difficult to listen to her complain.

"I loved Miri," I say. "It was wonderful and exciting to be with her, to watch her glow. I had a rosy childhood in that glow. I'm a professional because of her. I tried out for the scholarship because of her. I went to college because of her. Ada and Rabbi Mordecai were my true parents. They comforted me and loved me, and they liked Niall. I was a good friend, and, yes, I made mistakes, but I tried to be a good sort-of aunt to Tamar, whom I loved. Tamar confided in me."

"Are we so much less than they are?" Shirah's looking hard at me. "Miriam always seemed cold to me, Rache. You talked about her light, how she glowed. I never thought there was any warmth in it. You were always warmer than she was, and I kept waiting for you to figure that out, but you never did. I don't like Miriam, Rache; I never have, but I'm sorry about what happened to Tamar. It must have been hard enough to take the fear and the waiting you both went through without all the newspapers and TV jumping on it."

"It wasn't true what they said about Val." I feel some thickening in my voice. "He was a good man."

I stay at Shirah's all afternoon. I tell her about Rafael and World Wide. She's surprised. "I knew you were traveling—I thought you were going to pick up work. I guess I underestimated you."

"That wouldn't be so hard to do—I'm a kid sister, after all."

"Were you under a spell—not only with Miri and Tamar, but with their whole family?"

"Maybe I was, and waking up is very hard to do."

Courage has always been the prime virtue for me; Miri exemplified it. Without courage, I used to think, none of the other virtues can be realized. All the people I love and have loved had courage in plenty. What if that single virtue isn't enough?

Shirah's granddaughter has her bat mitzvah next week. The dream I've been in has lasted generations long. While I slept new lives were created and rose unacknowledged around me. Of course I'll go. I haven't been a good aunt to her mother or to all the others. I'll have to get to know them and to let them know me.

At that Sabbath service in the synagogue, I'll stand for the mourner's Kaddish, our prayer for the dead. In that synagogue, the custom is that only the immediate family of the deceased is acknowledged by standing when the prayer is recited. No one asks, of course, but in a tight community, everyone knows. I'll be standing as an act of defiance. Watch me. I hate the pain that has to be borne in secret.

About the Author

Joanne Greenberg was born in Brooklyn, New York, in 1932. She went to community school there, then to P.S. 9 in New York City when her family moved there. She earned a B.A. from American University in Washington, D.C., with summer school in London and the University of Colorado. Like most writers of her generation, she has had a large range of work experiences: horse herder, space control agent for an airline, EMT, teacher, and lieutenant on a volunteer fire department. For many years, she taught at the Colorado School of Mines.

Her husband, Albert Greenberg, has had professional experiences as a welfare department case worker, as a rehabilitation counselor, and as a psychotherapist that have furnished Joanne Greenberg with subject matter for many of her books.

The Greenbergs are the parents of two adult sons.

Visit Joanne Greenberg's Web site at:

http://www.mountaintopauthor.com/

Questions for Readers' Groups

1. Are all friendships absolutely equal? Rachel thinks that she owes Miri more than Miri owes her. Is this true?

2. More than once, Miri accuses Rachel of trying to usurp the mother's role. Is Rachel over-identifying?

3. Have you ever seen a friend walk toward disaster? Did you try to intervene? How? What was the outcome?

4. Is Tamara's willfulness a natural result of her upbringing, or are other factors at work?

5. Had Niall lived, would Tamar's willfulness have been less toxic? Would she have been less cosseted by Rachel? And if so, might she have learned more patience?

6. Both women turned against the orthodoxy of their upbringing. Miri adopts a new form of orthodoxy. What does Rachel do?

7. Miri has been accused of using people. To what extent is this true? To what extent is doing so wrong? What is the difference between using someone and playing to his strength?

8. Rachel and Miri were lifelong friends. Are such friendships rare? What causes the ruptures in long-term friendships?

9. Near the end of the book, Rachel notes, "Amazing, the pain that can be caused by wielding the sword of charm." What does she mean by "the sword of charm"?

10. To what degree is charm itself the force that drives events in the story of Rachel and Miri? To what degree is charm a sign of something else? If so, what?

About Montemayor Press

Montemayor Press is an independent publisher of literature for children and adults. To learn more about our books, visit

www.MontemayorPress.com

or write for a catalogue at:

Montemayor Press
P. O. Box 526
Millburn, NJ 07041

Also by Joanne Greenberg

Age of Consent
Appearances *
The Far Side of Victory
Founder's Praise
High Crimes and Misdemeanors (stories)
I Never Promised You a Rose Garden
In This Sign
The King's Persons
The Monday Voices
No Reck'ning Made
Of Such Small Differences
Rites of Passage (stories)
A Season of Delight *
Simple Gifts
*Summering (*stories)
Where the Road Goes
With the Snow Queen (stories)

*available from Montemayor Press

Breinigsville, PA USA
10 November 2009
227227BV00001B/1/P